Praise for Sam Lightner Jr.'s work

'*Heavy Green is a fascinating glimpse into a past that few people are aware ever existed.*'
#1 New York Times Bestselling Author Kyle Mills

'*Lightner's detailed account of his expedition and the climbing culture will enthuse readers who love to travel, and make those who prefer armchairs wonder what they're missing.*'
Carol Memmott, USA Today

'*Lightner's unadorned voice manages to keep both these incredible adventures very immediate and utterly affecting.*'
Kirkus Reviews

'*Heavy Green is one of the best researched and most entertaining books of historical fiction that I have read on this aspect of the secret war in Laos.*'
Carl A. Wattenberg, Jr. Army Intel Officer with Green Berets, 1963-1964

'*What Lightner does do is create a wickedly honest portrait of the pressures on the modern-day adventurer.*'
Fiona Cohen, Bellingham Herald

'*If you've wondered where the next Jon Krakauer is, Check out Sam Lightner, Jr. This is a climbing tale like no other.*'
Book Review, Third Place Books

'*This book has a down-to-Earth humanistic flavor and is a delight to read*'
Lynn Arave, Deseret News

'*The success of this book lies not in Lightner and Company reaching the top of Batu Lawi but in the historical references and vivid descriptions*'
Lindley Kirksey, Explorers Club Book Review

"*…a breezily told tale, one that will bring you as close to Borneo's bamboo vipers, foot rot, and sweat bees as you may want to get.*"
Caroline Fraser, Outside Magazine

"*…a real page turner… The writing achieves the excitement of a paperback thriller at times, which is no mean feat for a climbing book.*"
Cat Klerks, Wild Life

All maps are by Sam Lightner, Jr.

Cover Design by Elyse Guarino

Inside leaf art by Joan Dillon with help from Sam Lightner, Jr.

First edition July, 2017

Contents

Brunker, Cory, aka: "Large": Electrical engineer, maintains radar systems and generators for Operation Heavy Green. From Pampa, Texas.

"Burnie": Young Hmong soldier from Pha Thi village. Suffers accidental burns by US techs on Phou Pha Thi.

Dillon, Tom: Assistant to Laotian American Ambassador, William Sullivan. Work revolves around "secret" war being fought in Laos. Works in American Embassy basement, Vientiane.

Drakely, Brad: CIA case officer. Works with Hmong in defense of Lima Site 85 during Operation Heavy Green.

Dramis, Kyle: CIA case agent. Works out of Long Tieng/Lima Site 20, Northern Laos.

Ferris, Monte: Major; combat engineer; selects location for Operation Heavy Green.

Jum: Young Hmong soldier. Develops relationship with American technicians at Lima Site 85.

Keo, Quang: Major, North Vietnamese Army. In charge artillery unit, Vieng Xai cave complex, Houphan Province, Laos. Later takes charge of constructing Road 602.

Lilygren, John: First Lieutenant/Captain: Three-tour veteran South Vietnamese war, assigned to oversee operations and defense of Lima Site 85 during Operation Heavy Green. Originally from Wyoming; grew up in Thailand.

Lim Phou: Member, Hmong tribe who grew up on a French plantation. Works as coolie ferrying loads for the

North Vietnamese Army along the Ho Chi Minh Trail; later teaches rock climbing to Dac Cong; continues with them on mission.

Luang, Somporn: Member of the Thai Special Forces, or Police Aerial Reinforcement Unit (PARU). From city of Krabi, Southern Thailand. Commands PARU force assigned to protect radar facility, Phou Pha Thi, Operation Heavy Green.

McNamara, Secretary Robert: Secretary of Defense under presidents Kennedy and Johnson.

Milano, Richard: CIA regional security officer/attaché, assigned to American Embassy, Bangkok, Thailand.

Samsoum, Professor Phou Lim: Professor, history, University of Montana, Missoula, Montana.

Sears, Tom, aka "Raven-86": Forward air controller. Works with legendary Ravens out of Long Tieng, North central Laos.

Sullivan, Ambassador William H: American Ambassador, Laos, 1964-1969.

Sung, Thanh: Member, North Vietnamese Yao "minority" tribe. Lieutenant, special commando unit, Dac Cong, North Vietnamese Army.

Superchild: A Hmong pilot and the one character actually based on a real person. Most pilots thought of this man as the most gifted of Hmong pilots who fought in Laos; perhaps most gifted pilot in the entire war.

Tilden, Shep: Air traffic controller. Brother MIA in South Vietnam. Only African American in Operation Heavy Green.

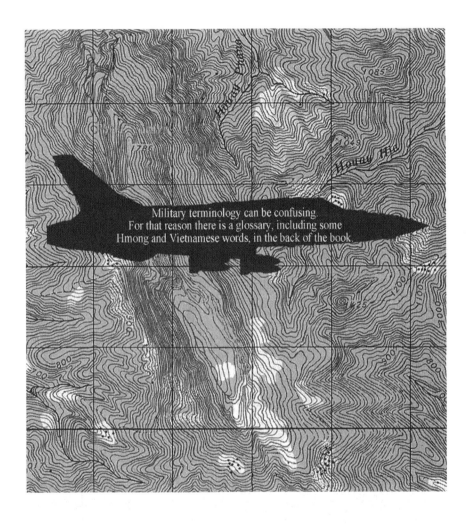

Military terminology can be confusing.
For that reason there is a glossary, including some
Hmong and Vietnamese words, in the back of the book.

MAPS

Southeast Asia circa 1967/1968

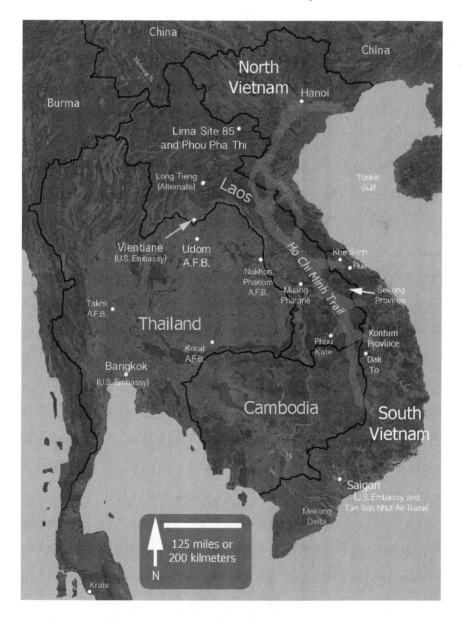

Northern Laos and Vietnam circa 1967/1968

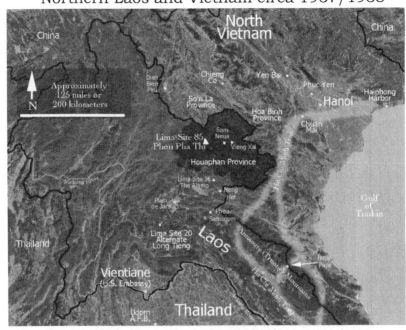

Lima Site 85 TSQ-81 installation

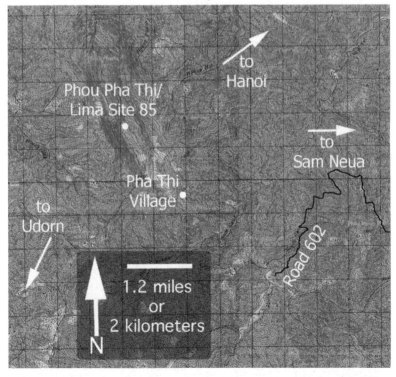

"Nature does not hurry,
yet everything is accomplished."
—Lao Tzu

Foreword

Without realizing it, I began work on Heavy Green some thirty-plus years ago.

My fascination with the First and Second Indochina Wars, and love of rock-climbing on the karst towers of Southeast Asia, led me to the discovery of this secret battle not long after it was declassified. I lived for much of twenty years in Southern Thailand, and have made multiple trips to Laos just to try to reach the battle site. All have failed.

I originally intended to write a non-fiction account of climbing Phou Pha Thi ("Poo Pa Tee") alongside a running account of the battle for the mountain, much like my first general-release book, All Elevations Unknown. Instead, unable to legally climb Phou Pha Thi, I decided to create a work of fiction.

It was always my intention to recreate the basic Heavy Green operation, but no character in this fictionalized account of the operation is based on a real person. There are a few political characters mentioned in the narrative, but none of the major characters who were a part of the battle are based on real people. Some might call this historical fiction, but I think a better classification would be "fictionalized history." Though the operation and timeline of the Vietnam War are facts, this is a work of fiction. I've made every effort to follow the basic history of the Heavy Green operation and the various programs that revolved around it, but the exact details of the daily operations, the specific timing of certain bombing raids, what ordinance was dropped, and the particular language between the controllers and pilots, for instance, have been fictionalized.

My efforts to garner the nature of the training of the North Vietnamese Dac Cong operatives never paid off. I know they had training much like what I illustrate here, but no doubt this fictionalized version differs in the particulars.

Names of places and events can be a difficult part of a book like this one as two different people, on two different sides of a conflict, may have two different names for the same thing. For instance, an American soldier would have referred to the enemy as North Vietnam, while a North Vietnamese soldier would have referenced his own country as the Peoples Democratic Republic of Vietnam. To simplify it, for the most part I stuck with the names that Americans are familiar with, as in North Vietnam Army, rather than The Peoples Army of Vietnam. If you find a name or term that you are not familiar with, there is a glossary in the back that should cover it.

Finally, I should point out the bigger picture of what was intended with Heavy Green. I was born in 1967 and some of my first memories are of news clips from the war in Vietnam. With Heavy Green I wanted to create a story that not only explained the once-classified battle, but also gave younger audiences a better understanding of how the Vietnam War was conducted. It is my hope that with this piece of historical fiction I have provided something that is both entertaining and educational.

Sam Lightner, Jr.

July 1, 2017

Prologue

"They had never really been friends, but the intensity of their differences wasn't apparent until the two armies met in Berlin," the professor said, reading from an unbound manuscript on what looked to be an oversized oak podium.

With a strong East Asian accent few could pinpoint, he spoke in a voice that seemed a little high-pitched for a teacher of history. Most of the professors at the university liked to bellow their words of wisdom as if they were Winston Churchill, but the young Asian was at peace with himself and his new life, and had no inherent need to sound impressive. His soft-spoken demeanor may not have been intimidating to the students when compared to the more tenured teachers in Missoula, but that didn't make him seem weak. There was an edge to the little man that was undeniable to anyone who encountered him, and the students focused on every word as he continued to read.

"On the one side were the Americans. The United States was a young nation, and through revolution, conquest, and commerce it had carved out a giant place in the world. Just on the sheer might of its economy, America entered World War II as the favorite. This economic strength extended from a populace of immigrants who had come to its shores believing their individuality would allow them to find success. Every man could own a home, be the king in his own castle, work the job he felt best suited him, and believe anything, provided it didn't infringe on his neighbors' rights to do the same. If one phrase could characterize the nation, it was, With hard work anything is possible."

The professor cleared his throat and adjusted his wire-rimmed glasses, then continued to read.

"On the other side was the Soviet Union, a brand-new political organization of very old nations. At its heart was Russia, the reclusive giant spanning from the European plains to the Asian shores of the Pacific. For centuries, its people had lived virtually hand-to-mouth, suffering through winters that were cold beyond description, and owing allegiance and all their efforts to the czar. The czars had been replaced by men who possessed a new political and economic philosophy that they felt would benefit all, but it came with a steep cost. For everyone to benefit, the individual had to pledge allegiance to the new system rather than to his own personal needs or wants. Total acceptance of the ideal that you worked for the betterment of the nation, and that the correct decision could only be made by looking at the needs of the many, was at its heart. It was a difficult concept for most to willingly accept, but when simplified it wasn't much different from the past: We used to work for the Czar, and now we work for the Soviet Union."

The professor closed the book and looked up to the

auditorium. The room could seat perhaps a hundred students in five or six rows that faced a stage, but only twenty-two had signed up for the course. The size and ambience of the space, combined with the distance between the students, felt formal and cold. The professor preferred a friendlier atmosphere.

"Class, that reading from the first page of a book that a friend and I are writing on the war in Vietnam, or more specifically, the war in Laos," the professor said as he stepped from behind the podium. "You are in Asian History 301 and I am Professor Phou. This is the first course I have ever taught, so we will both be learning this semester."

A large map of Southeast Asia hung to the left of the podium, and Professor Phou stepped behind it to find the prop that he hoped could help lend the gathering a little more intimacy. He pulled out a folding chair, opened it in front of the map, and took a seat directly facing the class, then continued with the course introduction.

"The standard way to teach Asian History is to ask students to memorize three or four thousand years' worth of Chinese dynasties and emperors, but I think that's boring."

The class laughed softly at the frank description. Asian History 301 was a seemingly unnecessary requirement for a number of degrees, and it had a reputation for being both dull and difficult.

"Let's put ancient China aside and just talk about something that illustrates why we should learn a thing or two about Asian history," Professor Phou said. "Since the war in Vietnam is something you students have grown up with, we are going to begin there and work our way back to China.

"Oh, and for those who signed up to memorize dynasties of China, don't worry; there will be twenty or thirty birthdays of Chinese emperors you will need to know for the final exam," he said with a smile.

The students snickered a bit more.

"The Vietnam War. What a mess, huh? Let's talk openly today about that war and how it all came to be. You guys in the back . . . come down here near the front so we can talk," he said, beckoning a few boys down from the upper rows of the theater.

They picked up their book-laden backpacks and moved down to seats closer to the stage as Professor Phou continued.

"So what kind of questions do you guys feel have never been answered by the news media? What do you want to know about America's longest war?"

A few uncomfortable seconds of silence passed, then a girl with long, straight brown hair and faded bellbottom jeans raised her hand from the front row. The professor pointed at her with a nod.

"It seemed like you were speaking about our arms race with the Soviet Union earlier," she said. "How did we go from trying to defend Europe to a war in Southeast Asia? I've never understood how we got to Vietnam in the first place."

"Good question," Professor Phou replied. "The answer takes us back to nineteen forty-five. At the end of World War II, the United States pressed all the countries of the world to give up their colonies. Germany of course gave up her colonies in Africa, the US gave up the Philippines, India and Pakistan got their independence from the United Kingdom, and so forth.

"President De Gaulle of France argued that the French had been humiliated in the war and thus should be able to retain their colonies. The French made it clear that if the US forced them to give up Indochina, which was the colony made up of Vietnam, Laos, and Cambodia, they would not be helpful to US interests in Europe.

"The United States was more worried about losing Germany to the Soviets than granting independence to a few little countries in Asia, so the Americans gave in and France retained its colony of Indochina. Of course, many of the people of that region did not appreciate this. A group known as the Viet Minh, which had been fighting the Japanese during World War II, revolted against French rule. They were led by Ho Chi Minh, of whom I'm sure all of you have heard. The United States was allied to France, and gave them support in their war against the Viet Minh."

"That doesn't make sense," said one of the boys who had moved from the back of the class. "If we didn't really want the French to keep the colony in the first place, why did we support them in a war for it?"

"Ahh, you are touching on the basis of most of the wars that have taken place over the last thirty years," Professor Phou said. "And that is what I was speaking of when reading from my book. Over the last three decades, what we now call the Cold War has essentially divided the world into two separate ideologies. When World War II ended, the United States and the Soviet Union began fighting an ideological war, and Ho Chi

Minh believed in the communist ideology. The US could not condone a communist leader in Indochina, so they had to help the French.

"Unfortunately, the French did not fight the war strategically well, and when they lost nearly ten thousand of their soldiers at a battle called Dien Bien Phou, the colony was surrendered to the Viet Minh."

Professor Phou pointed out Dien Bien Phou on the map.

"Here is Dien Bien Phou . . . it's in a very mountainous and beautiful part of Vietnam," he nonchalantly added. "As I was saying, the NATO countries, the Australians, the Koreans, and the Japanese all worried that the French surrender was going to be seen as a loss in the ideological war of communist dictatorships versus western-style democracies. Specifically, they worried that every country in Asia would be threatened by communist revolution. Rather than cede the entire former colony to communism, the United States and France pushed for a division of the colony based on borders that existed before the French took over. Thus, Indochina was divided into four separate countries: Cambodia in the southwest, Laos in the northwest, and a North and a South Vietnam in the east."

Professor Phou pointed out each country as he spoke. The brand-new map clearly showed four separate countries in bright colors, and it occurred to the professor that a correct map would now show Vietnam as one nation. The cartographers apparently had not noticed the Fall of Saigon.

"It was accepted by all parties that Cambodia and Laos would govern themselves," the Professor continued, "and the two Vietnams would come together or stay separate depending on how the people of the north and south voted in a referendum to be held in July, nineteen fifty-six. In the interim before the election, the United States and France put a member of the former Vietnamese royal family, a vowed anti-communist named Ngo Dinh Diem, in the presidency of South Vietnam. Immediately, Diem could see that he would lose an election to Ho Chi Minh, so before the election took place he declared South Vietnam an independent country known as the Republic of Vietnam. Virtually everyone in the world other than Diem referred to it as South Vietnam. The United States had to either back him or back the communist Ho Chi Minh, who was getting aid from the Soviet Union. As we all know, America's only choice was to back the non-communist."

"But everything we are talking about happened while President Eisenhower was in office," a boy interrupted. "Vietnam was Lyndon Johnson and Richard Nixon's war."

Professor Phou could tell by the boy's voice that he had strong feelings about the war. Many in the audience had family members who had served in the war, and he knew he had to tread lightly on the subject.

"Well, we are talking about policies that led to the war, and many of those policies were put in place by Truman, Eisenhower, and President Kennedy, even though most of the war was fought during the Johnson and Nixon Administrations," Professor Phou replied. "When John Kennedy took office in nineteen sixty, the United States had about a thousand advisors supporting South Vietnam's forces. At the time of his death, when Lyndon Johnson took over, there were over sixteen thousand American troops in South Vietnam and more committed for nineteen sixty-four. There were a hundred thousand troops in South Vietnam by nineteen sixty-five, but the war had really started for the United States while Kennedy was president."

A lanky boy with curly red hair raised his hand and the professor stepped forward and pointed to him.

"You mentioned Laos as the focus of your book," he said. "Why Laos, when we call it the Vietnam War?"

"Another good question," Professor Phou said. "The answer has to do with the geography of Vietnam, Laos, and Cambodia. The Soviet Union and China were supplying North Vietnam, through Haiphong Harbor near Hanoi, with the weapons it used to fight the United States. The ground war was taking place in South Vietnam, so the material had to be carried a thousand miles south from the ships to the battlefield."

The professor stepped back to the map and pointed to the Vietnamese coast.

"You can see that Vietnam is a thin strip of land that follows the coast of the South China Sea and that the coastline bulges to the east," he said, tracing the curve of the coastline. "Following the coast with supplies meant taking a much longer route south, and it also meant American planes on aircraft carriers could more easily attack the supply routes. The more direct route, and the one farther from the American Navy, went almost straight south from Hanoi. You have all heard of this supply line referred to as the Ho Chi Minh Trail. The majority of the Trail ran down the west side of the Annamite Mountains, which placed it in Laos. Almost one hundred percent of the munitions used against American and South Vietnamese troops passed through the mountains of Laos, and much of the war revolved around stopping the flow of those supplies. The end result was that more bombs were dropped on Laos than in all of World War II."

"Did you serve in Vietnam, Professor Phou?" the girl in the front row asked.

The professor paused for a moment and glanced back at the map, then replied. "Yes, I served in the war, but not in a manner most Americans are familiar with."

1

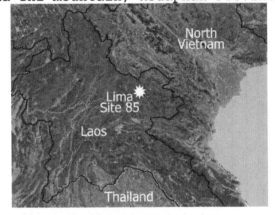

Major Monte Ferris of the 27th Combat Engineer Battalion hated helicopters.

He also hated flying over enemy territory.

Above all else, he hated thunderstorms, yet he was watching hail pummel the canopy of a Bell UH-1 Huey, in Northeast Laos, less than a hundred-fifty miles from downtown Hanoi, the enemy's capital.

Like it or not, Monte was enduring all three.

The engineer's aversion to flying in choppers had led him to ask one of the mechanics to rearrange the seats so he could see out the front canopy, which left him with little legroom, but a great view of the dark sheets of rain and hail battering the aircraft. Monte clenched one of the seat supports like a vise with his right hand, and twisted against the seatbelt to glance back at Kyle Dramis, who was calmly comparing a map to an aerial photo. How Dramis could read and keep from puking in the deafening roller coaster was a mystery.

A white flash lit up the leaden sky as Monte leaned forward to the young pilot, "Listen, is it really safe to fly this machine in this storm?"

Monte's question was rhetorical and easily understood as it was intended: A complaint.

The young Air America pilot, wearing Levi jeans and a red-and-tan Hobie Surfboards t-shirt, clenched the stick between his knees and adjusted an unknown knob on the console. The copilot pointed at an instrument that simply read CLIMB with a vertically running selection of numbers.

The pilot turned to Monte, "No, sir, it's not. But it beats exposing ourselves to 12.7 millimeter machine-gun fire. This bird is unarmored, sir." The pilot pointed to some dark figure out the copilot's window and said something into the radio, then turned back to Monte. "I flew a team in here last month and got shot at twice. Trust me, sir, if you don't like this ride, you'd really hate the roller coaster I'd put us on when I see the green tracers of a 12.7 millimeter anti-aircraft gun coming our way."

Monte leaned back and took a deep breath. They had tried to reach their destination for a few days, attempting the short airstrip in a souped-up Pilatus Porter, but the winds had been erratic and the pilot had bowed out. Apparently, the airstrip at Lima Site

85 was so short a plane could only take off under precise conditions. He and Kyle had waited, hoping for better weather but finally went with the helicopter option despite Monte's opposition.

"What do you have against helicopters anyway, Monte?" Kyle yelled from the back. He set down the map and began loading a third magazine for his M16. "I thought all you West Point grads feared nothin'."

"I dunno. Could be that they are so engine-dependent and have the glide ratio of a cinderblock. Or maybe it's because I got shot down in one last year near Pleiku."

"Hey, man, that glass sounds half full. You lived through it, right?"

"Sure, it's half full for me, but totally empty for the other three guys." Monte stared through the Plexiglas canopy. "I've hated these damn things ever since."

Kyle reached forward and patted the man's shoulder, now understanding just how serious the fear really was. "Sorry, mate. We'll be all right. This guy is probably the best pilot Air America has."

The nervous major nodded and gave a thumbs-up over his shoulder to say all was well. Though he had heard that most of the US Air Force brass at Udorn Air Force Base didn't like Kyle, Monte found him a breath of fresh air. He was a "crazy spook," as Colonel Holmes had complained, but how could you not be a little nuts as a CIA paramilitary agent who was only sent to the hottest and most secretive war zones in the world? If anything ever happened to Kyle, the US government would deny they'd ever heard of him. Perhaps it was that crazy, living-on-the-edge lifestyle that made Kyle quirky, or perhaps you had to be nuts in the first place to take the job. Either way, Kyle was friendly to Monte and seemed to deeply care for the tribesmen he was training to fight. Monte trusted him with his life.

"Sir, I'm pretty sure we are about to pop out of this squall," the pilot yelled back at Monte. "If we don't, we'll be turning back."

Within seconds, the gray clouds turned white, and then suddenly they were flying in smooth air, out of the mist. A broken ceiling of dense, alabaster billows hung above them, and a verdant sea of jungle covered the rugged hills below. The terrain was as rugged as anyone could dream up. Limestone peaks, separated by deep gorges, poked menacingly to the sky. Three layers of jungle canopy hid overhangs and caves in the rock that were incredibly effective bases for the enemy soldiers.

A few open fields stood out starkly in the continuous carpet of trees. Monte had been told the clearings were near the mountainside villages of the Hmong— the tribe working with the Americans to stop the North Vietnamese Army (NVA). He also knew that other than the Hmong, the communist Pathet Lao, who fought alongside the NVA against the Americans, were the only people who lived in this area.

"It's not all enemy territory, Major," Kyle yelled from the back seat. "The NVA and Pathet Lao stick to the valleys and canyons, but our friends the Hmong are on the ridges and summits. They own the high ground, and the Pathet Lao generally won't challenge them for it. If we crash, and you can get to a high point, a friend will likely find you."

Monte tried to spot an actual village on one of the open ridges, but his attention was taken by the limestone peak out the front canopy. It was the dominant mountain as far as the eye could see, slicing into the air like a giant axe blade. Gray stone cliffs, broken by occasional vegetation clinging to its vertical walls, dropped perhaps three thousand feet to steep slopes of jungle. Like ephemeral ghosts, wisps of water vapor rose from the big trees in the valley below, floating up along the face of the huge peak. The spine of the ridge between the north and south faces was broken in places, almost giving it the appearance of a serrated blade. The beauty of the peak was overwhelming, but there was also a sense of foreboding. Compared to the smaller karst hills, this mountain looked supernatural.

"That's Phou Pha Thi, Major," the pilot said. "The Hmong revere the place, but the Lao say it's haunted. Our LZ and the TACAN are on the ridge near the summit, just above that biggest cliff on the west face. Lima Site 85 airstrip is that cleared area lower on the mountain."

TACAN. Tactical Air Navigation, Monte translated to himself. These radio beacons were often all a pilot had to figure out where he was during a blinding monsoon. The TACANS had greatly helped the Air Force and Navy pilots, but the new equipment was going to be even better.

The "airstrip," if one squinted and could thus call it that, ran along a ridge for a couple hundred yards. Enormous trees bookended the runway, and a few clearings near one end showed the Hmong were eking out an existence below the peak. Seeing how short the runway was, not to mention that it did not look to be level or smooth, Monte was suddenly thankful they had gone with the helicopter option.

The young pilot turned the chopper to the west, then banked hard to the right and flew straight at the highest point of Phou Pha Thi. The Huey flew over the summit in a banking turn to the right. Monte looked out the right side window and saw a couple of children carrying AK-47s. They wore charcoal gray jackets and pants, with bright red sashes around their waists, and were waving to the helicopter from the rust-colored mud of the landing site. A van-sized, deep-green fuel tank sat on one side of the clearing; a small white flag strung to a shaft of thin bamboo fluttered in the breeze next to the fuel tank. A couple of huts huddled on one edge of the clearing; the other held the camouflaged steel shipping containers the army was so fond of. The hillside then dropped away in a series of cliffs and steep slopes that ran perhaps two thousand feet into the valley below.

The pilot turned the helicopter so it faced the spine of the mountain, then slowly brought it down to the muddy landing zone. Before the skids had touched the ground, one of the children was running up to the ship while the other uncoiled a hose from the fuel tank. It was at that moment that Monte realized they were not kids at all, but at under five feet tall, grown men. He now understood why all the Air America pilots and CIA operatives referred to the Hmong as "the little guys."

"Welcome to Phou Pha Thi, Monte," Kyle said as they both released the seat belts. "You may want this."

The paramilitary man handed him a weathered M1

rifle. Monte took the gun as one of the young Hmong soldiers, beaming a toothy smile that could not be an act, opened the side door. As Monte stepped from the helicopter and onto the mud and broken limestone, the man grabbed his left hand and shook it in an exaggerated motion.

"Allo, allo," he said through his smile.

"This is Mr. Bao," Kyle said. "We taught him the Western greeting of shaking hands, and as you can see he really likes it. He also only knows one word of English, which he enjoys putting to use. That's his son, Lek, getting the fuel pumping."

Lek turned and smiled but continued to uncoil the fuel hose.

The two pilots walked to the small hooch where a third man was stirring a pot over an open fire.

"I don't know him, but you can be sure he's related to Bao in some way," Kyle said.

"Lek doesn't look any younger than Bao . . . and Bao looks like he's twenty-five."

"Yeah, that's the norm up here. If these guys don't look old enough to have fallen off a charm bracelet, they look young. It must be the clean mountain living. The trail up the ridge is in front of the chopper."

Bao ran around the helicopter and onto the trail, his AK-47 slung across his back. The men walked across the red mud of the landing zone and onto a steeper bit of ridge. Glancing back, Monte realized the helicopter had landed on one of the few level places on the mountain. This was very rugged terrain.

They worked their way up a trail of ledges and broken cliffs, sometimes pulling on sharp, mud-covered spikes of limestone to get over sections of cliff. Monte heaved for oxygen in the thin air, but Bao was unfazed, running up the steep trail and then back to get the two men. Scrubby trees and bamboo had been cleared from the auburn-colored path, and a thick black cable ran over the limestone and mud. Monte understood the boxes at the landing zone held the generators for the TACAN radio transponder, and power to the machine had been strung up the ridge. After a few hundred yards of scrambling they reached a clearing. The TACAN, which looked like a camou-flaged box crowned with a round top hat, sat near the middle of the clearing. The green camo would have blended nicely with the verdant jungle but stood out against the light-gray limestone.

The jagged ridge of Phou Pha Thi continued beyond them, gaining and losing ground until reaching what appeared to be a high point perhaps a quarter mile away. The clearing was effectively the only area with enough level terrain on the entire mountain to handle what the military was planning. The mountain fell steeply to the east but on the west it was a complete cliff, dropping perhaps half a mile. To say the least, it was an airy location for a military installation.

"It's beautiful, Kyle. You didn't tell me it would be so awe-inspiring. This place would be a national park if it were back in the States."

"Yeah, well, when I introduced Elizabeth Billington to my dad the night of the prom, he pulled me aside, and said, 'Son, there is danger in beauty.' I wish I'd listened. She broke my heart."

Monte snickered. "Just how many Pathet Lao and NVA

soldiers do we think are in the valleys around this mountain?"

"The Hmong are adamant that there aren't that many, just the odd patrol from time to time. But the North Vietnamese border is only about twenty-five klicks to the north." Kyle pointed along the ridge. "The Laotian town of Sam Neua is maybe thirty-five klicks to the east, over there, and we're pretty sure the Pathet Lao base of operations is in the caves in that area. Beyond that, and a little to the north"—Kyle turned and pointed almost due east—" it's about fifty klicks to the border, and two hundred-forty to Long Bien Bridge in downtown Hanoi."

Monte recognized he was standing on a small island in an ocean of potential unfriendlies. He also realized how perfectly positioned and shaped Phou Pha Thi was for this mission. The radar unit the Air Force was designing worked through line of sight. The height of the peak added range, so it would no doubt reach well beyond the city of Hanoi, perhaps even to Haiphong Harbor.

"We'll need more space than we have here," he said. "That's gonna take blasting this rock into a platform. The North Vietnamese may notice all the hubbub."

"I'm sure they will, but they won't be able to form an attack out here for some time, and the attack they do put together will have to be big. That village down there is Hmong, and they don't like the North Vietnamese. The Hmong won't tolerate the NVA on their sacred mountain, and even the most disciplined communist troops won't want to fight their way up this ridge."

Monte looked down the huge west face of the

mountain and nodded. Operation Heavy Green was an outlandish idea that could change the direction of the war, and it was going to work.

Minutes later they were back in the Huey, airborne, and waving goodbye to Bao and Lek.

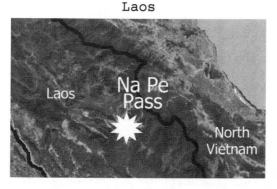

Young Lim Phou peered up through the hole in the canopy to look for the small American plane. He had heard the hum of the engine for perhaps ten minutes, but this was the only gap in the jungle that could allow a view of the sky. With only a few seconds of looking, he couldn't see the aircraft, but that didn't really matter. Experience told him that there was no real danger until the small airplane fired a smoke rocket. When that happened, the hundreds of people walking on the Trail would have to take cover and get as far from the smoke as possible.

Lim stepped off the muddy road and leaned against a rotting log to lift the weight of the rice sack from his shoulders. Like most members of the Hmong tribe, he was less than five feet tall, but his powerful frame could carry a big load. The North Vietnamese soldiers were well aware of the strength of the mountain people, and they had loaded him with a larger bag of rice than most porters could carry. They had also put two rocket propelled grenades (RPGs) on top of that bag, and as the bulk of the load lifted from Lim's shoulders, the grenades pressed against the back of his head. It wasn't comfortable, but for a couple of minutes the weight of the rice would be on the tree and the straps would no longer dig into his skin.

Lim had been looking for just such a place to rest for the last kilometer or so, but logs were hard to come by on the Truang Son, what the Americans called The Ho Chi Minh Trail. A solid teak log could be sawn into planks that could elevate a truck through a muddy bog, or serve as a bridge on a stream crossing. Usually, the maintenance crews only took foliage from a 100 meters or more away from the main road, but this tree had clearly been downed by an American bomb and could thus be used.

Lim took in a deep breath and glanced to his left along the trunk of the fallen tree, then spotted the reason the log had not been cut into planks. The tail end of a 120-kilogram bomb, dark green and perhaps a meter long, protruded from the mud next to the log. As was often the case, the bomb hadn't gone off on impact, but the tree could not be removed until a disposal team inspected and removed the unexploded ordinance. Within a day or so the bomb would be disassembled, its parts sent south for use in the war, and the tree would be sliced into useful pieces. For now, it made a good bench to rest upon and watch the Ho Chi Minh Trail in action.

Despite his feelings about working for the North Vietnamese cause, Lim always marveled at the work done by the cadres of the NVA's 559th Transportation Group. The network of paths and roads that wound its way south from North Vietnam to the battle zones of South Vietnam were constantly being rebuilt and rerouted to make transportation as easy and obscure as possible. The crater created by the blast that had felled the tree had already been filled in by men and women with shovels, while overhead, the hole in the jungle canopy, where the tree's crown had been, was being repaired with a thatch of leaf-covered branches. Some areas of the Trail actually passed through miles of imitation tree canopy, all woven together to hide the road from American bombers and spotter planes.

The NVA knew the Americans could tell the foliage was dead by its temperature, so crews of men and women worked in the trees overhead to constantly replace the thatch. Meanwhile, the ruts and craters in the road were being mended for trucks, bicycles, elephants, water buffalo, and men, women, and children. The procession of goods ran all day and night, everyday of the year, ferrying hundreds of tons per month of Soviet and Chinese-made war materiel to the battlefields in the South.

"You there, miao," said a stern voice. It was a Northern Vietnamese dialect, but Lim clearly understood the soldier. "Since when do porters for the Peoples Army get to sit whenever they want? That equipment is needed by our comrades in the South."

"I'm only taking the weight off my neck for a short time," Lim replied in perfect Vietnamese. "It allows me to walk that much faster and deliver the equipment sooner."

The young soldier, a private, raised his eyebrows at the answer. He glanced back at his fellow soldiers passing by, then walked to the log, set down his AK-47 rifle and RPG launcher, and leaned his canvas backpack against the log.

Lim looked down to a familiar tickling sensation on his foot. Like most porters on the Ho Chi Minh Trail, he wore sandals made from old truck tires. The open toes allowed feet to dry faster, but also left one exposed to leeches, centipedes, and snakes. Lim could see a tiger leech, with its black-and-orange stripes, inching its way across the arch of his foot. He pulled a small pouch of wet tobacco from his pocket, lifted his foot, and squeezed the liquid on the creature. It instantly coiled and dropped into the mud.

"Your people live in these mountains, right?" the soldier asked, making it clear he could see that Lim was Hmong. "I hear the miao hate not being high on the mountains."

Lim bristled slightly at the insulting, racist term miao, but held back an equivalent insult. Everyone was supposed to be equal in the eyes of the communist Peoples Republic of Vietnam, but that wasn't reality for members of the minority tribes. The Vietnamese, or Kihn as they were sometimes called, enjoyed a favorable position in the Army. The accepted inequality ran deepest for the Hmong as many of the mountain tribe did not recognize the supremacy of the Vietnamese. Lim didn't care for them much himself, and understood why many clans of the Hmong had joined forces with the Americans. Each time he heard the term miao, which stemmed from the Chinese word for barbarian, Lim questioned his future in Vietnam.

"Yes, the Hmong live in the mountains to the west," Lim replied. "But on the mountains and not in these soggy valleys. We refer to places like this as the Land of the Leeches."

"A fitting name," the soldier replied as he flicked a finger at a leech high on his leg. It didn't budge, so Lim reached over with his tobacco pouch and squeezed a bit more liquid.

"Thank you," the soldier replied. "I didn't realize—"

His words were cut off by the high-pitched hiss of a phosphorous rocket fired from the circling plane. They heard the distant whistles soldiers used to warn everyone along the trail of an attack, and Lim and the NVA soldier slid the heavy loads from their shoulders. Both men climbed to the opposite side of log from which the rocket had been fired, and waited for the blast.

"We will barely hear the plane before the bomb drops," Lim said to the terrified soldier. "The aircraft will be moving too fast to hear it coming. Keep your mouth open so the blast doesn't destroy your ears."

Within seconds they heard the rapid-fire thumping of an anti-aircraft machine gun from the ridge above. The gunner had not shot at the slow-moving spotter plane, probably because he didn't want to tell the American pilot he was over the Trail, but possibly because he just wanted the juicier jet target. There was a rumor among the porters on the Trail that any gunner who shot down an American bomber was given an immediate field promotion.

The sound went from barely audible to a painful scream in less than a second as the American jet raced overhead. Lim closed his eyes and opened his mouth, waiting an eternity for the bomb to detonate. After a couple seconds he felt the ground shake as the shock-wave rolled through the wet soil. Suddenly the air pressed in on his body, and then was gone in a deafening roar. Almost as quickly, all was silent, and he gasped for air that wasn't there. Leaves and branches fell from above, and Lim felt the sudden temperature increase on his skin. A slight breeze blew back on the two men as the atmosphere returned to the blast zone, and they could again hear the machine-gun firing.

"Stay down," Lim said to the visibly panicked soldier. "They may drop another one."

A few more seconds passed and the machine gun quit firing, but Lim and the soldier stayed on the ground. After perhaps a minute, the familiar whistles screeched in one long blow, indicating the planes had moved on. The two men stood and scraped mud and leaves from their chest as their comrades made their way back onto the road.

The bomb had fallen 200 meters to the west, completely missing everyone on the Ho Chi Minh Trail. Lim slid the straps of the rice bag over his shoulder and nodded at the good fortune that had just fallen on him and the terrified soldier. Usually someone died. For better or for worse, their supplies would get that much closer to the war in the South.

2

September 12, 1967, 2330 hours,
(5 months later)
4 kilometers north of Dak To, Kontum Province, Central Highlands, Republic of Vietnam

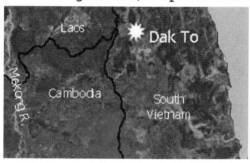

With the patter of raindrops no longer concealing sound, Li Tuan knew he had to move with extreme care. One broken twig could be enough to give away his team's position, and with that all three of them would likely die. The constant sound of hissing insects in the trees above helped to cover the noise of any rustling leaves, but crickets were unreliable. At seemingly random moments they went silent, often exactly when you broke a branch or cocked a trigger.

Tuan felt his elbows sink into the cold mud as he slid off a rotting log. The wet soil squeezed through a hole in his left sleeve as he leaned heavily to that side and looked back to his partners, Bam Sang and Dang Linh. The axle grease they had smeared on each other's faces hid their fair skin, and with the dark uniforms and their jet-black hair, the three Viet Cong blended into the dark night.

As planned, Sang slid over the fallen tree as well, while Linh waited on the backside of the log with his AK-47 aimed forward and just right of his partners. Tuan pushed his RPG launcher through the ferns and slithered silently toward a second, much larger log.

The Viet Cong, or National Liberation Front as they referred to themselves, had been the resistance in South Vietnam since just after the 1956 elections were cancelled. Tuan and his brothers-in-arms saw themselves as freedom fighters intent on ridding Vietnam of the influence of imperial America. As a child, Tuan had watched his father pay a tax to the French Magistrate after each harvest. It was money that went straight back to Imperial France. Under Ho Chi the Vietnamese people would decide their own fate. Together with the NVA, Tuan and his comrades were ready to give their lives so Vietnam could be independent and not subject to the whims of the West.

Cold water showered down on the soldier as he bumped each fern, and the pungent odor of decaying leaves filled his nose. The three men had scouted the area just five days before, and they knew the Americans had camped twice a mere 80 meters beyond the dead tree. A reconnaissance team had followed an American platoon from the base at Dak To earlier in the evening, and then watched them begin to settle in at this location.

Tuan and his partners were nearly certain the Americans had taken up defensive positions in the same spot they had been earlier in the week, and the Viet Cong soldiers knew exactly where those bunkers and foxholes were. The laziness of not digging new bunkers would cost the Americans tonight.

Tuan was considered an excellent shot with the B-40 rocket launcher, so much so that his commander had presented him with a brand new Soviet made RPG-2. The RPG was similar to the Vietnamese-made B-40, but the Soviet version was a little heavier, and felt more solid in Tuan's hands. The B-40 tube had been easy to run with, but fragile and thinner, and after just one launch it was easy to get burned by the hot metal. Tuan had once broken the trigger on one as well. The solid construction of the Soviet model inspired confidence that the same failure would not happen again. There was no need to get closer with the new weapon, and Tuan was happy for that. Any nearer and they would likely be inside the American perimeter and thus have to deal with the Claymore mine trip wires. In fact, the other side of the log they lay behind was a likely place for a mine.

Tuan leaned his head against the log and watched Sang's silhouette inch closer. He slid the wet sleeve of his shirt up and pulled a leech, thick with blood, from just above his wrist. Crawling on the forest floor for two hours during the rainy season made leech bites more common than mosquito bites. Tuan crushed the wriggling worm, then set it down a full arm's length away. He'd likely have a small infection where he'd been bitten, but it wouldn't itch like the mosquito bites. The leeches' bite didn't carry malaria. Of the two, he preferred the leeches.

Sang crawled to Tuan's feet and reached behind his head to pull the rocket-propelled grenade off his pack. Tuan turned the tube's firing end to Sang and held the weapon steady as Sang wrapped his fingers around the fins, folding them flat against the rocket's shell, and pushed the end of the projectile into the tube. Both men preferred to preload the weapon, but crawling through the jungle could inadvertently cock it and set it off, so they'd decided to arm it when they reached their firing location.

As predicted, the insects had gone silent right when the men needed the background noise the most. Tuan continued to hold the launcher steady as Sang slowly, and with almost no sound, finished twisting the rocket and grenade into the tube. Once fully inserted, the RPG was ready to fire.

Tuan rolled onto his stomach and ran the next few seconds through his mind. The seasoned soldier knew exactly what to do. He took in a deep breath and steadied the RPG, flipped up the range finders on the launching tube, pushed up onto one knee, keeping his head low, and lifted the weapon onto his shoulder. Tuan brushed some mud away from the hammer with his thumb, cocked it, and looked through the sight. It was too dark to actually make out the bunkers that lay just 80 meters away and left of the largest tree, but Tuan knew they were there. He took another small breath and, simultaneously as he squeezed the trigger, closed his eyes. This is where Tuan believed he excelled with the RPG. Many men closed their eyes and twitched a bit, but Tuan somehow managed to always keep the rocket aimed at the target even with his eyes closed. This skill kept him alive. The rocket's flames were bright, so keeping his eyes closed allowed him to retain his night vision and thus have a chance of escaping.

Tuan squeezed his right hand and the rocket instantly made a hissing sound as sparks and flame spewed from the back of the tube. The grenade shot out of the launcher, singeing the soldier's forehead as it raced over the ferns and stubby palms. Tuan and Sang jumped to their feet, spun, and stepped right as Linh opened up to the left with his AK-47. The grenade exploded on impact less than a second after launching, but Tuan and Sang were already hurdling over the first log when they saw the jungle light up with the blast. Linh fired for perhaps half a second more before turning and running with his partners. With memory of the lit forest in their minds, the three men ran as the Americans opened up on their original position. They could hear the chatter of a dozen M16s and a series of Claymore mines explode as they dropped into a stream drainage.

The three Viet Cong ran upstream for a couple hundred meters and then paused to catch their breath. The M16s had stopped firing and Tuan could hear the American soldiers' faint yells. The soldiers knew it was unlikely the American officers would give chase during the night as they didn't know the terrain well. Instead, the Americans would reform the defensive perimeter and attempt to remove their wounded by helicopter.

"You hit it, Tuan," Linh said through a whispering gasp. "I saw the rocket go into a bunker and I saw a man fly through the air from outside the bunker when it exploded."

Tuan nodded and pointed up the far side of the embankment. The mission was a success, and his team would live to fight another night.

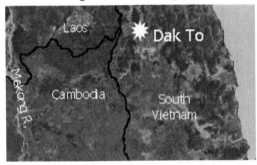

The rain had stopped, but it would soon begin again. First Lieutenant John Lilygren squatted between the roots of a giant mahogany and focused his eyes on the darkness of the black mud. The sweet, earthy smell of rotting leaves filled his nostrils, while a few inches away the drips of water falling from one leaf of an elephant ear palm to another set a rhythm above the din of millions of insects. Tree frogs chirped amid the hiss of the cicadas, both sounds you only heard in the rainy season, while miles away there was a low rumble of thunder. Or was it a bomb? One was as likely as the other, and neither was worth a second thought.

What was important now was taking care of his

33

men, and that meant focusing on the nearby jungle. Staring into the dark earth helped his eyes gain just a bit more night vision, and tuning his ears to the insects might alert him to a slight change near the platoon's perimeter. The bugs often went silent when someone moved under them, and that change in sound could be the difference between life and death.

The cold nights of the rainy season were the most difficult of the year. The air temperature might be 68°, but when you're soaked to the bone and unable to move for ten hours, it feels cold. The men were less vigilant when they were cold, and thus more likely to make a mistake. The nights of the monsoon also seemed to be the most likely for an ambush, perhaps due to a better flow of material from North Vietnam. The Viet Cong loved to move around on rainy nights.

John stared into the mud and remembered the words his CO said the day before: "You can't save all of them, John. It's a war," he'd stated, "and a damn bloody one at that. The other guys are trying just as hard as we are, and they are just as smart. It's inevitable that some of these boys are gonna die."

Earlier in the week he'd lost one of the brightest kids in the platoon. Like John, Private Mark Anderson's Scandinavian heritage had given him the blond hair and blue eyes of a Swedish movie star, and the sturdy six-foot frame of a complete athlete. Intelligent and hard-working, Anderson had had a lot of promise, but whatever might have been was taken away in a burst of AK-47 fire. Private Anderson was the twenty-fourth soldier to die under his command during his three years in Vietnam, and no matter what the CO said, John didn't want to lose another.

The location they'd been forced to use for a bivouac added to the stress brought on by the rain and cold. They'd used this same position just a few days before, and it was likely the VC knew about it. He hated sleeping in the same place twice, but orders were orders and Major Willis wanted 3rd Platoon here, perhaps because he knew extraction of wounded was possible from the nearby clearing. That was reverse logic to John, as bivying in the same place twice made it that much more likely they'd have casualties. Nevertheless, orders were orders, and they were here for the next six hours. John stood and walked to the first bunker, noting a poncho was slung over the logs that served as the bunker's roof.

"Gulley, Judge, where'd you two get the extra poncho?" John whispered from the entrance of the bunker.

"Hi, sir," Private Gulley replied.

Corporal Michael Gulley was from Los Angeles, and not the good part. He was sixteen years old in the summer of 1965 and had actually watched the traffic stop that led to the riots in Watts. To hear him tell it, there was no question the Los Angeles County Police Department hadn't read the Civil Rights Act, and a riot was long overdue. Gulley had never seen a forest before he arrived in Vietnam, and the natural beauty of the country often made him comment aloud, "This place is another world."

He was a good soldier and had the respect of his peers. With the intensity of combat the 3rd Platoon saw on a weekly basis, any racial bias against him that might have existed with the other soldiers took a back seat to his good decisions in battle. John had no doubt Gulley would be squad leader within a month or two, and perhaps a sergeant before he rotated home. The stability and successes that came with being a good soldier would likely be a positive thing for Michael Gulley, if he lived through the war.

"When the duster came in for Gomez, the gunner tossed a duffel out with some supplies. This was in the bag. The poncho has two holes and a little blood on it, but still helps with the rain," Gulley replied.

John nodded.

"Sir, earlier today I heard Sergeant Hayden say you once chased an NVA soldier for four days after he fired on you. That true?" Judge asked.

Private Aaron Judge was straight off a cattle ranch outside Broadus, Montana, and he'd never been more than a hundred miles from home before shipping out for basic training. Judge should have been in college somewhere as he was the most inquisitive kid in the platoon. Once he'd found out that John had spent much of his youth in Thailand, the questions had been constant. That was fine with John; he liked talking about life in Asia beyond the war. Aaron Judge had never seen a black man before he joined the Army and Michael Gulley had never met a cowboy, but the two had become best friends instantly.

"Yeah, I've heard that one before," John smirked. "You boys know Sergeant Hayden likes to exaggerate."

"He said you finally got the guy in Cambodia or something," Judge said, ignoring the brush off.

"Uh-huh." John hated this subject.

"Well, what's the truth, then?" Gulley asked.

"The truth is I only chased the guy for two days. When I realized I was halfway across Cambodia, I thought it prudent to run back to the base. By the way, Judge, I want you to remember that a man should never let the truth get in the way of a good story. Gulley already knows that."

"We can't believe you're calling it quits after only two years in-country. One might think you don't like this or something," Judge said, poking the barrel of his M16 into the underside of the bloated poncho. As he did the water spilled over the side of the log and ran down the bunker's mud wall.

"It's actually three years in-country, just two in this province," John whispered through a smile. "I'm in the army for another sixteen months, Judge. I just need a break from you."

"No chance, sir. . . . Major Willis says I'm to watch your every move for the rest of my deployment. . . . I'll just be hiding in the shadows."

"Well, I won't sleep well tonight with those thoughts," John replied.

Both men in the bunker watched the happy expression slide off the lieutenant's face. John leaned down and looked out the slit in the bunker toward the far clearing. The two young soldiers knew to be quiet and let the experienced man focus.

"Boys, it just went silent near our perimeter," John said. "The sudden silence might mean someone is out there. Stay focused. I'm gonna check on the other guys. Seriously, stay alert. I'll be back in a minute."

John turned and stepped away from the bunker

as the hiss of a rocket-propelled grenade overwhelmed the natural sounds of the forest. There was a white flash and he was airborne. As he slammed into the mud about ten feet from the bunker, John realized he had just spoken the last words Michael Gulley and Aaron Judge ever heard.

September 12, 1967, 2330 hours,
(same day)
CIA Lima Site 20, Alternate, North Central Laos

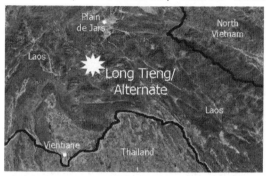

Kyle Dramis grabbed the half-full glass of lao-Lao off the bamboo table and downed it in one swallow. This batch of the local liquor, made by distilling rice and honey, had been given to him that day by Daeng, the Hmong woman who cleaned the hooch every morning. Each week she made two batches of lao-Lao; one for her family and her brother and sister's families, and one for Mr. Kyle. She brought Mr. Kyle a new bottle each morning, and he went through a bottle every night. If she brought two, he went most of the way through two and then was not up with the Hmong men the next morning, so she only brought one.

For his part, Kyle had tried a number of versions of lao-Lao over the previous five years, but it was Daeng's he liked best. He found that her recipe, which called for the poison-seething head of a centipede (or two), numbed his gut. No centipede, no numbness, and living without the constant pain in his bowels was the main reason he drank lao-Lao. Or that's what he told himself.

Kyle took a deep breath, grabbed the bottle, and droplessly poured another glass to just below the rim. He adjusted the flame on the kerosene lamp so it put out less smoke, and then turned on the radio. He found comfort by leaning back on two chrome legs of his Sears and Roebuck office chair until he was against the wall of the hooch . . . which is what he considered controlling one's liquor: You could pour a glass and not immediately drink from it.

Kyle had been assigned to Alternate for four years, which was commonly referred to as Lima Site 20A or "Long Tieng" by the other paramilitary guys stationed throughout Laos. It also went by the name "Alternate," as if it were an alternate landing strip. The runway had never been an alternate, but its designation as such was just one part of the elaborate plan to throw off the press corps. The CIA thought that if they referred to the base "Alternate," it would look less compelling to nosey reporters and thus they wouldn't stumble onto the Agency's secret. However, the ruse wasn't really necessary, as most of the press corps was perfectly happy hanging out in Saigon and only looking at what they thought was the real war in South Vietnam.

Kyle's first assignment in Laos had been to assist in vaccinating the local tribes against cholera. Together with the United States Agency for Development, USAID, they'd put off an epidemic in the northeast corner of the country. Within a couple weeks, Kyle was speaking enough Lao and Hmong to get along without an interpreter, so he stayed in-country and began building airstrips just south of the Chinese and Vietnamese borders. USAID was still using the airstrips to fly food and medical supplies into the various villages, and Kyle was now teaching the Hmong how to defend those runways from the NVA. The NVA didn't much care for the Hmong and hated that American supplies were assisting their highland enemies.

Kyle liked working out of Alternate. Granted, the constant smell of chicken and pig feces from the village permeated everything, the weather was iffy most of the year, and the enemy was never more than fifteen miles away, but it had its charms. Sunny days were never too hot, and the Hmong and Lao women made great larb gai, a chopped-chicken salad that pleasantly combined mint and chili. Virtually any supply he needed was in Udorn, just a short flight away. For a career CIA paramilitary guy who wanted to help his country hold back communist revolutions, it was the center of the world, with the added convenience that no one was looking.

More than anything, Kyle loved working in central Laos because he loved the people he worked with. The Hmong were sweet, good-natured folks who just wanted to be left alone in their mountain villages. They were energetic, intuitive, and friendly, all of which suited Kyle well. Most importantly, they were gung-ho about stopping the North Vietnamese advances into their country, something Kyle could completely get behind. Their leader, Major General Vang Pao, had molded the Hmong into a well-disciplined army, and Kyle and his associates had made sure they were well-trained and well-supplied. The NVA may have only been a dozen miles to the west, but he was safe in his hooch with 15,000 Hmong troops between them and Alternate.

"Whatz'ee say, Mr. Kyle?", Nao, a young Hmong who served under Vang Pao, queried from Kyle's hammock.

Nao was an excellent soldier and he understood English pretty well, but only if you spoke slowly and said things like, "Make sure there is no mud in the barrel of the M1-carbine when you fire it," or "Shoot that son-of-a-bitch on the 12.7mm machine gun." The reporter on Armed Forces Radio was speaking very fast about things Nao had never even heard of, but Kyle noted there was some progress; by saying "'ee", Nao had finally abandoned the concept that the spirit of the white box could talk and accepted that what he heard actually was a man's voice.

"Just a minute, Nao. . . . I'll tell you when there is a break," Kyle replied. Just like Kyle's college girlfriend, Nao always wanted to chat during the story, and usually at the moment the most important information was coming through.

"Remember, the break is when the funny music plays between stories," Kyle added.

Nao nodded and smiled.

"Nobel Peace Prize winner the Reverend Martin Luther King spoke earlier in the week at the American Psychological Association's annual conference. Though primarily about the civil rights movement in the United States, Reverend King's speech touched on numerous subjects, including urban unemployment and the war in Vietnam. He ended the speech by saying, quote, 'I have not lost hope.'"

"Nao, he said America is getting to be a better place to live," Kyle stated, currently contemplating the glass of tempting liquid on the table.

Nao smiled in appreciation of the importance of a good newscast.

"French President Charles de Gaulle was in Warsaw, Poland today for the first of a four-day trip to the Eastern Bloc nation," the voice continued. "President de Gaulle met with Prime Minister Cyrankiewicz to discuss how better relations could help exports from both countries."

Nao raised his eyebrows as if to ask for a translation.

"He said the assholes and the pussies are thinking about making one battalion," Kyle said.

Nao found that hard to believe. Every soldier who worked with Mr. Kyle knew an "asshole" was a North Vietnamese soldier who wanted to shoot you, and a "pussy" was a guy who was afraid to fight. Like so much of what the man in the white box said, it just didn't make sense.

"In a press conference in Saigon, General William Westmoreland reported that Operation Swift in the Khe Sanh Valley was in its eighth day and already a major success. The general said that numerous large weapons caches had been found in a bunker complex, and that to date there were one hundred ninety-six Viet Cong confirmed killed in action. And that's the news from Armed Forces Radio."

"Nao, he said way too much shit is getting down the Ho Chi Minh Trail every day," Kyle stated as he leaned forward and grabbed the glass. "He said you need to get some sleep so you can kill lots of cha gee tomorrow."

Nao nodded and smiled. He liked it when Mr. Kyle used one of the Hmong words, like cha gee, which was a nasty racial slur of the North Vietnamese. Nao then sat up from the bunk as the door opened and Kyle's partner stepped into the hooch.

Brad Drakely had not been in Laos for as long as Kyle, but he understood being a knuckle-dragger paramilitary guy as well as anyone Kyle had ever met. Brad had been training the Khumba of Tibet prior to coming to Southeast Asia. He had been sent to Laos in 1965 and was getting a little bored with Alternate. Brad preferred the smaller operations, where he could be in command and actually fight rather than oversee training.

According to Ambassador William Sullivan in Vientiane, it wasn't legal for CIA personnel to shoot at the NVA, but then neither was the CIA's very presence in Laos. It also wasn't legal for there to be 20,000 NVA troops building a highway through the country.

"Hello, dear, how was your day?" Kyle asked Brad, then gulped down the entire contents of the glass.

"You know, this country didn't even have glass

43

bottles three years ago," Brad said through a smile. He set an empty bottle on the table and continued. "Now I can't even walk across our lovely yard without tripping over two or three Mekhong whiskey empties."

"Well, I have to drink those so Daeng has bottles for the lao-Lao. For what it's worth, I had them nicely stacked under the hooch, but then Nao's kid started playing with them. From the sound of things, I'd say you might want to watch for broken glass when you step out to take a leak."

"Gotcha," Brad replied. Nao waved as he walked out the door and Brad continued. "I made some progress today on trajectory."

For years, the paramilitary guys had had little success trying to explain to the Hmong that a bullet would curve toward the Earth as it traveled. The Little Guys were deadly accurate inside 100 meters, but for some reason they could not come to terms with aiming higher for long-range shots.

"What'd you do?" Kyle asked as he stood up with a slight wobble.

"I told them that after a hundred meters the spirit of the bullet wants to return to the Earth," Brad replied as he poured some lao-Lao in the glass for himself. Kyle noticed he spilled a few drops and looked at Brad across the table with a hurt expression. "Just putting it in terms of the spirit world seemed to make them aim high at longer distances."

"Brilliant," Kyle slurred. "I don't know why we didn't think of that years ago. It always works better to put things in a spiritual context. And speaking of spirits," Kyle pointed his middle finger at Brad, "you need to be more careful with this lao-Lao. It's precious, and you always spill a bit."

"Will do," Brad replied. "But don't start with me. The day wasn't all fun and games. There was ugliness, too."

Brad emptied the remains of the lao-Lao into the glass, and picked it up before Kyle could reach it, then continued. "Remember those NVA cadres General Vang Pao put in the fifty-gallon oil drums last week?"

"Yeah... I doubt I want to hear this." Kyle clenched his teeth in anticipation of what Brad was about to say. Vang Pao's methods weren't all by the book.

"Well, he didn't have them flown to Udorn like he said," Brad went on reluctantly. "Apparently he'd gotten the intel he needed, so he left them there. They stayed in those steel barrels for nine days. I got to watch them get pulled out. One was still alive."

"I'm glad I missed that." Kyle sighed.

"Oh, no. No, no, no. You don't have to miss it at all," Brad said. "They took pictures with the new Polaroid. Vang Pao sent a squad out to hang the shots on a tree near the NVA line."

"Shit," Kyle exclaimed as he stepped toward the door. "I really would not want to have to explain that to Ambassador Sullivan, or a bipartisan Senate panel on illicit activities of the CIA, for that matter."

The arrogance of American politicians kept them from understanding how the agency actually worked. The politicians and public seemed to think the CIA ran every military operation it worked with, like American exceptionalism should just give American agents all the authority over the locals. The fact was, paramilitary guys didn't order the locals to do this or that. Ordering a Hmong around, like you were his boss, would get you nowhere. The CIA's model in Laos was to help the Hmong fight. If he or Brad yelled at General Vang Pao for all the torture he inflicted, they would just lose the general's respect. The general would lose face, which generals of all cultures hate, and he would be less likely to listen to the CIA's advice when it really mattered. To be a good paramilitary guy, you had to know your place in that netherworld between American values and the horrors of war. Politicians didn't get that.

"Also, I talked to Rich today," Brad said. "He came in on a C-123 with some supplies to do a little recruiting."

"You gonna take the Heavy Green assignment?" Kyle asked as he stepped out the door and onto the porch.

"Yeah, he really wants me there and I could use a change of scenery for a while," Brad replied.

"Sounds good," Kyle said.

Kyle stumbled down the steps and unzipped his fly, then stared up into the cold, dark drizzle. His best friend would be going someplace even more dangerous than Alternate. It was another step further from American values, and closer to the horrors of war.

3

September 14, 1967, 0655 hours,
(2 days later)
in flight over Northern Laos,
and Hoa Binh Province, North Vietnam

"Dingo, this is Raven-86," said a husky voice over the radio. "I have visual with you right now. I'm going to stay in this location, and if you don't find a good target over North Vietnam, I'd love to direct you on something here."

"Roger that, Raven-86," came the husky reply. "With all the predicted cloud cover over our target, there is a good chance we will have plenty of ordnance for you in about an hour. We will look for you here."

Aircraft returning to base could not land with live bombs, so the ordnance was generally dropped on some random, remote bit of jungle between the target and the base. Not only was it wasteful, but it was also hard on the jungle and made for an ugly, cratered topography. The simple exchange between the two pilots meant that today the United States wouldn't waste fifty thousand dollars' worth of good bombs on monkeys and snakes.

The hierarchal pyramid of any US Air Force Base placed fighter pilots at the very top, and that lofty position seemed especially pronounced at Udorn Royal Thai Air Force Base. Udorn was encircled by wire fences and landmines, and patrolled by sentries and dogs, to protect the runway and associated aircraft. The hangars were built to hold those aircraft, and staffed by thousands of men whose sole job was to keep the planes in working order. The mess halls, the officer staff, and everyone from the top general down to the lowliest airman pumping gas, were there so the fighter pilots could deliver ordnance on targets in North Vietnam. To be a fighter jock was to have status head and shoulders above everyone else on the base. Almost.

The most respected pilots in the entire Vietnam War didn't fly fast-moving jets loaded with bombs and machine guns. They weren't fighter pilots at all, but in an almost mythical squadron known as the Ravens. To be a Raven you had to be chosen from the exalted list of forward air controllers, or FACs, flying over battle sites in South Vietnam. The FACs were the eyes in the sky for both infantry and fast-moving jets, and they were coveted targets for the North Vietnamese.

If you did the job of a FAC well in South Vietnam, you might get a phone call asking you to accept reassignment. You weren't told where, just "reassignment." Taking the new job was a leap of faith; no one in Vietnam even knew of the Ravens' existence. If you said "yes," an Air Force colonel would be given the task of interviewing you, asking just a few questions, but the program was so secret the colonel was not even allowed to know where the pilot was going. If the answers were to the CIA's satisfaction, the Agency plucked you from the Army and had you "sheep-dipped." That is, they stripped you of any form of identity you previously had with the government, and then entered you into the Steve Canyon Program.

You were now in the most exclusive club of the war, but of course you didn't exist.

All Ravens shared the same call sign followed by a number. There was no "Maverick" or "Trojan," just your call sign that meant you were in this secret unit. The Ravens appeared in the air from a secret base that none of the Air Force pilots had ever identified. They flew 0-1 Bird Dogs, essentially a single-seat version of a civilian Cessna 170 equipped with a special wing that allowed the plane to take off and land with less than 500 feet of runway and to fly at incredibly slow speeds. The O-1 had no armor, and its only means of attack was to fire a white phosphorous rocket at a target as a marker and then hope the fighter jocks could blow it up.

The Ravens flew the most dangerous missions of the war, and accepted that there was over a 50 percent chance their name would have a "Wounded" or "Killed in Action" label next to it after just one year of service. While an F-4 or F-105 jet might hum past targets and antiaircraft gun batteries at 600 mph, a Raven would likely fly by at under 40 knots and just above the treetops.

Ravens flew low and slow so they could find the targets, and that was what separated them from other pilots. Speed didn't make you brave, it kept you safe, and the Ravens chose to fly without it.

They never wore uniforms, and often went into battle carrying only a 9mm pistol, in an aloha shirt, with khaki shorts and Stan Smith tennis shoes. The same garb might be worn on leave at Udorn, and no colonel would even think of complaining when that Raven irreverently strolled into the officers' club. Instead, he would likely buy the man a drink, and watch the cocky F-105 pilots say "sir" and salute the revered pilot. The other fighter pilots knew the real hierarchy of the pyramid was measured in bravery, and everyone in the sky came up short against a Raven.

Air Force First Lieutenant Kirk Brendan, who went by the call sign Railer, had only recently learned of the Raven program. His squadron, from the 355th Tactical Fighter Wing, was based out of Korat Royal Thai Air Force Base, and thus rarely ever saw a Raven. However, the legendary status of the forward air controllers was well-known to the 355th, and Railer was excited to hear that if they did not find their target over North Vietnam, Raven-86 would be directing them on runs along the border with Laos.

At 320 knots, Railer's fully loaded F-105D Thunderchief was only barely above its stall speed. With a thin, swept-wing design, the F-105, commonly called a Thud by its pilots, was capable of supersonic speed. Thuds were more like darts than airplanes, relying on a huge engine to keep them humming along above the speed of sound. The advantages of that sleek, high-speed design were problematic, however, when the aircraft had to slow down to refuel at the cruising speed of the KC-135 tanker. Add the bomb load and the drag of the spare tanks, and this was not an easy bird to keep in the sky. To hold the 52,000-pound Thud aloft, Railer had to adjust to every one of the slightest changes in the aircraft's attitude.

While Railer worked to keep the F-105 from stalling, the KC-135 pilot, call sign Milk Run, had his fully loaded aircraft flying at its highest speed. The big jet could pump nearly a 1,000 gallons a minute into the hungry Thud. Though it seemed like hours to both pilots, the tanks were topped off in under a hundred seconds, allowing Railer to unhook from the tanker and break off to the right.

"Milk Run, Railer is clear," the young lieutenant said in his calmest, most stoic voice. Refueling was stressful, and this would no doubt be a terrifying morning, but a pilot had to sound like a pilot: calm, cool, and collected.

Moving to the south of Milk Run at 480 knots, Railer put his Thud into a wide circle and took a deep breath. The leader of the squadron, Major Overgard, who went by Dingo, would be taking on fuel next. For Railer, this was one of the few moments in a sortie where he actually got to pause and mentally disconnect from what was happening that day. The mission had been planned out in detail: refueling order, approach pattern to North Vietnam, the objective, and of course all the known manmade obstacles that might pop up along the way. Railer unzipped a pocket in his flight suit and grabbed a baby bottle filled with water, noting the message he had scribbled on the plastic bottle months before: "No battle plan survives first contact with the enemy," the prophetic words of Prussian General Helmuth von Moltke. In his six weeks in the war theater, that had proven true on every sortie.

The battle plan for American pilots was, from a position of trying to win the war, pretty crazy to Railer. The rules of engagement specified what could actually be designated as a target, and often what was the obvious "target" was not something Washington would let the pilots attack. Supplies were pouring into South Vietnam via the North, and everyone knew where they could be found. Cargo ships from the Soviet Union docked in Haiphong Harbor, yet the pilots couldn't bomb anything within ten nautical miles of the docks. There were juicy targets all around the capital city of Hanoi, yet it had two circles of limitation: one twenty and another thirty miles in diameter. You couldn't drop on most would-be targets inside the thirty-mile circle, and a pilot wasn't even supposed to look inside the twenty-mile circle.

Railer had trained for over eight months in the F105, not to mention all the trainer flights prior to that, but nothing could completely prepare a man for aerial combat over North Vietnam. The Soviet Union had provided the North Vietnamese with the most sophisticated air defense system ever conceived. The sky over North Vietnam had become a test bed for surface-to-air missiles (SAMs) and radar-guided anti-aircraft-artillery (triple-A). However, certain triple-A sites could not be bombed, and unless they fired first, they weren't allowed to hit any SAM site. The pilots could see the defenses on the ground, but they couldn't do anything about it until after the enemy had fired the first shot. That first shot was often fatal.

To Railer, the most galling of the rules of engagement had to do with the MiGs. The North Vietnamese had MiG 17 and brand new MiG 21 fighter planes that helped to protect the supply lines to the south. However, the rules of engagement stated that American pilots could only shoot at the MiGs when they were in the air and attacking American bombers. Bombing them on a runway or tarmac was strictly forbidden. There were multiple times in the previous month and a half when Railer's squadron had flown over MiGs as they taxied to the runway. The planes would take off just to come up and take shots at him and his wingmen, but the Americans couldn't do anything until the MiGs were in the air and engaging in a fight.

Danger was part of combat, and Railer had accepted that fact before he signed up for the Air Force. The real problem with the war was not the enemy's defenses but that the targets were simply not worth risking a man's life for. Instead of bombing the source of the problem, like a Russian supply ship or the military headquarters in downtown Hanoi, they were given road crossings with a single truck, or areas where the listening devices picked up movement of "possible troops." When he'd shipped out of Nellis for Vietnam, Railer had promised himself he would not become embittered by the war, but these missions were already testing his resolve. He'd be risking his life again today in a plane that carried more bombing force than a

World War II B-17, and he'd likely be putting it to work on a single truck. That was a pisser.

"Thank you for the juice, Milk Run. Dingo is clear," Railer heard the lead pilot say over the radio. These were the words he had been waiting to hear as it meant all four planes had refueled and would now form up on Dingo and fly toward North Vietnam.

"Roger that, Dingo. Be safe," Milk Run replied. As Dingo banked his Thud to the north, the KC-135 turned south for safer airspace above Thailand.

Railer watched as Dingo swung his F-105 around to an 090 heading, due east, and slowed so the other three pilots could join up in formation. With multi-layered cloud cover over North Vietnam, the squadron would be relying on Dingo to find the right airspace.

The United States had placed small, tactical air navigation transponders, or TACANs, all over Southeast Asia that emitted signals aircraft could use for navigational assistance. It couldn't pinpoint a target, but it could get you into the general area. Dingo was the lead pilot, so the receiver in his Thud would be the one all the other pilots followed through the clouds. After finding that location, they'd have to spot the specific target based on aerial photographs and the terrain. If the cloud ceiling was too low, they'd have to abort the mission.

At the briefing that morning at Korat Air Force Base, the pilots had discussed the orders sent in from Saigon. The target was dubious at best, but the logic of the planners made some sense. A couple days prior, a B-52 had dropped its full load on a convoy of trucks. A follow-up aerial recon photo showed the road had been heavily damaged. The spooks planning the attack guessed there might be trucks stopped in that same location as the road was impassable. The brass at the briefing had also decided it was time for Railer to take the lead in the bombing. He had six weeks of combat under his belt, twelve sorties, and it was time for the young lieutenant to take the next step.

"Gentlemen, arm your Mark 84s and let's bump up to six hundred knots. Turn on your music, and we'll go silent until over the target. I've just been informed we will be without a Wild Weasel this morning," Dingo said over the radio. A slight chill passed through Railer as he listened. "Knockout had a mechanical and had to return to Korat, so Ho Chi Minh has another advantage."

The Wild Weasel was an F-4 Phantom that had been configured to target radar beams coming from the ground. The Wild Weasel's job was to fly over the target first and draw fire, whether triple-A or a SAM, then evade those shots and fire back on the radar site. If done in concert with an attack, the enemy often focused on the attacking aircraft or was outright destroyed before the bombing run was made. Without the Wild Weasel, the strike force was that much more vulnerable.

Each Thud had the ability to jam some radar, what Dingo had referred to as "turn on your music," but that was only so effective. Every time Westinghouse came out with a new version of the radar jammer, the Soviets tried out a new version of radar. One never knew if he was up to date or running the old equipment until he was in battle and the shit began to hit the fan.

Railer and the other three pilots diligently watched the cloud tops below them for the next fifteen minutes. They knew that by now Hanoi had seen them on radar, and they'd likely get alarms if a triple-A site or SAM locked onto the planes, but the possibility of MiG attack was also very real. Some days the NVA came up to fight, others they did not. This seemed to be one where evading a MiG-21 wasn't necessary—yet.

Dingo broke the silence the moment they'd passed over the possible target. "Okay, Railer, it looks like two cloud decks. Take her down and see if you can find something that's worth our efforts."

Dingo really has the cool-pilot voice dialed in, Railer thought.

"Gravel and Fargo, we will go Romeo and hold for Railer."

"Roger that, Dingo. Railer is in," Railer replied.

Knowing the plan was to run a few seconds over the target, Railer slowed out of the formation and rolled over to the right, starting a maneuver pilots know as a "split S." Dropping from 29,000 feet, the plane would roll and twist while it dove, and eventually end up flying in the opposite direction. It allowed a pilot to lose altitude quickly and fly in a pattern that was hard for a gunner to predict. Most important, Railer would come out of the dive with a lot of speed and hopefully get away from the target quickly and safely.

As he entered the dark clouds at 22,000 feet, the world suddenly changed from bright blue and sunny to dark and gray. The weather over North Vietnam really is crazy, Railer thought as he slid the sunscreen up on his helmet. The pilot glanced at his airspeed, now up to just over 620 knots, and noticed the gimbals on the plane's gyroscope had rotated into the dark. Though he was well aware of his flight attitude, the position of the gyro was unnerving. Ignoring the fact that anti-aircraft artillery would start coming at him any second, not to mention the flying telephone poles that were SAM 2 anti-aircraft missiles, the idea of flying straight at the ground at 700 mph while blinded by clouds was never comfortable.

Railer's F-105 suddenly popped through the cloud ceiling to a dark and foreboding North Vietnam.

"Visibility is at ten thousand, Dingo, with broken but heavy clouds below at about five thousand," Railer said in his calmest voice. The temperature in the plane hadn't changed at all, but he was now dripping with sweat as his heart beat like a snare drum.

"Roger that, Railer. Ceiling ten thousand," Dingo responded.

Railer could see a bit of the Song Da, or Black River, flowing from the northwest. Part of the river was obscured by clouds, but the stream's long, sweeping turn north was right under the F-105. Just southeast of the bend in the river was a large open plain with a few spindly karst limestone spires jutting 300 feet or so into the sky. The mosaic of square and rectangular rice paddies, all with rounded corners and in various shades of green, was split by a road. As far as Railer could tell, he was flying directly onto the target area. The only problem was he was going way too fast, and actually hitting a truck with one of the 2,000-pound bombs was going to be difficult at best.

"Railer is on target," he said coolly into the radio.

No sooner had the words left his mouth than an alarm went off in the cockpit and a steady stream of crimson dots came up from the edge of a stand of bamboo just south of the road. They were the distinct red tracers of a 57mm cannon, streaming up at his aircraft at around 3,000 feet per second. Railer pulled back a bit on the stick, angling left a tad, and the nose of the F-105 came up from the steep dive.

"We have fifty-seven mike-mike south of the road," he continued. The pilot no longer sounded so calm.

A second stream of red tracers angled from the west but didn't appear to have a lock on the plane so Railer focused on his presumed target. He still had not seen the trucks, but the rock outcropping with trees next to the small road seemed like the spot the NVA would hide them. The young pilot pulled the nose higher and flattened out the plane's trajectory at about 600 feet as green-and-white tracers streamed by to the left.

Railer noted the 37mm fire and toggled the bomb as he passed over the rutted, muddy road at 600 knots. The g-force pulled him deep into the seat and he could feel his suit come alive to squeeze the blood from his legs. Racing to the west, Railer turned on the afterburner and began to gain altitude, and in that moment the horrible sound of the missile alarm went off. Railer raced for the cloud, now accelerating away from the bombsite at almost the speed of sound. "Railer, we have a valid SAM launch," he heard over the radio as another stream of red dots shot up in

front of the plane. The young pilot banked right as he
entered the cloud and let the stream of 57mm shells
go off to his left, but the SAM warning went from beeps
to a continuous tone. He glanced at his instruments
and saw the air speed climbing closer to Mach 1 and
rate of climb at nearly 20,000 feet per minute. With
that, a bright white flash erupted just off the Thud's
right wing.

September 14, 1967, 0655 hours
(same day)
SA-2 Missile Defense Site 117,
Central Hoa Binh Province, North Vietnam

Despite the rain, Leh Duc stood outside the cave and
admired the menacing weapon. The missile, a Soviet
made S-75 Dvina, what the Americans referred to on
the radio as a SAM-2, loomed over him like a ten-me-
ter-long white dragon. The missile could reach speeds
over three times the speed of sound, and it could hit
targets as high as 60,000 feet above the ground. Even
if the proximity fuse on the missile detonated sixty
meters away, the 200-kilo warhead would destroy an

American bomber.

While delivering supplies near Mu Gai Pass the year before, Duc had lost part of his left foot to an American bomb, and it had left him thinking his efforts in the war were finished. Being given the job of guarding the new weapon, even if it was in the north and far from the front lines, meant there was possibly a little payback for the Imperialists. This missile, his missile, would someday bring down an American bomber.

The S-75 crew had only brought the weapon to the site a few days before. Weeks had been spent prepping the area, and the crew had spent nearly four months just north of Hanoi training with Soviet advisors. One of those Soviet men had come South with the crew, but he spent his time playing card games and drinking liquor in the back of the cave and had left most of the work on the weapon to the Vietnamese soldiers.

There were five other missiles arranged around the 100-meter-high limestone spire, but Duc's crew had been fortunate enough to be assigned to the side with the best cave. This made for more comfortable sleeping arrangements during the rain, and would make a great bunker in the event of an American counterattack. Be that as it may, Duc had no urge to be inside the mountain and away from the awe-inspiring machine. He was proud to be guarding the missile.

The sheets of rain hitting leaves and plopping into the puddles overwhelmed all other sounds. Duc only faintly heard yells originating near the No. 3 missile, and while he was trying to make out what the men were saying, the warning siren came to life. Within seconds Duc's missile crew ran from the cave to their assigned posts. Duc hobbled thirty meters or so behind the rocket while the crew ran through the various assignments of pulling flagged cords from the weapon and inserting power cables into the launcher.

The crew's leader, Lieutenant Kimh, spoke quickly into the radio and then waved Duc farther away from the missile.

With the siren and all the commotion around the weapon, Duc hadn't even noticed that the 57mm anti-aircraft batteries had begun to fire. Red tracers were arcing into the clouds, and moments later two 37mm guns opened up. With that, he heard the sound of the American bomber. It was actually to the south of the missile site when it dropped its bomb, so no harm was done to any of the new weapons. The plane was moving incredibly fast as it came out of its dive, and Duc saw a line of flame shoot out the back of the aircraft when the pilot turned up the power. As the plane disappeared into the dark clouds, the missile roared to life.

Overwhelming the five anti-aircraft artillery guns firing into the sky, a high-pitched hiss screamed from the back of the missile as flame and burning gas shot burning mud into the air. Almost faster than Duc's eyes could focus, the missile was gone, leaving only heat and a strange smell.

The crew watched for perhaps two seconds as it raced into the clouds behind the American jet.

September 14, 1967, 0655 hours
(same day)
one kilometer south of SA-2 Missile Defense Site
117, Central Hoa Binh Province, North Vietnam

"Hurry up, miao," Corporal Tan shouted in Vietnamese. "Or don't you understand our language?"

Tan muttered something to the other soldiers and Lim heard one of them laugh.

A steady, cold rain poured down on the porters and soldiers as they emptied the six trucks. The morning was dark for the hour, and Lim knew that meant there would be heavy rain all day. He grabbed the rope handle of one end of a long, green crate and slid it from the bed of the truck, then hefted the box onto his shoulder and plodded through the mud to a tethered water buffalo. The animal fidgeted and moved back and forth at the sight of the big box. This wasn't the beast's first time carrying a load.

An old man held the animal's leash as Lim slid the green box into a canvas sack that hung from the buffalo's side. The older man held much of the weight as Lim ran back to the truck and returned with a matching crate to counter the other side of the load. The buffalo bellowed with the weight, and another buffalo

62

moaned back from twenty meters away. It seemed no one liked the heavy loads.

"Is this too much for the buffalo?" Lim asked the old man. Normally Lim spoke in Vietnamese, but he could see by the black coat and red sash that, like himself, the old man was Hmong. It was a rare comfort to speak in his own dialect.

The North Vietnamese didn't recognize the Hmong language, nor had the French, despite the fact that the Hmong had been living in the region for over a thousand years. Hmong legends said they had once lived in cities and had fought for their own kingdom in what was now China, but had eventually been forced out by the Han. The tribe moved south into Southeast Asia and found the Viet and Lao controlled the fertile valleys and coast. What was left were the mountains, and the Hmong had made their home in the highlands. For the most part, the various tribes had coexisted by not coveting each other's land, but that had changed when the French colony collapsed.

"We are going to have to go through some deep rice paddies to get to the passable section of road," Lim continued. "It seems like a big load for a small buffalo."

An American bomber, a B-52, had managed to take out a bridge over the Song Da, as well as three trucks, eleven soldiers, and almost half a kilometer of the road. It would be repaired within days, but there was no stopping the flow of material south just because of a few 300-kilo bombs.

"No, son, he'll be fine with this," the old man replied. "And neither he nor I want to hear Corporal Tan complain that we aren't doing our share. Have you always worked in this area? You seem to know it well," the old man said in a change of subject.

"I spent most of my childhood on a plantation just a few kilometers from here," Lim replied. "This is my first time back to Hoa Binh in a long time."

The old man smiled in appreciation. It wasn't often a Hmong met a fellow member of the tribe who had lived such a cosmopolitan life. Hmong rarely left their home village or the mountains.

"My mother died when I was very young, and my father wanted to see something new," Lim said. "He put me in a basket and trekked north from our village, below Phou Samsoum, and ended up with a job on the tea plantation."

"I'm from Nong Het," the old man replied. "It's far from here, but close to Phou Samsoum. Hmong should not be so far from home; it's bad for the spirit. But I suppose that is part of war."

Lim nodded as he strapped the wooden crates to the buffalo.

"My father was not like most of our clan." Lim cinched the load down with a hemp cord. "I suppose that makes me a little different, too. My best friend as a child was the plantation owner's son. He was French. While my father was teaching me the Hmong ways, Dominique and his mother were teaching me to speak French."

Lim didn't mention he'd also picked up a little English from Dominique, and they had used it like a code to talk privately around the other French children. That he spoke Hmong and French was a bit taboo, and not something he let the Vietnamese soldiers know about. There was no way he could ever let them know he spoke some English, too. The Hmong had learned the hard way that too much education among members of the hill tribes was seen as a bad thing in North Vietnam.

"Where were you working before they moved you here?" the old man asked.

"I have been ferrying loads on various sections of the Trail for many years," Lim replied. "They have mostly kept me west of the Truong Mountains, but they pulled a group of us north yesterday. I never know why they move us around as they do."

As Lim walked back to the truck for another load, he thought about the happy days on the plantation. The French had not been good to most of the Vietnamese people, but Dominique's father had made sure Lim's father was happy in his job. Dominique had once told Lim that his father felt a bond with the Hmong because he had grown up in the Alps of France. He saw himself as a displaced man of the mountains, much like Lim's father. Dom's father had even taught Lim and his father the French skills of technical rock climbing, and the four of them had ascended many of the karst limestone towers in Northern Vietnam. For whatever the reason, Dom's father had made sure Lim and his father had good lives on the plantation, and this had perhaps come at a great cost.

As war between the Viet Minh and French colonials grew, so too did the dangers of being a European in Indochina. Dom's father had wisely chosen to send his son and wife back to Annecy, France, after the French defeat at Dien Bien Phou. The battle was a turning point, and Viet Minh patrols began to appear on the plantation within a few weeks. One afternoon, a squad of Viet Minh came and took Dom's father, leading him away with his hands tied behind his back. They returned the following day and took Lim's father in the same manner. That was the last time Lim saw either of the men. He left the plantation at age twelve and made his way back to the mountains. Years later, cadres for the People's Army had come to his village, recruiting porters to ferry loads on the Ho Chi Minh Trail. He'd been carrying military supplies for the Vietnamese for seven years now.

"Here, take this one," one of the soldiers said, lofting a 20-kilo bag of Chinese rice onto Lim's shoulder.

As Lim turned in the mud he heard the siren begin to wail in the distance. Immediately, the soldiers grabbed their pith helmets and AK-47s and jogged into the bamboo, putting as much distance as they could between the trucks and their fragile bodies.

The private standing in the back of the truck grabbed his rifle and jumped to the ground, then ordered the old man leading the string of buffalo away from the road. Lim calmly set the bag of rice down in the truck and followed the buffalo away from the road. Most of the soldiers were panicking; they had all been under air attack from the Americans before and knew just how horrible the bombing could be. Lim knew there was no rush. The siren was coming from the new missile launchers, and the new weapon seemed to see the American planes a few minutes before they were actually overhead. If all went as usual, the guns would start firing before the plane dropped its bombs.

Lim stepped around the buffalo and in front of the old man. He wanted to scout out just the right location for all of them to hide. Experience told him that would be a wet place. The low spots were safest, as the earth around you served as protection from the concussive effects and bomb fragments.

They settled in a paddy about 150 meters south of the road. The water went up to his knees, and the animals had a hard time walking in the mud, but it beat being cut in half by shrapnel. Lim leaned against the mud dike of the paddy and heard a ripping sound. When he pulled his shoulder away from the mud wall, another tear in his shirt was exposed. The cotton fabric had been wet for months and it was rotting off his body. He didn't know how he'd replace it when it was hard to even get a pair of rubber sandals from the soldiers, but he'd have to do something soon.

"If we're lucky, the bombs will miss everyone except that cha gee, Corporal Tan," the old man muttered.

Lim turned his head to the man and smiled to show he agreed with the sentiment.

Lim watched a string of red lights trace into the charcoal sky perhaps 500 meters to the north, then heard the thumping of the cannon as it fired dozens of shots. The shells snaked in a steady, curving line toward some unseen target beyond the murky ceiling of mist. With that, he heard the thunder of the jet, and could now locate the sound to the north. Two more guns began to fire, much faster and now with green-and-white tracers curving into the dark sky. The plane roared overhead and the clouds lit up in yellow light.

The bomb exploded perhaps 200 meters north of the road, and the concussion popped Lim's ears. The ground and air shook with the explosion, and one of the buffalo brayed and tried to pull away from the old man. The jet roared right over the men and they saw the flames of its engine spray out as it streaked for higher altitude. The yellow flame disappeared into the clouds, along with two more streaks of the red tracers.

Lim and the old man both turned to the north toward a hissing sound as a single, bright white light shot from the ground where the new weapons were. Until then, Lim had not seen a Soviet rocket launch. The fact that only one of them had been fired seemed to indicate it was a far more dangerous tool than the anti-aircraft guns. The two men leaned against the paddy and watched the area of dense cloud the rocket had just entered. Perhaps two seconds later there was a flash of white in the cloud. Another couple of seconds passed and the clouds lit up in orange. Lim knew the orange flash from experience: That plane and that pilot would not be dropping any more bombs.

4

October 9, 1967, 1120 hours
(25 days later)
525th Military Intelligence Group Headquarters,
Tan Son Nhut Air Base outside Saigon, South
Vietnam

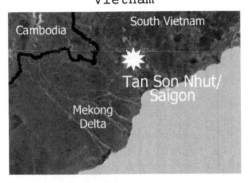

Lieutenant John Lilygren stood straight up and rubbed his eyes. He'd been leaning over black-and-white photos of jungle since 0600, and the ability to focus, both physically and mentally, was fading away. There were only so many "possible truck stops in southern Laos" one pair of eyes could handle. John took a sip of coffee and turned to look out the window at the naturally lit world beyond the air-conditioned Quonset hut. The airbase's sunlit runway seemed to immediately clear his mind.

"How long did you say you've been staring at maps and photos, Larry?" John asked the other lieutenant as he watched a C-130 touch down on the far runway.

"I'm in the fifth month of my second tour," the Brownsville, Texas native said in his Southern drawl. "I think I've grown muscles in my eyes that I didn't have in nineteen sixty-five. I've also lost a lot of hair. It's a stressful job, so pace yourself."

The young lieutenant was right about the stress, John thought. Figuring out where the bombs would go was difficult, but sorting out how the pilot might be shot down, as in where the anti-aircraft guns were, was what kept him up at night. If John missed something in one of the photographs, an American pilot would likely pay for it with his life.

In many ways, this aspect of intelligence work wasn't different from the stress of keeping his soldiers alive in the field. John regretted not seeing the Viet Cong RPG team before they'd fired on Gulley and Judge. Those were a couple more kids who would never see twenty-one, and there was another associated death the following morning when the side gunner on the evac helicopter was shot in the neck. The pain of his burns and the shrapnel in his shoulder had mostly faded, but the happy voices of those two kids in the bunker rang in his head every morning when he woke.

"Do you feel like we are doing any good here?" John asked after swallowing some lukewarm coffee.

"We are all cogs in the same machine, I suppose," Larry replied. "All of us have to keep doing our jobs. You and I spot trucks and guns, pilots drop bombs and slow the flow of materiel, and soldiers make headway in the field. If I question my role, I have to question the whole war, and General Westmoreland says I'm not allowed to do that."

John smiled and leaned back over the photos of the southeastern region of Sekong Province, an area of Laos he was quite familiar with. He'd secretly been in that area a year before on an advanced reconnaissance mission. The objective then had been to determine if the NVA's 324th Infantry Division was massing in southern Laos. It hadn't taken long to see the 324th were there, perhaps all 10,000 of them, but there was no way to tell it from aerial photos. John knew the Army's photos were as good then as now, and they hadn't seen a soul in the pictures. You simply had to have someone in the field doing the dirty work. An entire division could be hiding under the canopy, and you couldn't see them in a picture taken by an airplane or satellite.

"I know you're right, Larry," John replied as he passed a magnifying glass over the image of a karst limestone cliff. "That is certainly how the military, any military, has to work. But everything I've seen in the last three weeks has indicated we are blowing up more and more of Charlie's supplies, while the amount of equipment the enemy is receiving is actually increasing. We're making progress, but Ho Chi Minh is making more progress. We aren't hitting the supplies at the source, and that might be what it takes."

"Might?" Larry blurted, standing erect and pulling his shoulders back. "Might? Of course that's what we need to do. Listen, my father loves hunting rattlesnakes with a pistol. He has the record for largest Texas Diamondback ever taken. Damn thing is nine feet long and hanging on our living room wall. He always says: 'If you want to hunt a snake, you need to go for its head. Hittin' anyplace else just makes a mad snake.'" Larry leaned back over the photograph, then continued. "The way I see it, we're taking potshots at the tail end of the world's biggest snake. You and I can continue to try to save pilots, but until America goes after this snake's head, we won't kill it."

Hanoi. Larry was talking about bombing the supply depots around the North Vietnamese capital, and the logic seemed obvious. The problem was the politicians wouldn't let that happen.

"Lieutenant Lilygren, get in here," the commander bellowed from an adjoining room. The colonel never bothered to open the door. He just yelled loud enough for everyone in the building to hear. In John's three weeks with the 525th Military Intelligence Group, he was yet to see the man smile.

"Yes, sir," John said after opening the door to the CO's office.

"There's been a lot of chatter about you lately. Apparently you have friends someplace above. Or enemies," the colonel said. "It's hard to tell with orders like these. Your request for rest and recreation in Bangkok came through, effective immediately. Here are the travel orders." The colonel handed a manila folder to John. "Strangely, those orders came in two minutes after this," the colonel said, passing a single sheet of paper over his desk. "When you get to Bangkok you are to report to the chief intelligence office at the American Embassy."

"Yes, sir," John said, raising his eyebrows at the perplexing directives. He knew the chief intelligence officer in Bangkok, Richard Milano, very well, and would have stopped by for a visit anyway. Richard was more of an older uncle to John than just a friend.

"You spent some time in Bangkok as a kid, right?" the colonel muttered without looking up from his paperwork.

"Yes, sir. My father worked for the foreign service in the 'fifties."

"Must have been a strange place for a kid from Wyoming to grow up," the commanding officer said. "Anyway, you better get going. Those orders came from way up the food chain. CINCPAC, to be specific."

"I got R and R orders from Pacific Theatre Command in Honolulu?" John asked in a somewhat feeble voice. CINCPAC dealt with the big pictures, like where America's nuclear arsenal was aimed, and how many years the United States might want to fight the war in Vietnam. The comings and goings of one first lieutenant was way below their pay grade.

"Yes, and I don't want to get a complaint that you didn't show up soon enough, so get going."

"Yes, sir," John said in a low voice. "I'll be on the next flight."

First Lieutenant John Lilygren stepped out of the cool, dry Quonset hut and into the stifling humidity of the South Vietnam morning. As he looked over the orders, two fully-loaded F4 Phantoms shrieked down the runway in a tandem take-off. It was strange. He'd never even requested R and R.

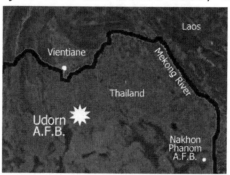

Brad Drakely stepped out of the Air America UH-1 chopper and strode across the new concrete tarmac towards the CIA's operation center. Known as AB-1, the rickety wood building had a leaky roof and two very loud air conditioners in its front windows. Brown paint peeled from the wood panels, and rats and two strikingly long snakes competed for the attic. The building's only redeemable quality was a somewhat inviting terrace that provided a clear and shaded view of the runway. As he stepped onto the porch, Brad noted a few Budweiser empties between the two chairs, probably left by Air America pilots the night before.

With all the commotion of the busy air base, most people would have never paid AB-1 any attention if it hadn't had a forest of antennas on its steep roof. That kinda said "CIA," but it didn't really matter because everyone on the base knew who worked in the building. Brad stepped through the doorway to see Richard

74

Milano, the CIA attaché stationed in Bangkok, leaning over a desk of aerial photos.

"Hey, Rich, when did you get here?" Brad asked as he tossed a jungle fatigue cap onto a bright red vinyl couch. As the hat left his hand en route to the ugly piece of furniture, he thought better of the placement. The couch had been borrowed, so to speak, a few months before from the Pink Pussycat Bar and Thrill in downtown Udorn. The owner of the Pink Pussycat liked to say his place specialized in "cheap Thai beer and cheap Thai love." As such, the couch had developed a soiled reputation with the Air America pilots. No one 'fessed up to how the couch had made it into the CIA office, though there were a few instant suspects.

"Hi, Brad," the gray-haired station chief replied. "I just flew up this morning to get your report. I have to head back this afternoon. Did you just get back from Lima Site 85?"

"Yeah. We had to make a stop at Long Tieng on the way home, but I was at LS 85 yesterday and this morning,"

"So whaddaya think?" Richard asked as he took a seat behind the desk. He reached into a small refrigerator behind the desk and pulled out two cans of Budweiser, then tossed one to Brad. "Is the mountain defendable?"

Brad turned to the couch and sighed. What the hell, he thought, and sat on the sticky vinyl. He grabbed an opener off the desk and popped two holes in the cold steel can, then took down a couple of gulps.

"Yeah, it's defendable," Brad replied with a raised

tone that said there was no short answer. "Of course it's vulnerable, too."

Richard nodded as Brad continued.

"I spent last night with the Phou Pha Thi village elders, and they are all on board with defense. Apparently the NVA patrols are taxing them, so to speak, on opium production. That sort of thing doesn't sit well with Hmong. They like the idea that they will be getting a lot of hard rice if they defend our installation."

USAID and Air America's original mission in Laos had been to support the locals with supplies like rice and medical supplies. As the North Vietnamese had exerted pressure on the Hmong, the Americans had increased their level of commitment to the tribe's security. That commitment had come in the form of weapons. Vang Pao, the general in charge of the Hmong forces, had begun using the term "hard rice" as code for the military supplies.

"So they understand this is a defensive position, and not the usual hit-and-run stuff they're used to?" Richard asked.

"Yeah, they understand," Brad said. "They've established trenches and bunkers that set the village and our facilities inside the same perimeter. The lower slope of the mountain will be the line, so the NVA would have to fight uphill. Throw in some American air power and it's a pretty good castle."

"Perfect. How goes construction of the facility?"

"The buildings are in place and have power. We should be ready to run the tests next week, as scheduled."

Brad twirled his cap on his index finger and glanced

out the window to the runway, then took a sip of beer. Richard and Brad had been working together in Laos for a few years, and the station chief could see his field operative was not completely happy with the strategy.

"Okay, so what's the downside?" Richard asked. "This is Laos, so there must be a caveat to the whole thing, and I can see you've already thought of it."

Brad took in a deep breath and let it out slowly. "The caveat, as always, is us. You asked if it was defendable, and it is, but only for a limited time. We will need to have an exit plan and we will need to stick with that plan. It's a defendable position, but only for so long, and the North Vietnamese are going to do everything they can to get rid of the place when they realize what it is."

Richard nodded. He knew it was important for Brad to feel he'd been heard on the subject.

"The Hmong are a militia fighting for their own independence," Brad continued. "They aren't mercenaries trained to hold a position, and we can't expect them to hold indefinitely against a well-trained regular army."

"I know," Richard replied. "The plan is to pull our guys when the NVA gets close. We will know when they're at the front door and we'll have choppers on standby. The Hmong can regroup with Vang Pao's people in Long Tieng."

"Rich, we've had mission-creep on this thing since the first day it was presented to me," Brad said, shrugging his shoulders. "Every day we add a little more to the plan, and that makes me think we're going to try to get more bang for our buck. We can't stay on that mountain forever."

"I know that, Brad. Ambassador Sullivan knows it, and I sent a memo directly to Secretary McNamara last week, so you can expect the President knows it, too. From bottom to top, we know we have to pull our guys when the NVA gets close."

"Okay, I just wanted to make sure my point was clear," Brad said.

Both men finished off the beer and threw the steel cans toward a cardboard box in the far corner. Toward, but not in. Richard pulled two more beers and tossed one to Brad.

"We still need to sort out how the Thai special forces are going to work as bodyguards at the facility," Brad said. "I'm not going to be able to oversee the Hmong and the Thais at the same time, and it's possible that a small group of NVA could get through the Hmong line."

"Yeah, don't worry about that," Richard replied. "I have a guy in mind who's perfect for the job."

5

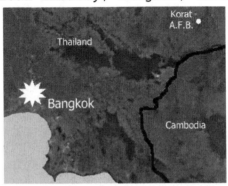

Lieutenant John Lilygren loved tuk tuks, the three-wheeled, motorized taxis that were a staple of Bangkok transportation. When he was a teenager and living in Bangkok, he and his two best friends had tuk tuk races. Each of them would hire one for twenty baht and tell the driver there was five more baht for the fastest to whatever destination in the city. This occasionally ended in a big mess on Sathon or Rama IV Road, but it was always exciting. Now back in Bangkok, he felt no need for any more adrenalin than came from a standard ride. John stepped out the back of the machine and paid the driver, then looked across Wireless Road to the American Embassy.

John Lilygren had grown up playing in the US

Embassy's garden, but the path he and his father had taken to get to Bangkok would have seemed unlikely eighty years before. Fearing a spread in the carnage of World War I, Lily and Magnus Lilygren had left Gothenburg, Sweden, for the United States. They had first settled in Minnesota, working on the dairy farm that had promised them jobs prior to immigrating. The Stock Raising Homestead Act of 1916 had made land available for ranching in the West, and they had taken advantage of it by resettling on 640 acres in central Wyoming.

Their son, Todd Lilygren, had been raised on that ranch near Sweetwater Station, and he'd returned to it after serving in the Burma campaign during World War II. Todd realized the day he got back to Sweetwater Station, in a whiteout blizzard, that he loved Southeast Asia and, coupled with the fact that his wife had died of cancer within days of the war's end, he'd applied for a job with the Foreign Service, contingent that it be in Southeast Asia. Wyoming's small population meant that virtually everyone in the state had political connections. An old family friend, US Senator John Hickey of Rawlins, assured him the position would be at whatever location Todd wanted. Young John Lilygren spent the next nine years with his father in Thailand.

John could see through the wrought-iron gate that the original residence, built in French colonial style in the early 1900s, had just been repainted bright yellow. It was surrounded by an expansive and lush garden, complete with fountains and bougainvillea-lined paths, which very much suited the laid-back feel of old Bangkok. The air was filled with the fragrance of flowering frangipani trees, a scent he'd woken to every day as a child. His heart warmed even more at the cries of the resident kakow birds which made a home in the old-growth trees around the ambassador's residence.

Some things hadn't changed, but others had. There was now a ten-foot-high whitewashed concrete wall around the embassy grounds. South of the residence, a modern building had sprung up with multiple floors rising above the perimeter wall. The big building had plenty of antennas on the roof and iron rods running horizontally over the windows. A Thai Army sentry stood about every fifty meters just outside the concrete wall and two brand new M113 armored personnel carriers with .50-caliber machine guns flanked the iron gate. The look of the Thai soldiers manning the big machines was deadly serious. It was just one view of Thailand that served as a stark reminder that there was a major war being fought for this corner of the world.

John waited for another tuk tuk to pass, then crossed the street and walked in front of one of the M113s and toward the gate.

The soldier manning the .50-caliber gun stared at John with steely eyes, and a Thai lieutenant stepped down and straight into John's path along the big machine. John saluted, then put his palms together in front of his chest, as if praying, and bent at the waist.

"Sawasdee kop, Tahan Pon," John said, reading the soldier's name on his uniform. "Pom Cheu Khun John." Translated, it was simply, "Hello, Officer Pon. My name is John, and I am a lieutenant, too," but the effect of saying it in Thai was immeasurably more polite than the formal introduction. As John expected, it completely changed the soldier's mood.

"Poot phaa sa Thai dai ma, kop?" The lieutenant asked, through a beaming smile, how John spoke Thai, then glanced at the soldiers, and back at John in disbelief.

Very few foreigners, or farang as they are called in Thailand, spoke the language. It was difficult for the Western ear to discern the various tones that could completely change a word's meaning, but John had been immersed in the language at a young age and somehow it had come naturally to him. Within just one year of living in Thailand, John had learned to read and write in the most respected dialect of the language. This skill had given him a clearer understanding of the culture than non-Thai speakers could ever hope to have.

"I lived here at the embassy for many years," John replied in perfect Thai.

"Khap khun kop, Pi Lieutenant John." The Thai officer thanked John and shook his hand.

The level of respect shown to the Thai by simply speaking their language was beyond measure.

As John had expected, military protocol had instantly been overwhelmed by Thai hospitality. The lieutenant gleefully yelled to the soldiers that the farang spoke Thai, and two more climbed down from the APC to introduce themselves. They had to meet this blond, blue-eyed farang who could converse fluently in the respected, higher dialect of Thai reserved for the educated class of Bangkok. One soldier remained aboard, but the look on his face revealed that he wanted to join the group, too.

"Go right in, Pi Lieutenant John," the lieutenant said in Thai. Despite being of the same rank and a bit older, the Thai lieutenant referred to John as "pi." Like the English "sir," it showed respect. John bowed again and walked to the gate.

Two young Marines saluted and the older of the two looked at John's military paperwork.

"I'm here to see Richard Milano. He's expecting me," John said. He was wearing his short-sleeve dress uniform, decorated with the merits of the last few years in the war. The Marines were obviously impressed.

"Yes, sir. Come right in, Lieutenant," the sergeant said as he opened the gate.

"That M16 ever jam up on you, corporal?" John asked.

"Only when I fire it, sir," the corporal said. It was a joke, but it also wasn't a joke. The new guns were very finicky.

"I'm trying to get my M1 back, sir," the young Marine added.

John nodded and smiled in appreciation of the opinion, then strolled across the garden to the large white building with all the antennas. That would be the one where Richard worked. He got directions to CIA assistant station chief's office from the Thai maid mopping the marble entry, then went upstairs and two doors down the hall. He stepped into the doorway of a drably painted room with a few pictures on the wall of President Johnson and Secretary of Defense McNamara. Below them was a framed photo of a person, silhouetted completely black, with an official nametag that read "Central Intelligence Agency Director Helms." Richard Milano's sense of humor stood out in even the simplest decor.

"So, Rich, you got time to run up to Katchanaburi for a day or two of climbing?" John asked of the dark haired man seated at the green metal desk.

"Johnny-boy. Damn-yer-eyes, how the hell are ya?"

The big man stood up from his chair, stepped across the room and gave John a hug. The two men hadn't seen each other in almost a year. Rich had always been very tall for a climber, but now he seemed to be adding a little width to the height. The strands of gray in his otherwise black hair probably weren't help-ing his rock-climbing passion.

"Watch the shoulder, watch the shoulder," John said as Richard went to give him a second hug.

"Right. How's that healin', anyway?"

"It's going to be fine. It's still tender from the burn, but the actual shrapnel didn't cut anything important. They took the stitches out last week." John paused. "Not much could be done for the other two guys. That's two more kids who never get to be adults."

"Yeah, that really is a bad deal. This war is damn costly. The figures I saw yesterday indicate we went over a thousand killed in action last month. I lost a couple of my guys this year, too."

"Whoa! Your guys?" John exclaimed in a more cheerful tone. Neither of them really wanted to talk about the death of American GIs. "Just what kind of job do they have the assistant CIA station chief doing these days, anyway?"

"Well, I'm wearing a couple hats now. It's a lot of pencil-pushing and paperwork, and a good bit of it is done out of the base at Udorn."

"Udorn. Isaan, Thailand is flatter than Bangkok. You're not going to get much climbing in at Udorn."

"True," Richard replied. "I was actually there yesterday afternoon."

Richard was originally from Laramie, Wyoming, about a four-hour drive from the Lilygren Ranch near Sweetwater Station. Like John's father, Richard had also gotten his assignment through Senator Hickey. Richard had been with the 10th Mountain Division in Italy during WWII and had come back from the war an avid climber. The rocky outcroppings at Vedauwoo, just east of Laramie, had been his home crag before he took the job with the CIA. He was stationed at the embassy in Thailand when John's father had been stationed in Bangkok, and the three Wyoming natives had become climbing partners. Together they had made dozens of trips to the karst-limestone spires of central Thailand in Katchanaburi Provence.

"I'm afraid I'm way too busy for rock climbing, my friend," Richard said, as he led John to a seat next to the gray, steel desk.

He pulled a cardboard filing box off the chair to make space, then stepped around to his own seat. "We have a lot going on here, but before we get to that, how's your Dad? I'm sure you hear from him more than I do."

"He's good. He's semi-retired, and back on the ranch and leading hunting trips into the Wind Rivers every fall," John replied. "Dad has a little more rosy opinion about how this war is going than I do."

"Well, that's not surprising. Anyone over here can see things aren't going the way we planned. It's only a matter of time before the politicians get sick of the protests and we get called home with a new record of ten and one."

"Yep, it seems like Ho Chi Minh has a better game plan than the USA."

"He always has. You know he worked for us during WWII?" Richard commented.

"What?"

"He was an informant and saboteur for the OSS."

Richard poured a couple glasses of water and passed one across the desk. John knew the OSS, the Office of Strategic Services, was the precursor organization to the CIA. It had been an effective counter-intelligence organization in Southeast Asia during World War II. John also knew that if Richard was pouring water, and not beer, the conversation was going to get serious.

"Yep, Ho Chi Minh was American OSS Agent 19. He went by the code name Lucius. Right after the war, when he stated he believed in communism, we ran him off. We refused to assist him in any way, and then helped out the French, instead."

"That's amazing," John said through a stunned look. "How is it the American people haven't heard about this?"

"Well, it's not something we like to talk about, Johnny." Richard laughed. "It's not just an egg, it's an entire chicken farm on America's face. This whole war might not have happened if we'd kept that guy in the fold."

John sat silent for a moment, still in shock, noting how the smallest change in history, or just one person, could have an effect on the entire world.

"This is where we are, John-boy," Richard said. "We can't go back in time, and there is a good chance he would have gone down the Soviet path anyway. No one can be sure just how history would have turned out if we had befriended Ho, but we are here now and have to take our lumps."

John nodded. This was definitely going to be a serious conversation.

"Let me get my accomplice in here so we can fill you in on the operation we're putting together," Richard said as he stepped out the door. Half a minute later, the CIA operative stepped back into the room.

"John, this is Major Henry Newcomb with the Air Force," Richard said as John stood. "Hank, Lieutenant John Lilygren, Rangers."

"Major," John said with a salute.

"Call me Hank," the major said, returning the salute and then extending his hand. "This uniform and rank almost seem surreal considering what we've been doing lately. Military protocol is not a part of the war up north."

"And I prefer to be called John," John said as he shook the major's hand.

"Obviously everything you are about to hear is strictly confidential, John," Richard said. "I had your record pulled last week and with your long-range reconnaissance missions, you obviously get to see classified stuff, but you should know this goes far beyond recon."

"Understood," John replied. "Considering how I got your invitation, if you call it that, I figured something secretive was on the agenda."

"By the way, Johnny-boy, did you really chase an NVA regular for two days after he fired on you?" Richard asked.

The major let out a chuckle.

"I'm always getting sold short, Rich . . . it was three days."

"You crazy bastard," Richard said, shaking his head. "Anyway, for the last few months, Hank has been handling a project we call 'Combat Skyspot.' It's done with us and the Air Force. Go ahead, Hank."

"Well, before we get to Skyspot, let me give you some background," Hank said. "First, as you probably are aware, the United States is in Laos."

"Yeah, the 'other theater' that nobody talks about," John said. "I just assumed we were there from time to time when I came across a kilometer-long section of jungle that had clearly been taken out by a B-52."

"Ah, so you've been in Laos, too," Hank said through a devilish smile. Everyone knew recon patrols were supposed to stay on the Vietnamese side of the border.

"We didn't want to be in Laos. But the NVA runs the Ho Chi Minh Trail through almost the entire length of the country. If we're going to stop the flow of arms to South Vietnam, we have to work in Laos."

Hank unfolded a map on Richard's desk.

"As you know, according to the Geneva Accords neither the US nor the North Vietnamese can operate in Laos," Richard said. "The Vietnamese admitted to having around seven thousand troops in Laos back at the Geneva summit, but when the mutual exit came in October of 'sixty-six, only about forty of them left the country. Obviously, they never intended to leave. Instead, they began building the road and path system that we now call the Ho Chi Minh Trail. We're flying approximately fifty bombing sorties against traffic on the Trail every day."

John's eyes widened. Fifty? Fifty sorties a day was a lot of bombs, yet the flow of weapons was increasing, not diminishing.

"The problem, as you know, is the Trail is hard to spot in the jungle, even for the forward air controllers who're looking for it at low speed," the major added. "It is especially difficult to see when cloud cover is thick, or when a 37mm gun is firing up at you. We have listening devices and a network of locals who can tell us what's going on, but the Trail gets moved every time we put a crater in a road. They must have tens of thousands of people working on it right now, including adding camouflage above. It runs for miles in spots, like a tunnel, under the jungle canopy."

"But it gets more complicated than the US dropping bombs, John," Richard added. "We have allies in Laos that are fighting on the ground."

"The Montagnards?" John asked. He had heard of the hill tribes that lived in the highlands of Vietnam. They didn't really recognize the border between the two countries, and also didn't recognize North Vietnam's leadership. As John understood it, they were ethnically different from the more populous Viet, and had not been treated well over the centuries.

"Yeah, the Montagnards, a generic French term for the hill tribes in Vietnam," Richard said. "The Chinese and North Vietnamese call the various tribes the Meo. There is one specific tribe in Laos, the Hmong, who are really taking the fight to the NVA. They aren't big guys, but I wouldn't want to tangle with one of them. They started fighting the Vietnamese right after World War II, and it hasn't stopped. Nowadays, we pay the soldiers a small salary and provide arms."

"We can't put American soldiers in there," Hank continued. "The White House and Joint Chiefs won't go for it, so we equip the Hmong as best as we can. They are fighting full-scale battles in an area called the Plain of Jars, about here."

Richard pointed to the center of the widest part of Northern Laos. "The CIA's forward air controllers, the Ravens, are also based there."

"We actually have an army on the ground in Laos?" John asked.

"We'll come back to the Hmong," Hank said. "You should have some idea of our operation."

"Okay," John said. "So what is Combat Skyspot?"

"Skyspot is a program we have to increase the accuracy of our bombing runs. We've put these beacons, six of them, actually, in various places in Laos. The beacons are called TACANs, which stands for Tactical Air Navigation system," Hank said. "Essentially, the TACAN uses high-frequency radio waves to communicate with a transponder in various aircraft . . . mostly F-105s. It can give them a pretty good idea of where they are at night or in bad weather."

"Who maintains these things?"

"They sort of run themselves most of the time, and we just have to do some maintenance," the major replied. "Hmong soldiers are stationed at each site to keep other locals away and let us know if the Vietnamese get wise to it. So far they haven't seemed to notice anything."

"These things have a downside, John," Richard stated. "They aren't that accurate."

"Well, they improved our effectiveness quite a bit," the major countered, "but not enough. Before the TACANs, our bombs were falling sometimes a quarter-mile from the target. With it, we are averaging between three hundred and four hundred feet from the target. It's an improvement, but in thick jungle, or in these rocky hills, it's not good enough."

John was again in a state of shock. Everyone in Vietnam suspected Americans were bombing the occasional target in Laos, and everyone knew they should. But what he was hearing, and he assumed he wasn't getting the whole picture, was that there was a secret war being waged in Laos. Not a few bombing runs, but a couple of secret armies fighting over control of the Ho Chi Minh Trail.

"So John, the deal is this," Richard said, "we are looking to upgrade one of the TACANs to a fully functioning radar facility. It will be like an air traffic control center at a major airport, but rather than direct landing aircraft, the new system will line up bombing sorties. This program is called Operation Heavy Green"

"The specific equipment to be used is a completely independent radar unit called a TSQ-81," the major said with some pride. "And it will change the war."

"The location for this thing is on a limestone mountain less than a hundred-fifty miles from Hanoi. The TSQ will be manned by air traffic controllers who can pinpoint the F-105 drops," Richard said. "The controllers will actually be civilians, not soldiers, so we can keep up the plausible deniability that Ambassador Sullivan is so fond of. He really likes being able to say there are no American soldiers in Laos."

"So the US ambassador to Laos, Sullivan, is opposed to this thing, but you guys are going to do it anyway?" John asked.

"His boss likes it," Hank replied, pointing to a picture of President Lyndon Johnson on the wall.

"The ambassador is all right," Richard said. "He has to play the role of the guy who pretends we aren't in Laos, but he's not a career politician, so he feels uncomfortable about lying. If I had to talk to reporters every day, I'd feel the same way. In any event, the White House wants this operation to happen, so Sullivan is reluctantly going along with it. However, he'll be part of every decision. You can count on that."

"We're going to put a Hmong force on the mountain for security," Richard continued. "And I'm putting one of my guys in there who's been working with the Hmong for a while. To help with radio communications, and to have just plain-old bodyguards, we'll have a couple squads of Thai PARU commandos at the site."

John knew about the PARU. They were the cream of the crop of the Thai armed forces, and the Thais took their military training seriously. Every man in the

PARU was known to be an excellent shot, but they excelled in hand-to-hand fighting. Muay Thai was brutal for a national sport, but the licks eight-and ten-year-old kids took in phys-ed class paid off later in close combat.

"Ahhh. It's coming together," John said. "Orders for me to come see you, and someone is needed to liaison with the Thais?"

"That's right," Richard said. "The Hmong are good fighters, but they are better at guerrilla tactics, hit-and-run stuff, than anything else. Holding a specific spot is not their forte. I want the PARU force guarding the TSQ-81, and I want one of our Special Operations guys assisting the PARU. Your understanding of Thai and the Thai culture, as well as your Ranger background, makes you perfect."

John appreciated that America was putting together a mission that would actually hit the North Vietnamese Army more accurately. But the scale of the mission, this secret war, was an enormous departure from what he had known about when he'd walked into the room.

"Okay, so when are you going to put this plan into action?" he asked.

"It's already in action," the major replied. "The facility is built. We are doing a test run in a few days on a target in Laos. If that goes well, we move in by the end of the month."

John sat silently staring into the distance, trying to absorb it all. Richard and the major understood the shock John had to be feeling. The war was far bigger than he had thought. They waited quietly for his next question.

"Okay," he said. "I like that we are taking the real fight to the enemy, so I'm on board. But I just got transferred to G2 at Tan Son Nhut and my CO is a real hard ass. He probably isn't going to let me leave my job after just three weeks."

"Yes, he is," Richard said through a grin.

"What did you do, Rich?" John asked through a chuckle.

"I called him last week to arrange your transfer," Richard replied. "I tried to speak reasonably, but that SOB is a hard ass, so I had him softened."

"How?"

"He got a phone call from Robert McNamara last night. At home. The Secretary's involvement is how you got R&R in Bangkok, which technically isn't real." Richard reached into his desk drawer and pulled out a bottle of Maker's Mark bourbon.

"So I'm here on falsified orders and the Secretary of Defense knows my name?"

"He knows you, but you are not here on fake orders. Actually, Lieutenant John Lilygren isn't here at all. We can only have civilians in Laos, and that includes on this mission," Richard said. "You got sheepdipped this morning and aren't in the Army. You can go back to it when this mission is over and it will look like you never left. I think you'll come back as a captain, if that helps."

"That's great, Rich. What if I hadn't wanted to take the mission?" John asked.

"I'd just put you back in there," Richard stated. "You'd have never known it happened. But, I knew you'd want this job."

"Okay. Let me see if I understand Operation Heavy Green," John said. "We are putting a hyper-accurate radar site in a country we claim not to be in, and we are manning it with civilians."

"Yeah, go on," Richard said.

"And from this we will bomb the road we can barely see and that moves daily?"

"Almost," Richard replied, pouring the bourbon into three glasses. "The Laotians have a proverb: 'You cannot kill a cobra by beating on its tail.'"

John immediately had a sense of déjà vu. That was the second time he'd heard that proverb in as many days.

"This program isn't about the Ho Chi Minh Trail," Rich continued as he passed out the glasses of bourbon. "We need this level of accuracy because we're going to start bombing the supply depots and MiG bases around Hanoi. That's why it will change the war."

The phone rang.

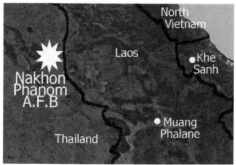

Captain Somporn Luang stood in the waiting room, sipping tea and admiring the giant map of Southeast Asia. The details the Americans possessed were amazing. Lengths of string ran from photographs to various points on the map to add important visual information. Luang knew most of the photos had been taken on missions to retrieve downed pilots; he'd personally been where five of the pins were placed.

One couldn't help but be thankful for the wide, brown Mekong River that separated his country from Laos, Luang thought. The American pilots referred to it as "the Fence"; the name suited the wide waterway. Without it, the occasional skirmish and light insurgency spilling into Thailand would be the full-on war that existed in Laos. Luang was also thankful that his current home, Nakhon Phanom Royal Thai Air Force Base, was sixteen kilometers from the west bank of the river. Those sixteen kilometers were populated by people who would gladly notify the Thai authorities of

96

anyone who looked out of place.

If a Vietnamese insurgent managed to get through the gauntlet of Thai villagers, he then faced a barbed wired fence fifteen feet high, a wide expanse of concertina wire, some anti-personnel mines, guard towers next, as well as almost three hundred members of the Thai military. All of this guarded the various bombers, recon aircraft, and American military personnel, not to mention Luang and his fellow commandos. The Americans had even begun using dogs to patrol the perimeter at night.

It all helped Luang get to sleep, but was probably making him soft.

Luang was from Krabi, one of the southernmost cities in Thailand. Like all Thai boys, he'd learned Muay Thai, the martial art of kickboxing. He excelled at the sport, winning every tournament he had entered. Luang had joined the military a little young, at age sixteen, and had immediately been taken in by the company commander for his Muay Thai skills. He was soon paraded to various fights with other units, which he easily won. In 1962, when his commander was offered a position in the Police Aerial Reinforcement Unit (PARU), the most respected of the Thai Special Forces, Luang went with him.

The political and cultural epicenter of Thailand had been in Bangkok for centuries. Southern Thailand had been considered a cultural backwater, so Luang's background had been a bit of a drawback in his military career. One of the officers at the PARU base in Hua Hin had once said that the dialect Luang spoke sounded like the runny farts of a water buffalo. From then on he'd been nicknamed Kwai, the Thai word for buffalo.

Even though the Thais thought of the buffalo as slow and dumb, Luang liked the moniker. It was an ironic joke on how fast he was in the ring. However, he also knew the chiding went a little deeper and had a sad bit of Thailand's reality to it. Like most people from Krabi, Luang was Muslim. He wasn't a religious man and had only gone to mosque when his father had forced him. But he knew that due to his Southern dialect and not having been raised a Thai Buddhist, some of the insults were serious. The other men of the PARU weren't just kidding him.

Luang excelled under the American teachers at Hua Hin and he was eventually sent to Fort Benning, Georgia, for further training with US Army Rangers. He took immersion classes in English as part of the military training. The Rangers taught him how to use every weapon in their arsenal, as well as how to work from helicopters and parachute from planes. After six weeks of training, Luang had graduated with his jump wings. He was not only a member of the Thai PARU, but also an honorary Army Ranger.

One unpleasant event in America had produced an unexpected outcome. The evening after his graduation, Luang got shoved out of the line in the mess hall by a very large instructor from Louisiana named Sergeant Billy Macon. This man was perhaps two meters tall and weighed over a hundred kilos, and most of the other Ranger students feared him.

"You chinks can get in the back of the line with the niggers," Sergeant Macon said in a strange accent.

Luang knew he was being challenged, and it was not in his nature to simply back down from a bully. He said nothing but stepped back into his rightful place in line. The giant man grabbed him by the neck. In one motion Luang jumped while lifting his left knee into the big man's rib cage. Luang felt a couple of the bones give as the force of the blow pushed him back to the ground. As his feet came under him, Luang's elbow flew over the big man's arm, now suddenly only barely holding the Thai's neck. Luang's elbow caught the giant just behind the chin. Billy's jaw broke and dislocated instantly. Half a second later, Billy was on the ground and unconscious. His size had been intimidating, but his skill as a fighter: horrible.

Luang and every other man in the room realized only one more blow from the hundred-thirty-pound Thai would have ended the giant's life.

A whistle blew and Luang stepped away. A wide circle, well out of arm's reach, had formed around the Thai soldier. Luang was taken to the stockade minutes later by two muscular members of the military police. Thinking he might be thrown out of the PARU, or even executed by the Americans, Luang was terrified when Colonel Maestas showed up at the jail. Colonel Maestas was in charge of Ranger training, and he was known to be a serious man who did not allow rule violations. Luang jumped to attention and made no eye contact with the officer or his assistant.

"Corporal Luang," the colonel asked sternly, "are you the man who knocked out Sergeant Billy Macon twenty minutes ago?"

"Yes, Colonel. I am very sorry, sir."

Colonel Maestas turned to a military policeman and said, "I want this man released immediately. That ignorant racist Macon has already been in my office twice this year, and he no doubt had it coming. Eric," he continued, turning to the lieutenant who'd followed him into the room, "I want Corporal Luang transferred to hand-to-hand combat, and I want him teaching tomorrow." Maestas turned back to Luang. "Corporal Luang, like it or not, we are going to be fighting a war in your part of the world very soon. I want you to teach the Rangers how people fight in Southeast Asia. I don't want them to learn it in the field."

Luang was ordered to spend the next eight weeks teaching Muay Thai to American drill sergeants at bases around the country. He ended up with a merit award from the Americans and a jump in rank in the PARU.

His time at Fort Benning, and flying across America to various Air Force and Army bases in Texas, California, and Hawaii, had made a lasting impression on Luang. The country was enormous, with every conceivable convenience, and its military was far superior to anything Luang had ever imagined. He'd come away from the United States with one certainty: The Americans could never lose a war to the Vietnamese. As long as the United States was helping defend his country, the people of Thailand were safe.

"Captain Luang, you may come in now," Captain Subhait said in perfect Thai.

All the PARU at Nakhon Phanom knew of James Subhait. His parents were very close to the royal family and his father had been the Siamese ambassador to the United States at the outbreak of World War II. His father had been opposed to an alliance with Japan and, with the Japanese occupation of Thailand during the war, his family had been unable to return. Subhait was thus born in Washington, D.C., and was a citizen of both Thailand and the United States. His family returned to Thailand after the coup in 1949 and Subhait had attended the American school. After graduation he had attended the US Air Force Academy. He was now an assistant to Colonel Weaver, who was in command of the 634th Combat Support Group.

Luang stepped into the room and came to attention in front of Colonel Weaver's desk. Though he was not a large man, the Thai's physique was impressive even in his loose-fitting uniform. Bands of muscle in his cheeks and forearms revealed the Thai soldier was all muscle. Luang stared into the distance with his salute but noticed with his peripheral vision there was another American, wearing a white, short-sleeved dress shirt, a thin black tie, and horn-rimmed glasses, standing a few feet to the left of the colonel.

"Sawasdee kop," the colonel said, casually leaning back in his chair behind the desk.

Luang noted his accent was similar to that of Sergeant Macons.

"That's 'hello' in Thai, if I pronounced it right," the Colonel continued, "And about as much of your language as I know, so we should probably let Captain Subhait start translating right now."

"Sir, if I may?" Captain Subhait asked.

"Yes, Jimmy?"

"I believe Captain Luang speaks English every bit

as well as I do. I'm not sure you need my translation slowing the conversation."

"That true, Captain?" the colonel asked.

"Yes, sir. I speak English, sir."

"Okay then, at ease, Captain," he replied.

Luang relaxed his stance and put his hands behind his back.

"I saw in your file that you commanded a Special Guerrilla Unit of PARU in nineteen sixty-five on multiple missions inside Laos. One was long-range reconnaissance at Vang Muang near the Vietnamese border, and the second was later that year on the Plain of Jars near Long Tieng. Did we get that correct in the translation?"

Luang glanced at the man in the dress shirt and tie.

"It's okay, Captain," Subhait said. "You can speak freely in front of Mr. McKenna."

"Yes, sir," Luang replied. "Both missions were to gather intelligence on the North Vietnamese's 559th Division. On the second mission we were diverted to rescue a downed A-4 Skyhawk pilot from the US Navy. I believe he served on the USS Intrepid. We actually had to trek to Long Tieng after he was lifted out by helicopter."

"The reason I bring this up, Captain, is we have another mission in Laos, and not one that is related to your daytime job," the colonel said.

"Sir?"

"I mean, most of the work the PARU do is retrieving our downed pilots from the woods before the NVA grabs them. This mission will have a bit more pizzazz, shall we say. We will need people who know just how deeply involved we have become in the war in Laos, and your résumé makes you perfect for the job."

"Thank you, sir," Lung replied.

"Captain, this is Irvin McKenna with USAID," the colonel said. "The Air Force, in conjunction with the Army, USAID, and Thai PARU Squadron 333, is putting this operation together."

Luang knew that when someone was introduced as "USAID," he was usually in the Central Intelligence Agency. Many educated Thais feared this clandestine American presence, but not the Thai military, not the King of Thailand, and certainly not Luang. He understood what was necessary to stop the North Vietnamese. Luang put his hands at his side and nodded to the man almost in a traditional Thai wai, the bow of reverence and respect.

"Nice to meet you, Captain Luang," the man said with a weak smile.

"Captain Luang, the operation is top secret so we can't tell you any details until you are actually in the program," the colonel continued. "What we can tell you is that it is extremely dangerous, which is why you're being asked if you want to join instead of being assigned to it. We believe this operation will hit the NVA where it hurts. Feel free to speak your mind."

"Sir, I understand the secrecy, but may I know something about what my duties would be?" Luang asked.

"Jimmy, tell him what he needs to know for Heavy Green," the colonel said to Captain Subhait.

"You would be in control of perhaps three squads of

men who are being chosen by General Yasawat of Squadron 333 in Udorn," Captain Subhait said. "You will be under American command, but will file an oral report with Major Phanu each week. Nothing will be in writing."

This shed a little more light on the program. For Major Phanu to be involved, it would have to be in Northern Laos. Luang had worked under Phanu on the Plain of Jars. He knew Phanu to be smart and very tough, but not the most open-minded officer. Phanu was from Chiang Mai, and always felt the Thai way of doing things was the only way. He hadn't always been receptive to orders from American superiors or General Vang Pao. Luang had heard that Phanu had been transferred to Lima Site 36, what the Americans called "the Alamo," in North Central Laos.

"Mai pen rai, Phan Tri Phanu," Captain Subhait said to Luang. "Kohn farang choi dai."

"In English, Jimmy," the colonel said with a sigh.

"Sorry, sir. I was just explaining that Major Phanu would not be in command."

"That's right," the colonel added. "Phanu will be filing a report with General Yasawat of the Three Thirty-third. We will probably send Phanu to you rather than have you leave your post."

The major is going to love that, Luang thought in jest. Phanu didn't like answering to anyone, and having to travel to meet a Southern Thai Muslim who he outranked was going to no doubt infuriate the man.

"Sir, thank you for the honor and privilege of this offer," Luang said. "I very much would like to take this assignment and will not fail you. If I may, sir, I do have two questions."

The colonel nodded.

"Should I file the transfer request with the Three Thirty-third? And do you know who will replace me with my squad?"

"General Yasawat has already arranged it," Subhait said. "He is also choosing your successor. His assumption was that you would want the assignment. All you need to do is grab your gear and meet Mr. McKenna on the flight line at eleven-hundred hours. The boys at Udorn will fill you in on Operation Heavy Green when you arrive."

An hour later Luang was seated next to the "USAID agent" in a Sikorsky S-61 helicopter en route to Udorn Royal Thai Air Force Base.

October 10, 1967, 0940 hours,

(same day)

American Embassy, Vientiane, Laos

Tom Dillon quietly pulled the heavy teak door to Ambassador Sullivan's office shut and took a deep breath. The ambassador's secretary glanced up from her typewriter, raised her eyebrows, and smiled as if to say "that sounded like a tough meeting." They were always tough, but this one had been particularly tense. The voices grew loud again behind the door, propelling him through the hall and onto the stairway.

Tom ran athletically down the stairs, skipping a step with each stride, and passed out of the old colonial embassy building and into the new, modern-designed concrete block the embassy staff referred to as AB-1. He descended a dull, white stairwell to the basement where his office had been for the previous year.

The enormous square room had little airflow besides the deafening air conditioners, and there were no windows for natural light, but the fluorescent tubes kept it bright. Black filing cabinets were packed into the corners next to desks, and a large steel table sat in the middle of the room. The wall decors were huge aerial photographs and maps of Southeast Asia. Detailed maps of particular areas, including three from Military Zone II of Northeast Laos, were roughly framed with handwritten notes and smaller photos. The room was not decorated for comfort; it was built for war.

As Sullivan's assistant, Dillon understood where the ambassador's anger was coming from. William Sullivan had been sitting with Averell Harriman, across the table from the Soviets and North Vietnamese during the Geneva Agreements of 1962. Because of those negotiations, Sullivan had quoted the portion of the agreement that read that the two parties "agree not to impair the sovereignty, independence, neutrality, unity, or territorial integrity of Laos" so many times that Dillon could recite it himself. Sometimes the ambassador yelled it, just to make sure the air attaché, the CIA station chief, and of course his young assistant, never forgot the treaty.

Ambassador Sullivan had served on a Navy destroyer in WWII and had seen the horrors of war first hand. He had watched through the blaze of the ships' guns as Americans charged into German machine-gun fire at Normandy, and had later seen hundreds of defeated and distraught Japanese soldiers commit suicide by jumping off Okinawa's cliffs. He recognized that most military decisions were not based on clear cut-and-dried facts, but on educated guesses, decisions that usually led to the stark reality of life or death. He did not want to see American soldiers die for Laos, and felt the Laotians themselves were better suited to defending their own country.

The failed invasion of Cuba at the Bay of Pigs had helped to get William Sullivan the Laos ambassadorship. The Kennedy Administration felt America looked weak in world opinion, which made it a bad time to turn their backs on the insurgency in Laos. Under the Geneva Agreements, the United States had admitted that it had about a hundred-fifty people working in Laos. By Hanoi's own estimation, North Vietnam had about 7,000 cadres building roads, bunkers, bridges, and so forth, to help ferry supplies to South Vietnam. The US pulled virtually all its paramilitary agents from the country, but left two behind to monitor the NVA: Would they keep to their agreement? At best count, forty NVA soldiers crossed the border back into North Vietnam. They'd never had any intention of leaving, and everyone knew it.

Sullivan knew it best, and as the ambassador he had been assigned to "fix it." His job was not just diplomacy with Souvanna Phouma, the Laotian prime minister, he was also the functional military leader of all US forces operating in the country. The nickname "Field Marshal Sullivan" was now in common use.

Just after Sullivan's posting in 1965, Prime Minister Souvanna Phouma (also the Laotian crown prince) had let the vampire in the door. Under political and military pressure from his brother, who just happened to be the leader of the communist Pathet Lao, Souvanna gave the North Vietnamese permission to traverse the country as long as they did not threaten his leadership. When the US recognized what had happened, they asked for and received the prime minister's permission to bomb any military supply routes going to South Vietnam.

The two policies were an attempt to appease both sides but had a horrible effect on Laos. The US Air Force was running Operation Steel Tiger and Barrel Roll, bombing campaigns in Northern and Southern Laos, that hit North Vietnamese targets daily. The little Kingdom of a Million Elephants was on its way to becoming the most heavily bombed country in the world.

"Good morning, sir," James Chang said as Tom entered the room.

Chang, whose first language was Mandarin Chinese, had received his Harvard diploma just sixteen months before getting the Laos assignment. His parents had immigrated to the US in 1946, and they had not let their son squander the family's first chance at an education. Chang excelled in all academics and had gone to Harvard on a full scholarship. With a double major in Asian history and foreign affairs, the ambassador had personally plucked him from the list of possible diplomats for Vientiane. "He is a whiz kid," Sullivan liked to say, "and we need more of those."

Chang stood up and leaned over his desk to hand Tom an over-stuffed manila folder.

"Here are the Operations Orders for today's requested targets and aerial recon shots from the Air Force. I don't have the updated list from Saigon yet, but it should be here any minute."

"Anything new here?" Tom asked as he paged through the paperwork.

"No, sir, it's the usual stuff. Most of the requested targets are SAM sites and the MiG base at Phuc Yen," Chang said. "And of course the usual request for the Presidential Palace in downtown Hanoi."

"Of course." The Air Force hadn't yet realized that the "downtown Hanoi" joke was getting old, Tom thought.

"We also got another nasty phone call from Colonel Embry at Korat. It looks like we lost two more F-105s south of Hanoi this morning. He screamed there were surface-to-air missiles sitting on the docks in Haiphong Harbor and by not allowing his pilots to take them out, we were just killing Americans."

Dillon let out a sigh and looked up from the tan folder. "Colonel Embry is too deep in the war to see the bigger picture. Those are Russian military personnel delivering the SAM systems and escorting supply ships into Haiphong Harbor. The second to last thing the President wants to hear over his morning coffee is that some Soviet Politburo member's son was blown up by an American bomb."

"Yes, sir. What is the last thing he wants to hear over his morning coffee?" Chang asked.

"That Secretary Brezhnev and the Soviet Union have declared war on the United States. To Colonel Embry, losing a pilot is the worst thing possible, so he screams at the ambassador. To Lyndon Johnson, losing New York City is the worst thing possible. Johnson appointed William Sullivan not only as ambassador, but also as the de facto leader of all military operations in Laos. His job is to win the war and not get us into World War Three."

"Yes, sir."

"Let me look this over. You should have tomorrow's Frag Order in half an hour or so. In the meantime, I want you to call Richard Milano in Bangkok and get a firm number on how many civilians will be on-site in this Heavy Green operation. Ambassador Sullivan likes details. He is not going to accept the CIA's 'estimate.'"

"Yes, sir," Chang replied.

Tom Dillon laid the contents of the folder across his desk and grabbed a few large, black-and-white photos from a file in the top drawer of his desk. He then picked up a magnifying glass and began comparing the photos to those that had come in with the Operations Order.

James Chang picked up the black phone on his desk and dialed zero on the rotary, then said, "Hi, Trisha, it's James. I need a secure line to the embassy in Bangkok.

6

October 18, 1967, 1520 hours,
(7 days later)
Udorn Royal Thai Air Force Base, Thailand

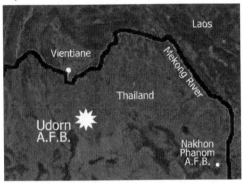

John Lilygren, now civilian John Lilygren, raised his hand and extended two fingers to get the bartender's attention. It was a noisy afternoon in the B-29 Bar, but Tex, the Thai bartender, always kept "Pi John" in the corner of his eye. John mouthed the words "sawng beer, kop" so Tex could see, and the young bartender tipped his cowboy hat in acknowledgment.

A forward air controller from Dallas who was part of the shadowy squadron known as the Ravens had given the Thai bartender the hat after hearing how much he liked John Wayne movies. Tex and his hat were instantly inseparable. Tex called his favorite waitress over and put two cans of Budweiser on her tray. She started for the table and he grabbed her hair, pulling her back for two chilled glasses. John had told him all week that he and his friends were drinking from the can, but the hospitality gene overpowered all else in the Thais. Tex was not going to send beer to a table without a chilled glass.

The B-29 Bar was in an old Quonset hut just outside Gate 3 at Udorn Air Base. Its decor consisted of photos of various aircraft in action in Laos, emblems of the units stationed on the base, and a few examples of unexploded Soviet ordnance that had been found in the Laotian mountains. An undetonated TM-46 anti-tank mine hung over the door. A stereo had been donated by a group of Air America pilots who'd flown some planes to Taiwan for maintenance. Sadly, they had only been able to buy two albums: "Walk Don't Run" by the Ventures, and Pat Boone's "White Christmas." As the CIA paramilitary guys had a standing "No Pat Boone" rule, the surf hits by the Ventures played all day and night, all week.

"How was the morning run with the PARU?" Brad Drakely asked as he wiped the sweat from his forehead. The tin building was air conditioned, but the machine did a better job of tainting the room with the smell of mold than it did of actually cooling the air.

"Totally destructive to my ego," John said to his new friend. "Those guys are animals. I've been humping loads in Vietnam for three years and it was still all I could do to keep up with them in running shoes. Not sure, but I think Luang had them run slower than normal, too."

"Yeah, I had two of them run into Alternate from a

downed chopper last year," the young CIA operative said. "I figured from where their helicopter crashed, those two guys averaged six kilometers an hour over thirty-six hours. No trail. Honestly, I don't know how you do that in Laos. They are tough as nails."

The young waitress, Nong Mee, stepped between John and Brad's chairs and set the beer and glasses on the table.

"Thank you very much, Nong Mee," John said, making sure to make eye contact as he spoke. She knew John was fluent in Thai, but she had asked him to use English as much as possible. Her husband was part of the PARU and had been injured during a rescue, so she was the breadwinner of the family. Speaking English, she'd decided, was vital to her future.

"You aRRe welcome, Pi John," she replied. Pronouncing R's was challenging for the Thais, and John had gotten her to overstate them for practice. He smiled and nodded in approval, and Mee returned to the bar.

"All right, John, before the air traffic control guys get here, hit me with it," Brad said. "You've been building me up for this question all week, and I've been busting my brain-pan trying to figure out what might be so horrible that you'd only ask me over a beer." He and John had met the previous week when they'd both arrived on the base. They shared a room in the Air America compound, and had instantly become friends. John had been asking about how the war was fought in Laos, and Brad, in a weak moment brought on by a few shots of Jack Daniels, had agreed to answer any question John had, provided the Ranger buy

113

the drinks.

"Nah, I have another question before we get to the doozy," John replied. "You get two today as we will be working with the technicians until we all fly in to Laos."

John had read most of the files the CIA had on the Hmong. They had first been united as a fighting force just after World War II by a French colonel named Trinquier. Colonel Trinquier called them the Maquisards, and with almost no scrutiny from Paris, he came up with unique ways to win their allegiance. The colonel lived for six years with the Hmong in the northern highlands of Laos and Vietnam. He recruited only single French soldiers to serve in his officer corps, and then required them to marry into the tribal hierarchy of the Hmong. There were about 250,000 Hmong in Laos, and within eighteen months he had 20,000 of them fighting the Viet Minh.

Vang Pao, a bold officer from Xieng Khouang Province, was one of the Maquisards. Vang Pao had risen through the ranks of the Colonel Trinquier's army through personal acts of bravery in battle, and then brilliant military decision-making. Most Hmong disliked the cha gee, but Vang Pao really hated them. He knew the Vietnamese's long history of dominating the Hmong, and Vietnamese incursions into Xieng Khouang Province had killed some of his family. When the North Vietnamese started using Eastern Laos as a route to supply the war in South Vietnam, it helped unite the various Hmong clans under Vang Pao. He was now a respected general in control of 20,000 troops.

John had learned the CIA had been in Laos since the late '50s, which explained why his buddy Richard had made weekly trips to Vientiane when John was a kid. Besides military training, they had built a network of airstrips, which everyone referred to as Lima Sites, all over the country. Their airline, Air America, had been used to fly rice, medical supplies, even Western educational supplies, into various Laotian villages. Per capita, the people of Laos received more in aid from the United States than any other nation on earth. The CIA, Air America, and USAID, with no more than a hundred total employees, had all worked in unison to help the Hmong against a growing communist insurgency from North Vietnam. Military equipment was part of the aid, but until the Vietnamese had really ramped up their efforts on the Trail, rice and antibiotics had been the standard freight, and bombs and bullets had been minimal. This hill tribe, which didn't even have a word for the wheel, really was being treated like an ally of the United States, and the entire operation was in the dark.

"Okay, shoot," Brad replied. "Tex, I'm gonna need a shot of Jack Daniels," he yelled to the bar. Tex tipped his hat and called Mee over.

"All right, what is Project Waterpump?" John asked with a sly grin.

"Sweet Jesus! How the hell did you find out about that?"

"It was written down on a notepad on Rich's desk. I couldn't miss it."

Mee dropped off two shots and went back to the bar.

"Okay, the whole plan has been to make sure the Hmong have ownership of the war, right? I mean, it's partially their country, and we won't be here forever. If they don't win it their way, it won't last after we leave."

John nodded, and Brad continued.

"So the Hmong have this legend called Chao Fa, about a mystical prince who can fly. He is the 'Prince of the Sky,' they say. In the various stories he always comes to save some Hmong village or individual by flying in and vanquishing the enemy." Brad downed the whiskey and took a deep breath. "So we thought it would work well, culturally and militarily, if we trained some of the Hmong to fly fighters and bombers in support of Vang Pao's ground forces. Training the Hmong to fly airplanes is Project Waterpump."

"What?" John exclaimed. "If you've made anything clear to me it is that these guys are only half a step out of the Stone Age. You said yourself they don't even know how to drive Jeeps."

"Oh, they are lousy drivers. But there is one of them who can fly the T-28 better than we can. The American pilots say the airplane is like an extension of his body. He's been bombing the hell out of the Vietnamese this year."

"Wow. It really is their war."

"Yeah, well, it is, but it seems to be going in the direction the war in South Vietnam took. This Operation Heavy Green is a bit heavy-handed for Laos in my book, but we shall see. . . . Hell, let's keep this conversation positive," Brad added in a jovial tone. "It's time for my questions."

"More than one?" John asked.

"Yeah, you get two, I get two. I'm sure the answer to my second one will have a lot of buckshot in it, but the first is more important." Brad took a sip of beer, then said, "When I've worked with the PARU, I try to explain things to them, then they put it into effect, then I explain what went wrong. As soon as I do that, they seem to lose focus. The more I teach, the more they seem resentful. Since they are good soldiers, I have to figure it's got something to do with my teaching." Brad took a sip from the condensation-covered red-and-white can.

"Well, without seeing you actually teach, I can't be sure," John replied. "But a common communication problem between our cultures is that we Americans are very direct, and that can make the Thai lose face."

"How?"

"Well, if you begin your explanation by pointing out that they did something wrong, especially if it is in front of other people, you are being rude. In a friendly setting, which is how you've explained the CIA tries to operate in Laos, they would never do that to each other. You're an equal, but you're making them lose face by pointing out a flaw."

"All right. That makes sense, but how do you get around it? They have to be able to see the mistake so they don't do it again."

"A boss or a higher-ranking officer could directly point out the mistake, but not someone who's thought to be an equal. The better approach would be to point out what part they did right, then put yourself in the position of the person who made the mistake. Say it like, 'When I was in training, I loaded the howitzer this way and it was a mistake.' That way you are being self-deprecating. Do it with a smile and they will respect you even more."

"That's probably it, and that's what I'll do." Brad nodded. "Now hit me with your big question."

"Okay." John took his shot of Jack Daniel's and looked his friend in the eye. "Tell me about the opium."

There was a pause in the conversation.

"Brad, I want to know everything."

This was an important question to John, and one he had wished he'd thought to ask Richard when they'd first talked about Heavy Green. Rumors abounded throughout the war theater that the CIA was in the heroin business, and he knew that opium poppies grew in Laos. John was still in a position with this mission he could get out of if he didn't like Brad's answer.

"Opium? Right, that makes sense," Brad said, suddenly serious. He glanced around the room, concern clear on his face. "First, I'll say this: For the last thousand years, no army has won a war in this part of the world without ruling the opium trade. Opium is to Burma, Thailand, Vietnam, and Laos what oil is to the Middle East. That said, the CIA isn't in the opium business, and neither is Air America." He took a gulp of his beer, then continued. "Opium's been a major part of the medical business in eastern Asia for centuries. Of course it has a recreational use, too. The locals mostly smoke it, but it's primarily used for pain, for surgery, for cataracts. It is a kinda cure-all for these guys. They use it for religious ceremonies, much like our Indians did with marijuana. The poppies only grow above about three thousand feet, and virtually all that terrain in Laos is controlled by the Hmong. Consequently, the Hmong have controlled the farming of the plants for hundreds of years. Hell, they even got along with the French because the French paid a better price for the stuff than the Chinese or Vietnamese."

John nodded. He raised his hand to Tex and pointed at the two empty shot glasses. Tex poured two more and handed them to Mee.

"Again, the war in Laos does not belong to us. We are assisting as best we can, and we love that they are sticking it to the NVA, but it really is their war, and it's in their country. We can't force our values on these guys. Their only cash crop for buying produce and rice is opium, so we turn a blind eye to it. Out of sight, out of mind."

Mee delivered the whiskey and both shots went straight from the tray to mouths.

"But in the interest of being honest, something difficult for a paramilitary CIA man like me, I'll add a bit more," Brad said. "Last year. No, in January of this year, one of the Air America kickers, what the Air Force calls a loadmaster, watched a couple of Hmong soldiers load three M60 crates on a C-123. The plane was flying from Lima Site 20/Alternate to Vientiane. Some Lao army guys unloaded the crates when it got to the capital. Now, this load is suspicious because weapons never go out of Alternate. They always go in. My partner, Kyle, looked into it and found that the general was using old gun crates to ship opium. I had to calm Kyle down that afternoon. He was ready to shoot General Vang Pao, which would not have helped the American position in Laos."

"No, I'd guess not," John said drily.

"So Kyle calmed down, and then he laid into Vang Pao in a polite manner. The general denied anything had gone onto any Air America planes, but we just don't know. In any event, Kyle made it clear to Vang Pao that if we ever did find it on our planes, we were pulling out. The CIA can't risk that. Vang Pao can't risk that either; it could jeopardize all the support he gets from the USA. So really, the honest answer to your question is opium is the single biggest cash crop in Southeast Asia, and we are sure our allies sell it. However, we don't let them sell it through us. We don't ask questions, and they don't tell us anything. It's their business."

"Okay. I can live with that," John said, nodding. "It is their country. You know there's a pretty big problem with it in Nam, and it must be getting back to the States because I had a new kid show up in my platoon last year with a taste for the stuff."

"Yeah, it's a problem. But we can't make these people be Americans. If we're going to be here, we have to accept some of their values. The use of opium is one of those."

"I agree. Thanks for being straight with me. Now what's your second question?" John saw the door to the bar open as he spoke. Two of the air traffic controllers who'd flown in that morning stepped into the doorway and looked around the room for familiar faces.

"Okay, here it is," Brad asked. "Did you really chase an NVA regular for five days from your base in

Quang Tri?"

"Oh, Jesus," John said, shaking his head. "Is that actually in a file somewhere?"

"Maybe. I'm CIA. I have my ways."

"Well, I'll tell you about that later. The TSQ-81 techs just walked in."

John raised is hand to call them over, then held four fingers up to Tex, and mouthed, "See beer kop."

October 18, 1967, 1520 hours,
(same day)
Vieng Xai Cave (base of operations for
Pathet Lao/NVA),Houaphan Province, Laos

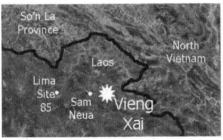

"Corporal Truang, find Lieutenant Sung and send him in here," Major Keo said into the darkness.

Besides killing seven soldiers and wounding another eleven, the American bombs the day before had taken out the generator that kept the lights working in the caves. Given their limited amount of kerosene, they could only light the workstations with lamps, which was just as well as the deeper parts of the cave had limited airflow. Keo would be thankful when a new generator was in place.

Keo was a major, or Thieu Ta, in the People's Army

of Vietnam, what the Americans called the North Vietnamese Army or NVA. The artillery company under Keo's command was made up of both North Vietnamese cadres and Pathet Lao guerrillas who were united in the fight against the Americans and the Hmong. They'd spent the dry season battling for control of the Plain of Jars and would likely be there again this year when the rain stopped.

The southwest monsoon had come early the previous year, turning the road running south through Houaphan Province into a quagmire of mud; Keo's company had lost a number of weapons with the early change in conditions. The trucks used to move the big guns to and from the Plain of Jars could not pull back when the Hmong commander, General Vang Pao, had attacked. Two Katyusha rocket launchers, a 122mm howitzer, and two 37mm anti-aircraft guns had gone to the enemy in the early monsoon. Keo's position was overrun—with the help of American bombers—and fourteen cadres had died in the battle. Pulling back, they had also lost two 12.7 Dushka machine guns and another eleven men.

The current assignment was to get the new equipment in as soon as the road was passable, but a new wrinkle in the war had appeared and there was no denying its danger to Keo's company. Lieutenant Sung and his Dac Cong Commando squad had just returned from a recon of the area in question and Keo needed answers from Sung.

As Corporal Truang and Lieutenant Sung approached the desk, the ground shook, depositing a rain of dust from the cave's ceiling onto Keo's desk. All three men winced; they knew what was coming.

The sound of the bomb blast and compression of the air in the cave were simultaneous, and the sudden popping in their ears was temporarily disorienting. Cadres new to the bombing often panicked, but the higher-ranked men under Keo's command had been through many aerial attacks. Keo took in a deep breath before the cavern filled with dust and raised his eyebrows in respect for the bomb; it had come much closer than most.

Keo immediately dusted off the work surface. He liked the French furniture, and this desk and these chairs occupied a special place in his heart: Both had been in the old French jail in Sam Neua town until Keo had had them moved to the cave complex at Vieng Xai. He kept the smaller, more rickety bamboo chair for his seat and let others take the carved teak chair that had been used by the French commander. Fifteen years before, when he'd been with the Viet Minh insurgency against the French, Keo had been seated in that same bamboo chair with his hands bound behind his back. He'd been arrested under suspicion of being in the Viet Minh.

Keo was only sixteen then, and had denied any association with the illegal organization. The French commander recognized his post was a long way from the French garrison in Hanoi, so he didn't like to make waves with the local population. After a short interrogation, he'd let young Keo free. The young Viet Minh cadre later heard that the French commander had been killed at Dien Bien Phou, perhaps by a shell fired from the artillery Keo had helped put in place. Now, as a major fighting for his country, the old chair reminded him how far he'd come, which kept the fire burning to continue the fight.

As the dust settled, Lieutenant Sung walked to the desk, executed a perfect salute, then stood at attention in the light of the kerosene lamp.

Keo unfolded a large map of the province on the desk. He glanced up and was immediately reminded that Sung was not Kinh, or pure Vietnamese, but Yao. The Yao had come to Vietnam from Southern China, and they had a similar language to the Thai, or people of Thailand. The official communist party line made all people of Vietnam equal, but like most of the PAVN officer corps, and most Vietnamese for that matter, Keo was not a fan of having these other races in his country. More to the point, it did not seem right that a member of the Yao was allowed to run a squad of the elite Dac Cong.

At the moment it was Sung's dress that was bothering Keo more than anything else. Rather than wearing the standard issue tan uniform with pith helmet of the Peoples Army, Sung was wearing the more traditional black pants and black fold-over jacket, much like the Viet Minh had worn years before, and what the local Hmong population wore now.

"I take it from your dress you have not had a chance to change clothes yet, Lieutenant Sung?" the major asked.

Keo liked the newer uniform, and wasn't impressed with the commando outfit. The uniform distinguished the person wearing it as a member of a united force, fighting for a revolution. The uniform meant the Vietnamese had arrived in the 20th century. While Sung's position in the Dac Cong may have required he dress as a guerrilla for some missions, Keo wanted to see him in the modern uniform, anyway. It was a matter of respect for how far they had come in the past twenty years.

"Sir, yes, sir," Sung replied. "We returned only about twenty minutes ago, sir. We encountered a Hmong force yesterday two kilometers west of Sam Neua. I admit, sir, both groups were surprised. They moved quietly. The resulting skirmish delayed our return."

"Any casualties?" Keo asked.

"One, sir," Sung replied. "We were greatly outnumbered, and retreated to the northeast. They followed for a few kilometers, then broke off."

"I see," replied Major Keo as he stared in the dark eyes of the commando. "Tell me what you learned about the American installation on Phou Pha Thi."

The ground shook again and more dust rained down, now on the map laid across Major Keo's desk. This bomb barely caused their ears to pop, and both men knew it had fallen much farther from the cave.

Sung waited for the rumble to dissipate and then continued. "Sir, first off, the Americans are referring to it as Lima Site 85, or LS 85. This is the name they gave to the air strip they created at the base of the mountain in nineteen fifty-eight."

Keo wrote the American name on the map.

"The explosives that were detonated on the mountain two weeks ago made for a much larger platform than we originally thought," Sung explained. "We have since seen twenty helicopters or more bringing large loads to the mountain. Many from the twin-rotor, CH-47-style helicopter. There are now multiple buildings near the top of the peak, and artillery has been installed at the base. Here are the photographs we took of the mountain from one of the smaller hills to the west."

Sung placed a roll of Chinese black-and-white film on the desk.

Keo glanced at the film canister, then stared at the floor and nodded in deep thought. This was disturbing news. As he feared, and as had been discussed with the divisional commander the previous week, the Americans appeared to be creating a new base north of the Plain of Jars.

"There is more, sir. It appears that the Hmong from the village on the mountain have been mobilized by the Americans to be defensive. We could not get close enough to see clearly, but in spots they were digging in the south and east faces of the mountain."

"Show me where, Comrade Sung," Keo said as he leaned over the western portion of the map. Produced by the Soviet Union, the map was far more accurate than the one he had used during the French war.

Sung located Phou Pha Thi as Keo pulled a black-and-white photograph of the mountain from a file in the desk.

"We could see men here, and here, through the trees, Captain," Sung said, pointing at the contour lines of the map.

Keo placed the photo in front of the young lieutenant.

"Yes, sir, that is about here," he said, pointing at spots on the map.

"Do you have any idea how many of these miao there are on this side of the mountain?" Keo asked.

Sung had heard that word from the major before, and he did not appreciate it. The same slur could be used for his tribe, the Yao, as it was for the Hmong.

"Sir, we had an obscured view and thus could not see. However, one of my men knows this region well. Comrade Foua believes there are perhaps seven hundred to a thousand Hmong living in the village on Phou Pha Thi. My guess is there is a company of men on that mountain, and they have dug into a very defendable position."

Keo stood and walked around the desk, still staring at the floor and occasionally nodding with his own thoughts.

"Sung, I'm going to speak freely with you," Keo said eventually. "Despite some of the barbaric ways of your people, you have been a good soldier and you understand how the Americans think."

Sung was a bit taken aback by the jab, but he had to let it go. Keo was his superior, and there were simply sad realities to life in the Peoples Army of Vietnam. One was that his tribe did not rule North Vietnam.

"Earlier this year our forces managed to retake much of this area around the Bam Bam River Valley, here," Major Keo said, pointing on the map to the hills north of the Plain of Jars and south of Sam Neua and Phou Pha Thi. "That has been part of the Hmong stronghold before, and its loss might be motivating their change in tactics. Before we can extend ourselves back onto the Plain of Jars, we need to be concerned with Houaphan Province. If the Americans can build a base on this mountain, they will have a decided advantage in the region."

"Yes, sir. Without question, sir."

"And then there is this," Keo said, his voice trailing off as he searched a pile of papers on the right side of the desk. "Last week I received a message that the American Air Force has placed some new radio equipment in Southern Laos and that the equipment seemed to help their bombers with navigation. The improved accuracy of the raids we've seen in the last six months or so on this base may be related to these devices."

"Sir, it would then make sense that the unit we know was placed on Phou Pha Thi earlier this year is the same as the ones you are speaking of," Sung affirmed.

"Yes, it sounds like they are preparing to defend it, and creating a new base of operations north of the Plain of Jars. One has to remember that the enemy is always trying to think like you, lieutenant, but one step ahead. If they assume we want to destroy it, they will fortify the position. Apparently you have seen these fortifications."

"Yes, sir," Sung replied. "And one more thing, sir. That force we encountered yesterday . . . I have not fought a group quite like them. We are trained to move quietly, and clearly they are, too. We walked right into them. If not for some terrain advantages, we would have likely lost the entire squad."

"That can happen," Keo replied. "One squad often

misses another."

"Yes, sir, except this wasn't a squad. I believe they were in company strength, perhaps three hundred men. One moment we were in a quiet part of the forest, and the next we were engaged with at least two hundred soldiers, sir."

"They aren't ghosts, Lieutenant. They just know how to use the forest, just like you. This is their forest and they know it well."

"Yes, sir. Anyway, sir, the engagement was in this drainage here," Sung said, pointing to a canyon west of Sam Neua. "I got the impression they were making their way up that drainage to where we'd been."

Keo nodded and smiled grimly. That meant there were at least two companies of entrenched men on Phou Pha Thi. Maybe more. They would not be there if it wasn't something important.

"Lieutenant, I need you to go back out there and report back to me in fourteen days. Observe and don't be seen," Keo said with a dismissive wave of his hand. "And send Truang in here on your way out. I need to draft a message to Hanoi."

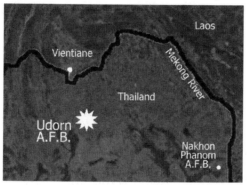

"Welcome to Udorn, Thailand," Brad said as he stood and offered his hand to both technicians. Brad had brown hair and brown eyes and was distinguished by being over six feet tall, with broad, muscular shoulders. His size often intimidated others, but he looked small next to one of the technicians.

"My name is Brad Drakely. I guess you guys met John earlier."

The air traffic control officers looked out of place in a bar full of military personnel. In blue Bermuda shorts and white, button-down shirts, it was as if the CIA was trying to give them easily distinguished disguises. Add to it that one of them was well over six feet tall, and the other an African American, which was not a common sight in the Air Force officer corps, and they truly stood out. Both had thick, horn-rimmed glasses, common for men who spent so many hours a day staring at video screens.

"Hello. Thank you," the young technician replied. "I'm Shep Tilden and this is my friend, Cory Brunker."

"Everyone calls me Large," Brunker said with a Western drawl as he shook Brad's hand. Like John, he had short, blonde hair shaved from the sides. "It's an easy name for everyone to remember. Good to see you again, John."

"I love a fitting nickname," John said. There was no question that Large was the biggest man he'd ever seen in the Air Force. Shep wasn't a small guy, either, probably over six feet, but he looked small standing next to Large. "Take a seat, fellas. Nong Mee is bringing cold Budweiser, and we can even order hot dogs from Tex if you're hungry."

"I could sure use the beer, but no food. They fed us on the flight between Subic Bay and here," Shep said.

"I'd take that beer, too," Large said. "If nothing else, it will help me quit trying to figure out what time it is. My body feels like it's the middle of the night."

"It is the middle of the night for you," John replied. "I think it's one a.m. in Los Angeles right now. Is that where you flew out of the States?"

"Let's see. The base at Bolling outside of Dallas, then Ontario, California," Shep said. "We were in Honolulu for a day, then on to Subic Bay. We hung out there for an evening and then flew here this morning."

Nong Mee placed the four Budweisers and four glasses on the table, then took an order from two tired-looking pilots in flight suits at a nearby table and returned to the bar.

As they sipped the cold beer, John explained the inner workings and layout of Udorn Royal Thai Air

131

Force Base. The technicians of Operation Heavy Green would be working in two-week shifts, and they'd have the option of using the base facilities if they wished when they weren't at the radar site.

Original construction of the base had begun during World War II by the Japanese, but it had grown by leaps and bounds since America entered the war in Vietnam. Not only was there housing for the personnel of 7th/13th Air Force at Udorn, there was also housing and offices for the Thai Air Force, Thai Army, and of course the Thai PARU Special Forces. Air America and the CIA had their own compound inside the original base. Ordnance storage facilities, maintenance hangars for aircraft, motor pools for trucks and Jeeps, officers' quarters, radar facilities and support equipment, and an enormous fuel storage facility, lined the 9,000-foot runway.

To make everyone more comfortable when they weren't fighting the war, there was a hospital, library, hobby shop, swimming pool, and a movie theater. If you didn't like the food at the new mess hall, you could buy your own at the PX. The single-story wood buildings that had sprung up on all sides of the perimeter housed Thais who worked or served on the base. Essentially, it was like its own little American city.

Brad filled in the two technicians on the plan for getting the men to the radar site. He explained that it was at a point known as Lima Site 85 on a mountain known as Phou Pha Thi, in the very northeast corner of Laos. All their equipment had been flown in over the previous months, and the CIA had completed the assembly just like the Reeves Instrument Corporation had laid it out on paper. There would be flight tests all week on Laotian targets; the Hmong would verify. Once they were sure everything was working correctly, which would probably be in the next five days, Brad and John would fly to the site with the PARU commandos. They'd make sure the Hmong forces were properly in place and that the site was secure enough for the technicians. That done, the techs would fly in and take the war to the North Vietnamese.

"We have a few questions for you guys," John said. "Like, where are you from and how did you get involved in this program? I mean, Large, you don't exactly look like a typical Air Force guy."

"Nope. At six-foot-eight and two hundred and fifty-five pounds, no one is gonna mistake me for a fighter pilot." Large grinned and said in a western drawl. "I'm from Pampa, Texas, in the panhandle east of Amarillo. I got a degree in electrical engineering at Texas Tech, then joined the Air Force to work on radar systems in B-52s. I got a letter inviting me to join the program. There were about fifty of us at Barksdale Air Force Base, and I think only two didn't take the job. It's better pay than the regular Air Force work."

"Yeah, Large is married, so he gets the big bucks. Six grand a year," Shep said. "I just get four and a half. The ongoing joke is that it's a 'black thing' but, nah, the military pay scale is fair. I get less money because I don't have any dependents, but it still beats what the Air Force was paying me before. I took the job because I thought I really might be able to help. My brother went missing in the Mekong Delta last year; he's listed MIA. When that happened, I was doing air traffic control at Holloman Air Force Base in New Mexico. You don't feel like you're making a difference directing trainers on touch-and-goes, but with this operation maybe I could."

John and Brad nodded. Shep and Large went on to explain how the process of joining the Heavy Green operation had taken place. The men had gotten a basic explanation of the program at Barksdale in Louisiana. They were then discharged from the Air Force with the promise they could be brought back in with no change in rank or pay. Everyone then accepted jobs with Lockheed, who agreed to pay the men on behalf of the Air Force and CIA. Like John and the Air America pilots, they were technically civilians and could work in Laos without violating the 1962 Geneva Accords.

"Well, I know you guys aren't bunking on the base," John said. "Where are they putting you up?"

"Some of the guys are at the Dreamy Hotel, and Large and I have rooms at the Charoen Hotel," Shep said.

"The Dreamy," Brad said through a laugh. "I thought they only offered hourly rates."

"Yeah, it seemed like a nice building from the bus, but the girls out front looked a little rugged," Large said. "I think it's safer for a single man like Shep to be at the Charoen."

"And speaking of safety, just how dangerous is this going to be?" Shep asked. "I mean, we got a rough description before we shipped out, but you guys know this stuff better than anyone we met back in the States."

"Well, you can think of it as being on an island a

hundred miles behind enemy lines," John said. Shep's eyebrows rose as if this was new information. "The island is totally controlled by friendlies, but if you leave it you may end up at the Hanoi Hilton."

The technicians looked a little confused, and John realized the best information they could have was what he'd learned two weeks before when he'd walked into the American Embassy. It was only fair they be brought into the know, and since he was a civilian now, what was the worst that could happen? John added what he'd picked up in the various monthly reports Richard had loaned him.

The war the technicians knew about in Vietnam was also being fought in Laos, but the press corps just wasn't bothering to report it. The reporters couldn't see it, and no one talked about it, so they didn't make an issue of it. If over a thousand American bodies were flowing out of Laos every month, as they were in Vietnam, someone might have raised a stink.

Hmong General Vang Pao, the ranking Laotian leading a fight against the North Vietnamese, had about 20,000 men under his command. The entire army received its pay and training from the CIA. Thailand also had troops in Laos that supported Vang Pao and helped find downed American pilots. The Ho Chi Minh Trail ran down the remote, east side of the country, and the US was putting a steady stream of bombs on anything that moved along it.

"And these Hmong guys," Large asked, "they can hold back the enemy?"

"Well, I should tell you, I haven't even been in there yet, but I'm not too worried," John said. "I'm in charge

135

of a team of Thai Special Forces, the PARU. We'll essentially be your Praetorian Guard. The PARU will be stationed all around the facility."

"I was in there yesterday," Brad said. "The mountain is about the most defendable position in Southeast Asia. The north and west side of the mountain are sheer cliffs about twenty-five hundred feet high. The east and south slopes are very steep, and we have eight hundred Hmong dug into trenches and foxholes. The truth is, the Hmong are guerrilla fighters who like to do hit-and-run and ambushes against the Vietnamese. For that reason, we have some reservations about them trying to hold a fixed position for extended periods. The plan is that they never have to hold the mountain against a frontal assault for more than a few days.

"To get up the mountain to where you'll be, the NVA would have to attack with an enormous force. The Hmong will know about this long before the enemy gets there, and we'll be able to whisk you away before any attack comes."

"Yeah, keep in mind that Brad and the CIA have been operating in Laos for years," John said. "There's an entire network of landing strips and small bases in the country to support the Hmong."

The technicians made glancing eye contact with each other. Both Brad and John could see they weren't completely convinced.

"We may be behind enemy lines and only a hundred fifty miles from Hanoi, but we're also only fifteen minutes from LS 36, what you'll hear the other paramilitary guys and the Hmong refer to as 'The Alamo,'"

Brad said. "The Lao town there is Nha Kang, and it's an important base for Air America. We have rescue helicopters there on standby 24/7."

"When an American pilot is shot down over North Vietnam, he has about fifteen minutes to get rescued or the NVA gets him," John said. "Air America is on duty at The Alamo to pull out the pilots before those fifteen minutes are up. If the Hmong tell the Air Force that the NVA are about to attack, those choppers will be there for us in minutes."

"Yeah, and add to that the fact that Alternate, Lima Site 20 at Long Tieng, is only half an hour away," Brad said. "There are twenty thousand Hmong there who don't want the Vietnamese near Phou Pha Thi."

"Okay," Shep replied. "It sounds about as good as can be expected. We did sign MOUs stating we could be killed, so this isn't a total shock."

"Nah, it's about what I expected," Large said. "But I have a favor to ask: Can you guys refer to LS 36 as Nha Kang, and not The Alamo? As I recall, The Alamo didn't go that well for the Texans."

7

October 30, 1967, 0820 hours,

(12 days later)

Lima Site 85, Phou Pha Thi, Houaphan Province,

Laos

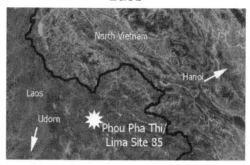

Captain Luang sat with his feet hanging off a limestone ledge, staring thousands of feet down to a jungle that spread to the south as far as the eye could see. Like a thick, bumpy carpet, the mosaic of green trees covered the hills, valleys, and in spots hid the rivers that flowed from the rugged terrain. Thin, wispy lines of fog, a bi-product of the heavy rain that had fallen the night before, rose from the lowest areas of the jade carpet. It would rain again later in the day, but for now the mountain was dry. Luang had found a comfortable section of rock just in front of the bunker with the Dushka 12.7mm machine gun. It was the perfect spot to relax before John brought out the "funnies," as he called them, from Udorn and Vientiane.

The damp morning air was cool on the Thai captain's skin, but with no breeze and the sun's rays getting through the broken cloud cover, the summit of Phou Pha Thi was pleasant. Luang took a sip of coffee from his tin cup, then offered it to Jum, a young Hmong who had been spending lots of time at the radar site.

Jum sniffed it and handed it back to the smiling PARU leader with a sneer. The Hmong boy then stood and looked off into the distance.

"Plij ploj," Jum said, pointing to the southwest.

"Helicopters," Luang replied with a nod.

The PARU leader had fired way too many machine gun rounds in his life and his hearing had suffered a bit from it. Young Jum, who was maybe thirteen, simply had better ears. Plij ploj was the Hmong term for the sound a large bird's wings make when it takes flight. For the Hmong, birds had become less common than helicopters, and the term had been adopted for the loud machines. The plij ploj were pretty far out, but within a minute he could clearly make out the sound of cool air getting chopped apart by the rotors of two brand new MH-53 Jolly Green Giants.

John Lilygren stepped out of the radio communication building with a pad of paper and his own cup of coffee. "Khun teknik thi kalan ma ni,"—"The technicians are coming"—he said to two PARU soldiers in a bunker, then strolled over to the 12.7mm Dushka and sat on the stacked rocks of the bunker wall.

"All right, Luang, do you and Jum want the good news or the bad news first?" he asked, glancing across a sheet of yellow legal paper. He knew Jum couldn't understand, but the kid liked to hear his name in conversation.

"I am enjoying the moment, Pi John," Luang said. "I prefer the good news first."

"Well, I shouldn't have offered. I think I'm going to give you the bad news first. The choppers are getting closer and I don't think our technician friends are going to want to hear bad news the moment they arrive."

"Yes, that order will be fine, too," Luang said. He looked at Jum and nodded.

Jum smiled. He hadn't gotten a word of it, but he felt he was an equal.

"Well, first, Udorn says that a couple days ago the NVA were seen near TACAN transponders at Muang Phalane and Phou Kate," John said. "PARU engaged 'em. There were casualties on both sides, and two more Thais are missing in action. Your old squad is currently looking for the missing guys."

"Do you know who was killed in the PARU?" Luang asked. He maintained his usually stoic voice with the question, but John knew it hurt to hear you might have lost friends, and certainly fellow countrymen.

"Richard didn't have their names, but he told me they were stationed in Udorn. That's all he knew."

Luang nodded, then took another sip of coffee. The helicopters were much closer now and there was no mistaking the sound of an MH-53 Jolly Green Giant.

"There's more," John said. "A Raven flying east of here yesterday confirmed what the Hmong seemed to be saying earlier in the week. There is construction equipment, including at least one bulldozer, about two klicks west of Ban Tham. That puts it about fifteen klicks northwest of Sam Neua, and twenty-five kilometers from here. For what it's worth, General Vang Pao's people confirmed all this."

Luang turned to John and shook his head as the first of the two big helicopters flew perhaps three hundred feet over the radar facility in a wide, banking turn. This was indeed bad news as it indicated the North Vietnamese were coming toward Phou Pha Thi. They likely had a pretty good idea what the TACANs were for. He stood and then poured the rest of his coffee on the ground and tossed the cup into the bunker.

"Does this mean our mission is over before we even get it started?" he asked in jest as he stood.

"No," John replied in an artificially upbeat tone. "We get to stay. Richard, the Embassy, General Vang Pao, and the Air Force are all in agreement that the road is being built to bring in heavy ground forces. That's going to take some time, and they plan to harass the NVA the entire way."

Without talking about it, the two men began walking down the wet, rocky trail toward the helipad. Jum followed, and then Luang pointed to the AK-47 leaning against the bunker. The kid ran back and grabbed it. He was continuously forgetting where he put his rifle, and the Hmong leaders were tired of it. Luang didn't want to hear the young soldier get reprimanded again.

"It may even work out to our advantage," John said. "If they are bringing in armor and artillery, not to mention a lot of troops, our listening equipment in the jungle is going to pick it up. For what it's worth, Richard said Vang Pao was ecstatic. This meant less artillery for him to have to deal with in the dry season, and he intends to focus his efforts on taking Sam Neua this year. Ho Chi Minh could find his forces in a pincer movement between Sam Neua and the Plain of Jars."

"Is that the good news?" Luang asked.

"No," John answered as they strolled down the path. "I'll give you the good news after we get these guys unloaded."

As the giant helicopter slowed just above the helipad, its rotor wash fanned the shrubs and small trees until they were almost flat on the ground. The rear ramp opened and two Hmong pulled the refueling pump and hose toward the big aircraft. Perhaps thirty other Hmong soldiers stood around the perimeter of the helipad, some in brand new camouflage fatigues the CIA had given them. The uniforms were trimmed to their arm and leg lengths, but the overall fit left lots of fabric flapping in the wind.

Brad Drakely whistled and waved off the refueling with a swipe of his extended arm. The Hmong didn't know it, but the plan was for the big choppers to refuel at Lima Site 36 for the return trip; there was no reason to waste Lima Site 85's precious fuel with so many dependent on it.

Large was the first of the technicians to step off the helicopter's rear ramp, followed by Shep and the other technicians. The pilot kept the rotors spinning while the Hmong unloaded duffel bags and crates. Meanwhile, the second helicopter circled about half a mile to the north, waiting for its turn to unload. Walking from opposite sides of the helipad, John and Brad met the technicians just beyond the rotors, while Luang spoke with the side gunner through the open gunport, pointing to a ridge east of Pha Thi.

"Welcome to Commando Club," Brad yelled over the whine of the turbines as he extended his hand.

"Commando Club?" Shep replied. "I thought we were Operation Heavy Green."

"We are," Brad said. "But you know the goddamned Air Force. They like giving code names more than blowing shit up. The brass is now using Commando Club as our call sign for missions, while the overall operation combined with the TACAN's used in other parts of the country is Heavy Green. It's some silly technicality that uses up fifty pounds of paper. I was told to mention it, as if that changes anything for us while we do our jobs. Anyway, welcome to Phou Pha Thi and Lima Site 85."

"Is this our security contingent?" Large asked, waving his hand toward the armed Hmong soldiers. "They aren't big, but they do look tough."

"Yeah, they look especially small in those oversized American uniforms, but don't let it fool ya," John yelled as the big helicopter lifted off. As if in one cho-reographed motion, the second chopper set down within seconds in its place and began to unload. "These guys know what they're doing, and they're fighting on their home turf. There are about five hun-dred more of them from the local village dug in along the south and east flanks of the mountain. Another three hundred marched in from Alternate last week. This place is better defended than Udorn."

Twelve men made up a full contingent of technicians for a two-week rotation on Phou Pha Thi. Besides a few general maintenance technicians, there were two who specialized in running the TACAN that had been installed the year before. They hadn't previously kept the TACAN specialists at Phou Pha Thi, but as long as there were living quarters for the men on the radar unit, it only made sense to keep people near the machine rather than fly them in daily. Another technician handled the computer that ran the TSQ-81 radar system. The computer was complex and only a few people in the world knew how it actually worked. There was a teletypist and a cryptographer who could each communicate with Udorn, and there was Large, who was there to keep it all powered correctly with the MB5 generators. Finally, there were four radar technicians who, like Large, understood how to repair some aspects of the TSQ-81, and of course how to direct American bombers to their targets.

The twelve men grabbed their duffels and followed John up the hill as he laid out various facts about Lima Site 85, like the geography of the area. Phou Pha Thi summit was about 5,700 feet above sea level and soared 3,000 feet above the surrounding terrain. It wasn't the highest peak in Laos, but its appearance, like that of a wedge pointed into the sky, did distinguish it from the others. The Hmong village at its base was also called Pha Thi and had about a thousand residents. Near the village was a 600-foot airstrip the CIA had built for Air America.

After a couple hundred yards of hiking, they reached what looked like a windowless mobile home. It was a green steel box about forty feet long, ten feet high, and ten feet wide. There was a wooden door on one end, and steel plating and sand bags had been added to the roof. Some sand bags and rocks had been stacked along the base.

"This is home," John said. "It's going to be a little cramped, but just pretend you're in the Navy and on a submarine. Toss your bags in there and I'll show you the operational buildings."

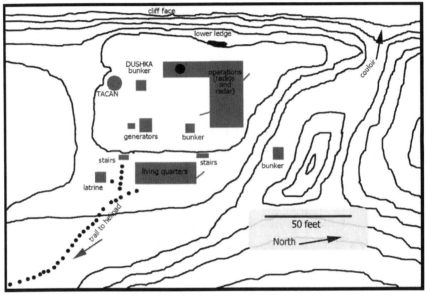

A rough map of the Lima Site 85 radar installation in 1967/68. All topo lines are approximations and roughly ten feet in elevation change.

The technicians filed into the building and had a short discussion over who got what bunk, with Large taking one that allowed his feet to hang off the end, then quickly came out to finish the tour. It seemed everyone was excited to learn the actual layout, but there was palpable tension.

"They seem a little tense, John," Brad said as they walked up the steps toward the Operations Building.

"Yeah, I get that impression, too," John replied.

Both men knew the technicians had never been in combat, and being only a few miles from the North Vietnamese border, was something new. They marched up a six-foot set of stairs and were greeted by two PARU sitting in a bunker with M16s.

"This is Eik, and this is Boi," John said. The two Thai soldiers nodded and smiled at the technicians. "There are seven members of the PARU guarding this immediate area. That's Soley and Boon in that bunker on the spine of the ridge. Ya-ya and Lek are on that 12.7mm machine gun, and, oops, I forgot to introduce you to Pon and Bundit on the trail over there. You probably didn't even see them. Of course everyone met Luang last week. I think he's still talking with Brad down at the helipad. By the way, Brad's hut is down there at the helipad so he can be closer to the Hmong."

John stepped next to the wall of the larger building atop the stairs as the technicians ascended to the next level of the complex. They had been training and preparing for this mission for almost two months, and he knew they were interested in the equipment.

The TSQ-81 had been built by the Reeves Instrument Company of Long Island, New York. The company had been building radar equipment for years, but the Air Force had added a big hurdle to this order. Every component, from the computers to the radar dish to the buildings, had to weigh less than 5,000 pounds, the lifting capacity of the new tandem rotor CH-47 Chinook helicopter at Phou Pha Thi's altitude; if it was any heavier, they couldn't get it on the mountain. Reeves had come through, and the technicians were marveling at the advancements in engineering. In total, helicopters had moved 150 tons of equipment from Thailand to Phou Pha Thi.

"So these units were put together as one, but they are separated into large compartments on the inside." The technicians stepped into the clearing above the living quarters. "We've been referring to this bigger unit as the Operations Building."

They could easily see that three of the container-shaped buildings had been put together, two into a double-wide unit, with the third running lengthwise from its end like a giant L.

"This wider portion of the building is for maintenance, storage, and the communications equipment," John said. "It's compartmentalized inside. Obviously, the radar equipment is under the radar dish, in what we're calling the Mission Room."

The generator shed, converters, and original TACAN unit stood just east of the courtyard and away from the newer radar equipment. It was a lot of technology crammed into a tight space. Between the various outer buildings lay a bunker with the Soviet-made 12.7 mm Dushka machine gun the Hmong had taken from the NVA. The modern equipment may have been key to the mission, but the twelve men walked past John and the buildings and stood in awe of the view.

"I don't think I've ever seen that much green," one of them uttered.

"Jesus, John, what's the drop-off here?" Shep asked.

"Well, if you go up to the edge, you can see down about twenty feet to another ledge that's about ten feet wide," John said. As he spoke, Brad and Luang came up the stairs and joined the tour. "It's easy to access that lower ledge with a few easy climbing moves. From that ledge, it is something on the order of twenty-five hundred feet to the jungle below."

"Any of you guys sleepwalkers?" Large asked.

There was an uneasy chuckle from the group.

"Yeah, I guess we're pretty safe on this side," Shep said. He leaned forward and saw rolls of concertina wall lining the edge of the cliff. "Nobody is climbing up a wall like that."

As he spoke, Shep noticed John's expression change.

"Well, I'm not so sure," John said. Shep stepped back from the edge. "That wall is big and it is steep, but from a climbing standpoint the rock has a lot of useful features. In my estimation, someone who knows what they're doing could scale it. There's a steep couloir, or gully, to the north. Soley and Boon are in the bunker guarding it."

Shep, John, Brad, and Large had spent a few evenings out on the town before the military men had flown into Lima Site 85. They'd met Richard Milano one evening in Udorn and had been told that John had once been an exceptional rock climber. Richard said John had been chosen for the Phou Pha Thi mission in part because he understood how people could move in the mountains.

"Is that why there's all this concertina wire along the rim?" Large asked.

"Yeah, there is concertina wire encircling this area," John replied. "Yesterday, Luang and I strung the wire along the cliff and placed some trip-wired Claymore mines at the top of the couloir. We'll add some more mines in the coming days. For the record, fellas, don't go beyond the concertina wire. Getting blown up is not part of your job description."

There was another muted round of nervous laughter from the group.

"John, I think I speak for all of us when I say that some of the Air Force's actions in the last few days have been a bit disconcerting," Shep said. "They made us give up our wallets and American magazines so we wouldn't look American if we were overrun. They even took away the letters we'd gotten from home. It's not exactly how they sold it in Louisiana. Being overrun by the North Vietnamese was not one of the options we were given."

John knew that Ambassador Sullivan's office had been leaning on the CIA and Air Force to make sure the operation did not look military. Sullivan had to view this as just one mission in a larger war, and as such he had to think about conditions if it did go bad. His actions were probably just precautionary, but certainly would make anyone uneasy about living in enemy territory.

"I understand that, and I understand your concern," John said. "They're just covering their asses for the worst-case scenario."

Brad said, "Look, guys, the Hmong live on this mountain; Phou Pha Thi is sacred ground to them. They know where the NVA are, and they won't give up the place without one hell of a fight. On top of that, you have the seven toughest men in Southeast Asia on guard up here. These Thai soldiers make John and me look like Girl Scouts. If things start to go south, the Hmong will know about it and we'll bug out."

"Lima Site 36 is on standby and is just fifteen minutes that way," John said, pointing south. "We'll know when we have to leave, and they'll pull us out."

The technicians looked at each other and nodded a bit.

"I think we can have faith in that," Large said.

"Why don't you guys go unpack and then we can go over the operations center," John said. "I'm sure you're going to want to see exactly how it was installed since we have a mission tomorrow."

The technicians went back down the steps to the living quarters. Brad and Luang walked to John at the edge of the cliff. They waited for the technicians to disappear down the steps before talking.

"Pi John, they seem pretty scared," Luang commented.

"Yeah, I would be, too," Brad said. "They are totally dependent on us. I think a couple of them have never even fired a gun."

"What was that good news you had this morning?" Luang asked.

"Oh, right, the good news. Remember the two Buddhist monks the Hmong found taking pictures in Pha Thi village last week? The ones who said they were from near Sam Neua?"

Luang and Brad nodded.

"They were interrogated in Udorn, and their film was developed. Richard talked to them himself. He says they were coming to bless someone's wedding or something. I think that confirms what you were told by the locals, right?"

"Yeah," Brad affirmed. "The Hmong elders said there had been a wedding."

"Richard developed the film and it was all shots of monks and people at a party. No worries."

"Hmmm," Luang mumbled with a nod. "Were the men released?"

"Yeah," John said casually. "They got flown to Alternate so Vang Pao's people could take them back to their village."

Luang's eyes opened wide and Brad clenched his teeth as he quickly looked away. He instantly remembered seeing the two NVA soldiers being pulled from the oil drums at Alternate. Both Brad and Luang realized that John didn't really understand how Vang Pao fought the war.

"What? Nah," John said in disbelief. "They're Buddhist monks."

"Too bad for the monks," Luang said solemnly.

"Don't forget, John; it's their war." Brad said. "I guess either way we really don't have to worry about them giving intel to the NVA."

October 30, 1967, 1020 hours,
(same day)
Chuan Mai, North Vietnam

A meeting of this magnitude had rarely been called
by General Giap for the obvious reason: One well-
placed American bomb could change the entire command structure of the North Vietnamese Army. However, the latest moves by the Americans in Northeast
Laos demanded the attention of the highest-ranking
officers. General Siphidon, in command of Pathet Lao
and Vietnamese forces in Northeast Laos, General Van
Tien Dung of Military District Two in Northwest Vietnam, and the great general Nguyen Giap himself, had
all convened at the 305th Commando Headquarters in
Chuan Mai.

At just thirty kilometers from the center of the
capital, and inside the outer perimeter of what the
American bombers had been targeting, it was closer
to Houaphan Province than Hanoi but still reasonably
safe enough to conduct such a meeting. It also allowed
General Giap to later meet with the commanders of the
Dac Cong, North Vietnam's Special Forces, to discuss
an alternative means of dealing with the new American

presence in Northeast Laos.

Soviet General Anatoli Hiuppinen's office had confirmed that radio transmissions from Muang Phalane and Phou Kate in Southern Laos, had been made by navigational equipment, probably for F-105 bombers. This meant the improved accuracy the Americans had shown in the last year was not just blind luck. Intel taken off Hmong prisoners, as well as reports from Major Keo and a Dac Cong recon team, had made it clear a similar navigational device had been placed on Phou Pha Thi. The generals agreed that this alone was reason enough to attack the Hmong stronghold, but the American improvements to the area posed an even bigger threat.

An election year was coming in the American political system, and history had shown the US often changed tactics in its wars with a new leader. If the Americans "took the gloves off," as they liked to say, and put a firebase in Northern Laos, it would change the war. It was conceivable they could build a base similar to those found in the South, with long-range artillery and hundreds of troops. Such a base could be completely supported by helicopters from Thailand.

This would go against the position the Soviets claimed Ambassador Sullivan held, but with a new president could come a new ambassador. There could be a whole new front in the war if the new base was built. General Siphidon pointed out that the new base would be able to thwart his attacks on the Plain of Jars and could also exert pressure on the northernmost transport routes for the Trail.

General Giap, an avid chess player, saw it from a

different angle: The Americans could essentially put North Vietnam in check by having a base within striking distance of the capital. It had to be destroyed at all costs.

November 3, 1967, 0720 hours,
(4 days later)
Sam Neua, Houaphan Province, Laos

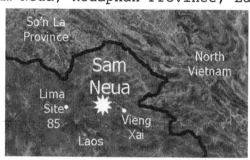

Major Keo had received the honor of constructing the road and moving artillery into position for the coming battle. He suspected he'd be given battle command of the artillery as well, though the generals had not made that decision at their meeting. Keo had immediately moved his office from the cave at Vieng Xai to the old French garrison command building in Sam Neua, and he'd have to move farther west to a field office in the coming days. It was the same brick and stucco building he'd been interrogated in twenty years before, though a bit more green mold had crept up the whitewashed walls, and a number of red roof tiles were broken.

The major had decided the change in surroundings went hand-in-hand with a change in times, and he'd arranged the desk and chairs back to their original positions. This meant he was now out of the bamboo chair, the one that reminded him how far he'd come, and was in the more comfortable teak furniture. It suited. The French were gone, and there was no reason to keep their ghosts alive in his mind.

The first order of business had been to begin construction of a new road, now deemed R602. Heavy equipment and a construction battalion from the NVA 559th had been transferred to Keo's command, and he had split the battalion into four separate units. This allowed a 24-hour work cycle and also prevented the loss of the entire road crew to American bombers. Major Keo had also reassigned all artillery destined for the Plain of Jars to be moved to various camouflaged placements along the road's length. No two pieces were kept in one location out of concern for the American bombers, and nothing was placed within a mile of the road construction equipment. All material would be moved forward when the final battle plan was drawn up.

Corporal Truang stepped into Keo's new office and cleared his throat. "Major, Lieutenant Sung is here as you asked, sir."

"Send him in, Truang," the major replied without looking up from a map.

Moments later Lieutenant Sung stepped through the wood-framed door of Keo's new office. Sung had been in the field for over a week and his black pants and jacket were lined with the salty residue of perspiration. The grass in front of the colonial building was wet, making his rubber sandals wet as well, and his shoes squeaked as he walked across the brown tile floor. Sung stepped to Keo's desk and saluted, then stood at attention.

"At ease, Lieutenant," Keo said. "Did you lose any more men this week?"

"No, sir." Sung really didn't like the major's arrogant tone. "We operated on both the east and southwest sides of the mountain. I believe we went undetected by the enemy forces, with the exception of one Hmong hunting party. Two Hmong men managed to walk into our position. We interrogated them and then killed them both."

"It seems a bit reckless for a Dac Cong lieutenant to keep a squad in a place that a couple of miao locals could so easily stumble into," Keo said.

This was the fifth time Sung had reported to Major Keo, and the third time the major had used miao in that manner. It was insulting, and no one in his position should use it. The rude connotations of the term could be applied to many of the people of North Vietnam, and he was pretty sure Keo intended that to be understood.

"Sir, with the exception of the open poppy fields maintained by the Hmong villagers, the forest is very dense around Phou Pha Thi. My men and I were positioned in one of the few clear vantage points of the west face that is not a Hmong farm. There are no trails into the clearing. We concluded from our interrogation that the two men were tracking a sika deer and had not followed us. In any event, they cannot report our presence."

"Very well," Keo said casually. "What did you see?"

"Sir, the Hmong are dug in on the flanks of the

mountain and their perimeter is very defendable and difficult to penetrate. The village of Pha Thi falls inside the Hmong lines. Under cover of darkness, one of my men made it to the helicopter landing area. There appears to be one American in that area with the Hmong. The new facility the Americans have been constructing is above that by perhaps two hundred meters. There are Thai soldiers stationed along the ridge there, and my man did not feel he could reach the position without compromising the mission."

Major Keo nodded in thought. "What about the east side and the area east of the mountain?" he asked as he pulled out another Soviet map. "How steep is the base of this ridge?"

"Sir, that ridge has clearings for poppy fields that have just been planted. I personally approached the fields three nights ago. It is not a steep area and did give me a line of sight to the secondary Hmong positions and the helicopter-landing zone. It may also allow a view of the new facilities higher on the ridge. However, the local villagers will know of our presence if we move into that area."

"It would be incidental at that point," Keo replied, "but so noted. You went up this drainage here, yes?" Keo pointed to a small canyon that ran east toward Sam Neua.

"Yes, sir. We followed it for a few kilometers, then the terrain got very steep and we turned north and back east in this next stream. I'm not an engineer, but in my opinion the road could follow the path we took."

Major Keo marked the spots Sung identified on the map. He made some notes in the corner of the map, and then pulled a file from a desk drawer.

"Your mission has changed, Lieutenant," Keo said in a stern tone. "I'm not sure why, but I was sent an order for you and your men to transfer to a Dac Cong operation center in So'n La. They want you there in ten days, so you better get going. Here are the transfer orders."

Keo stood and walked past Sung to the door. "Corporal Truang," he called in a louder voice. "Come in here. I need your help in assigning someone from the 959th to take up Sung's recon job. Lieutenant Sung, you are dismissed."

Sung turned and passed the young corporal on his way to the door. No more orders from Keo, he thought. A smile washed over his face as he stepped into the morning sun.

November 11, 1967, 1020 hours,
(8 days later)
Phuc Yen Air Base north of Hanoi,
People's Republic of Vietnam

In the past six weeks Cha Lim had been transferred between so many bin trams, sections of the Ho Chi Minh Trail, he didn't know where he was. Lim knew he was entering Phuc Yen Air Base, but he wasn't sure whether that was northeast or northwest of Hanoi. One thing Lim was sure of was that it was nice to finally get a little rest. The back of the Soviet-made MAZ-200 truck wasn't exactly comfortable—in fact, Lim was sure the Russian beast didn't have shock absorbers—but riding was better than walking after six straight weeks of carrying loads.

Lim and another courier, who had introduced himself earlier as Ang, sat up and let the sentry look them over so the truck could be cleared onto the base. The truck pulled past the checkpoint and drove onto the wide, new concrete tarmac past two rows of fighter jets. At the far end of the line of jets a MiG sat in the shade of a hangar. Foreign men in one-piece uniforms were performing some sort of maintenance on the aircraft. Lim had heard that the faster the plane, the more men needed to work on it, and that the fastest planes of the Vietnamese Air Force were only worked on by men from the Soviet Union. That plane was clearly very fast.

The truck drove past the tin hangar to a twin-engine transport aircraft and came to a stop. Two European-looking men, in gray pilot's jumpsuits, stood in the shade of one of the plane's wings, smoking cigarettes.

Lim didn't know it, but the trip that had brought the pilots and their Antonov 24 transport to Phuc Yen had taken three days. It had begun in Tashkent in Soviet Uzbekistan. From there it was a hair-raising flight over the Himalayas to Delhi, India. This had pushed the aircrafts fuel supply far lower than either pilot was comfortable with. From Delhi, they had gone on to Calcutta where supplies had been added to the original load. The next stop was in Kunming, China, where they'd picked up another small load of equipment. From Kunming it was a relatively short flight to Hanoi. They would be flying back via a safer route that avoided the Himalayas by crossing the deserts of Western China. Both men were happy to not have to repeat the Himalayan leg of the journey.

A captain, wearing the North Vietnamese Army's heavy dress uniform, and a sergeant in typical tan fatigues, walked out to greet the truck as it pulled up next to the plane.

Lim listened intently to make sure he didn't miss any orders.

"There are three crates in the Antonov," the sergeant told them. "You need to move them to the truck. If you can't lift the crates, you can empty the contents and then refill them in the truck. Private Ban," the sergeant addressed the driver, "the captain and I need to speak with you in the hangar. Let's go."

The sergeant and driver followed the captain to the hangar, while Lim and Ang stepped down from the truck and then climbed in through the aircraft's rear cargo door. The three crates weren't that big, but being made of wood there was no doubt the contents would be heavy. Assuming so, the two men pulled hard on the first box to get it to the door, and unexpectedly, it slid easily. Granted, it was too heavy for the two men to lift down from the plane, so some of the load would have to come out, but it was lighter than they'd expected for military supplies. Using a pry-bar from the truck, Lim and his partner lifted off the lid. Lim was instantly shocked by the word he saw: "Mountaineering."

It was part of an English phrase, "Mountaineering Club of Hong Kong," written onto a large, heavy canvas sack. The bag looked strangely out of place in a plane loaded with war supplies. The two men lifted the white sack from the box, then Lim dropped from the plane to the tarmac and his partner lowered the bag to him. Feeling the bag in his arms, he was again stunned. He knew that bumpy sensation from his days with Dominique on the plantation. There were ropes inside that canvas bag.

Lim hefted the bag onto his shoulder and carried it to the truck, then lifted the bag into the back of the lorry and jumped in to pull it forward. He looked to the hangar and the pilots to make sure no one was watching, then opened the bag a little to see the contents. There it was: A Goldline rope, the same style of rope Dom's father had taught him and the young Frenchman to use so many years ago, and Lim's heart warmed with a flood of memories from happier days.

He thought of a Hmong saying: "Fish swim in water, birds fly in air, Hmong live on mountains." Lim had felt accepted, even applauded, for being part of a tribe that lived in the mountains. His days climbing with his French family were the happiest of his life, ones that had become all but a faint memory during the years of working for the North Vietnamese Army.

Lim closed the sack and ran back to the plane to help his partner unload more gear. Another very heavy box inside the crate contained various pitons from

Austria, and iron carabiners with a stamp that read "US." Only the one large crate held climbing equipment, but what it held was astonishing to Lim: four alpine-style hammers and half a dozen canvas backpacks. Lim loaded it all into the truck with care, noting exactly where the gear was so he could perhaps get another view of the equipment later.

The two men then unloaded the other two crates, both heavily laden with light infantry weapons. New AK-47s, new black Dac Cong uniforms, six Soviet made flak jackets, and a number of boxes of grenades and other explosives, eventually filled the back of the truck.

It was an odd assortment of climbing and military equipment, with an even odder procurement process: Two of the older ropes and many of the carabiners had been confiscated by a Soviet KGB agent in Northern India, which had been used on a CIA mission to a mountain in Uttaranchal Province of India. A Soviet agent had purchased the gear from a group of porters and it had been loaded onto the plane in Delhi.

A second KGB agent stationed in Calcutta had purchased the pitons and hammers from a janitor who worked in the British Consulate. He had known that certain members of the British contingent had climbed in Nepal, and the janitor knew some of the equipment was in a box in the basement of the consulate. It had been fairly easy to get it out of the British building without being noticed.

The Goldline ropes had been purchased in Hong Kong by an agent of the Chinese Ministry of State Security, then taken through Guangzhou to the air terminal in Kunming.

Just before everything had been tucked away, the sergeant reappeared with the captain, the truck driver, Private Ban, and two other men in black jackets with AK-47s on their shoulders.

The sergeant walked to the truck and gave the crates of equipment a quick look. "You two are to accompany this equipment all the way to its final destination at So'n La. Private Ban will drive you and the gear northeast to the outer bombing perimeter, at Viet Tri, then you will take it out of the truck and haul it on push-bicycles. Corporal Den of the Dac Cong is in charge." He pointed to one of the men climbing into the front seat of the truck. "That's it. Get going."

With that, the MAZ-200 engine turned over. The truck made a wide turn around the plane, and headed for the dirt road. Lim stood in the lorry and looked back to the plane as they drove off the concrete tarmac. The captain and sergeant were walking back to the hangar as the two European pilots climbed into the aircraft.

Half an hour later, Lim and the three other men were unloading the truck and strapping the various packages onto the push-bicycles. Lim managed to get the sacks with the ropes and climbing gear on his bicycle.

8

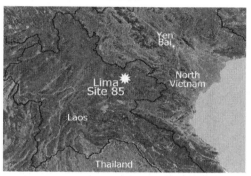

James Bechtel, the cryptographer on duty at Lima Site 85, decoded the day's orders at about 0345. He couldn't believe what he was reading, so he redid the whole decryption. Like all the technicians, he knew the Air Force had been complaining about having to bomb worthless targets along the Ho Chi Minh Trail. The politically safe operational orders had become such a farce that Air Force pilots joked that you were an Ace if you got five water buffalo. After confirming he had decrypted it correctly, James figured the morning's order was going to get a cheer from the pilots, not to mention the technicians. He could have gone to sleep after decrypting the orders, but decided to stay awake and watch the bombing raid take place.

John Lilygren stepped into the dimly lit Mission Room after receiving the daily report via radio from

Richard in Udorn. The shape of the room was almost like that of a hallway at nine feet wide and forty feet long. With all the equipment jammed along the walls, there wasn't much room to stand, but still most of the technicians had packed themselves around Shep and Alex, who were looking at the black-and-green radar screen and the plotting board. Large stood in the back as he could look over everyone and still have a good view of the screen.

Seeing Large reminded John of why on the previous evening he'd finally been able to sleep. It was pretty cold in the middle of the night in the PARU bunker, and with his lighter sleeping bag, he'd been forced to snuggle between Luang and Eik to keep from shivering, but it had also been quiet. Large snored so loud that Brad joked he might give away the American position. A night with only the sounds of a light breeze rustling the leaves had left John very well rested.

"What's up, bud?" John asked Large in a hushed tone. "You guys nervous about something? You don't usually all congregate in the Mission Room during a raid."

This unit of technicians was on their last day for this cycle and would be getting two weeks off for the effort. Another team of technicians would be coming in to pick up where they left off. This meant the current technicians had gone two weeks without a shower—very evident in the cramped and poorly ventilated Mission Room. As much as he loved the guys on the first rotation, Brad was looking forward to the fresher-smelling bodies of the incoming group.

"Yeah, well, we wanna see this one," Large replied.

"When I read the frag order this morning, I checked the generators twice to make sure nothing went wrong. We're going to hit the MiG base at Yen Bai with four F-105s out of Takhli Air Force Base."

Commando Club had been in operation for just over two weeks. The radar techs had directed missions all around the outskirts of Hanoi, including one on the railyard just outside Hanoi at Lang Dang. Air Force Reconnaissance had reported very successful targeting, and the listening devices along the Ho Chi Minh Trail indicated a reduced flow of goods. But this was the first mission where the F-105 pilots had been cleared to attack the men and equipment that were regularly shooting them down.

Shep had realized early on the mission was going to draw a crowd; he'd put the radio transmission on speaker so all could hear it being called in.

"Trojan, I have you at the I.P.," Shep said into his microphone. "You're at twenty-nine-k and five-two-zero k-t. Adjust to heading to 0-4-5 for target. Stay high."

"Roger that, Commando," the pilot replied in a deep, relaxed voice. "Twenty-nine at five-two-zero. Go to O-4-5. We are I.F.R."

John had watched most of the attacks of the previous two weeks and had learned much of the jargon the pilots and radar technicians used. "Trojan" was the call sign for today's lead pilot. He and his fellow pilots, who were collectively part of the 357th Tactical Fighter Squadron, had already refueled and reached the initial point of radio contact with Lima Site 85, that being the "I.P." At this point the aircraft went into formation and were given directions by the ground controller, in this case Shep. From here on out they would follow his commands to reach the target.

The radar equipment would pick up the speed and altitude of the squadron, and at the moment they were at 29,000 feet and flying at 520 nautical miles per hour. That translated to 598 regular miles per hour, just 65 miles per hour below the speed of sound at sea level. The pilot confirmed the radar with the numbers, and let Shep know that he was under I.F.R, the acronym for Instrument Flight Rules, meaning the pilots were in cloud cover heavy enough that they could not see the ground below or sky above and could navigate only with the plane's instruments. As Shep was now navigating for them, this didn't matter; he would be guiding them to the target.

They might have been able to locate the target using the signal from the TACAN, but often under these circumstances the mission was cancelled. The TACAN would get them to the area, but the pilots would have to see the target to drop their bombs. With the new radar on Lima Site 85, they'd be guided right onto the MiGs whose pilots had no idea there'd been a change in the American rules of engagement.

"I'm going to keep the squadron high until they pass this point here," Shep said, covering the microphone with one hand and pointing to a spot on the plotting board with the other. "That peak right there, Phou Loung, is about ninety-eight hundred feet high. I could put them below it and then they'd be shielded from radar units around Hanoi, but we got a report the other day that said the NVA were putting triple-As on these mountains. If the guns were close to the peak's summit, our pilots would be easy targets."

As far as bomb accuracy, the missions had gone well to this point, but they hadn't been without controversy. From the very first mission against the Yen Bai railyard, communication between the pilots and the radar technicians had been terse. Many of the pilots had complained that by following a line laid out by ground-based radar, they didn't have the ability to evade triple-A and surface-to-air missiles. It was hard to balance the two, as staying focused on the target had probably had a lot to do with the previous inaccuracy. So far there hadn't been any higher rate of aircraft loss, but when the Vietnamese understood that they could count on a straight line in the direction of attack, there likely would be.

The technicians and pilots went to radio silence, and suddenly John felt the tension in the room. It was impossible for the men in the relative safety of a heavily defended mountaintop not to imagine what it was like for the pilots. They were racing across the sky toward an enemy that knew, virtually every day, they were coming. Moving at 600mph, but in thick cloud, the pilots could probably see no more than fifty feet in front of their aircraft. At any moment an enemy shell could explode in the white mist and rip apart any plane in the squadron.

Despite the feeling of exposure any pilots had, this mission had been planned to try to throw off the North Vietnamese. Shep was guiding them in on a line from just east of Sam Neua toward Tam Dao Nord, a small massif about 5,000 feet high that rose above some of the best targets. So many F-105s had been shot down along Tam Dao Nord that the pilots had dubbed it Thud Ridge. The previous attack on Yen Bai railyard had flown down the northeast slope of these small mountains, and by flying toward them again, the Air Force hoped to catch the NVA off guard.

Unlike those previous targets, today's objective was not on the east side of Thud Ridge and it had never been attacked before. It lay on the west slope of Thud Ridge, but the formation was flying as if they were aiming for the east slope. Just to add to the deception, a Wild Weasel had been sent over the east side of Thud Ridge to draw SAM fire. It would be monitoring the radio communications and would turn to Yen Bai to support the pilots' escape.

The men heard the far door to the communications room swing open and then slam shut. That was Brad, and everyone knew it. The door on his hooch at Alternate had been difficult to shut, and he'd developed a habit of slamming every door he used. Large had accused him of having been born in a barn for the excessive noise, and Brad had taken it as a compliment. He'd also decided he'd just let everyone know he was there by continuing to slam doors.

"Hey, bud, what's up?" Brad asked John in a hushed tone. "You've squeezed everyone in here."

"We are about to hit the air base at Yen Bai with four F-105s. They'll be on the final leg any second."

"Well, that's good news. You talk to Udorn this morning?"

"I did, and that's not good news. From what Richard said, I don't think we have to worry about our transmissions being routed through a C-130 over the

Tonkin Gulf anymore. This place isn't a secret. I'll fill everyone in after the mission."

Brad understood. All the transmissions to pilots from Phou Pha Thi were routed through a plane circling off the North Vietnamese coast. The Air Force knew the Vietnamese could track the radio transmissions going from Phou Pha Thi to the attacking aircraft. It had been the hope that by sending the transmissions through a plane off the coast, the NVA would not get wise to what was going on at Phou Pha Thi. To them, it would just look like a plane off the coast was directing the bombers. However, from what John had said, it sounded like that charade might be over.

"Trojan, go to three-three-zero and five-k, fast, then go to five-zero-zero knots," Shep said, breaking the radio silence. He quickly repeated the command so the pilots were certain of the change. Alex confirmed the course change on the plotting board, and everyone could see how the mission had been constructed. The planes were brought in high as if they were headed to Thud Ridge, then made a hard turn to the north and descended on to the final bombing run. The Thuds would be flying lengthwise down the runway, making a hit more likely, and they would be aimed for home when the bombs dropped.

"Roger that, commando, three-three-zero, five-k, five-zero-zero knots," the pilot replied. His voice was pitched a little higher, and his words came a little faster this time. They were no doubt feeling the stress of being over enemy territory. A few seconds later the radio cackled again. "Commando, ceiling nine-k and we have visual. Will wait for your command."

Brad raised his eyebrows as if to ask John what the message meant.

"The planes have broken through the clouds at nine thousand feet and can see the Yen Bai runway," John said.

"Trojan, go to three-k and five-zero-zero k-t," Shep said.

"Roger."

"Trojan, ten seconds to target," Shep said. "Five, four, three, two, one, bombs away."

"Roger, commando, bombs away," the pilot said quickly. "We have 57s mike-mike to the north. Trojan, taking evasive action. Whoa, two 37s, too."

The technicians could hear the high-pitch whine of the radar alarm in the pilot's cockpit. Both 57mm and 37mm guns could be fired with radar guidance.

"Trojan, this is Weasel," everyone heard the Wild Weasel pilot announce. "We currently have no SAM launch here."

"Roger that, Weasel," Trojan replied. "We are back at twenty-two-k and climbing, no losses. Looks like we had one secondary explosion on the ground, and there is a new crater in the middle of the runway."

The technicians erupted into cheers and began shaking hands. Their portion of the mission was over and the lead pilot would be in charge of the squadron's flight back to the base. Shep and Alex put down their microphones while one of the other technicians began powering down the computer and other electronics. The entire group walked outside into a bright but overcast morning. The cloud cover above was thin, but another band of clouds hid the valley below. Mist swept over the limestone ridge to the north.

"That's how it's supposed to go," Large said as he took in the view.

"It's still stressful," Shep said. "It would be terrifying being one of those pilots."

John walked to the Dushka machine gun bunker. Luang and Soley had been there breaking down and cleaning the big gun since sunrise. Burnie, a Hmong fighter from the village yet to see his twelfth birthday, sat and watched the two PARU work on the Dushka. Burnie was one of the Hmong who, like young Jum, really enjoyed the company of the technicians. His only word of English was "Allo," but he seemed to enjoy just listening to the Americans' conversation. His mother had died in the 1961 cholera outbreak, and his father was later killed in battle. He had no other family, so the technicians had sort of adopted him. Granted, he had people who watched over him in the village, but the Americans liked having him around.

Burnie had gotten his nickname a month before when Brad had started prepping the local fighters for Operation Heavy Green. The CIA operative had been explaining how to fire an RPG, and for some reason Burnie had decided to stand right behind the launch tube. When the rocket fired, it scorched off Burnie's eyebrows, eyelashes, and half of his hair. The kid's face had only been singed and the burns quickly healed, but a nickname was born.

"Good job, you guys," John said as the technicians gathered at the Dushka bunker. "I think that's why we all signed up for this operation. I don't want to ruin the mood, but I have a few other things I think we should talk about before you guys fly back to Udorn."

A few of the technicians sighed with the obvious signs of bad news.

"Heads up on what's going on with the NVA in this area," John said. "Construction on the road, what Udorn is calling R602, has continued; it's definitely coming here. We've monitored almost twice the truck traffic into Houaphan Province compared to this time last year, but very little on the approach route to the Bam Bam River Valley and Plain of Jars, which means the NVA is massing heavy equipment for an assault on something in Houaphan Province, and as we are the only installation in Houaphan, well, you get the picture."

"Jesus," Shep said. "So does this mean we're already finished here?"

"No, not at all. In some ways this is good news. We always knew this facility would be discovered and we'd have to abandon the mountain, we just didn't know when. This simply confirms they know we're here. But it's also a good indicator of how they'll attack. The fact that the NVA is bringing in heavy equipment tells us they'll be attacking with that equipment. Bulldozers, trucks towing artillery, so forth, all make a lot of noise. Building the road makes a lot of noise. Our intelligence will know when it begins to get close. For that matter, we'll be able to see when the road is within the range of their heavy guns. I'm guessing the Air Force will pull us out then."

"Yeah, guys, remember that the listening devices we've dropped all over this province aren't our only source of information," Brad said. "The Hmong are watching the NVA because this little army in the trenches below you doesn't want to be caught off guard, either. I actually came up to tell you that a Hmong squad followed an NVA recon force up that ridge yesterday." Brad pointed to a high point about a mile east of Phou Pha Thi.

"If they're that close, we should have called a strike in on them ourselves," James, the cryptographer, said.

"Well, yeah, but we didn't have to," Brad said. "Like I said, the Hmong followed them. When they follow the NVA, it's not to have tea and cookies. I have five sets of NVA ears down in my hooch. I didn't think you guys would want to see them—these guys haven't seen a Q-tip in a while."

"Ears?" Large asked in a shocked tone.

"Yeah, the Hmong like to bring me trophies. Until I start seeing kids without ears in the village, I'm gonna believe they're off the enemy."

Large and Shep looked at each other and smiled, while shaking their heads.

"Shiiiitttt," Large said in his Texan drawl. "There's another little nugget that wasn't in the Air Force's travel brochure. This is the resort that just keeps on givin'."

"Guys, the point is the enemy does know we're here, but they've shown their hand," John said. "That means everything is going to plan. Have a good rest in Udorn. Don't have too much fun. You need to be rested and ready to go in two weeks so we can run more missions like today."

9

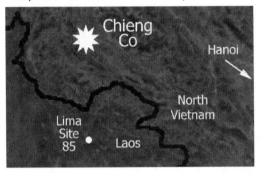

The two-week trek from Viet Tri to So'n La had been relatively easy for Lim, Ang, and the two Dac Cong. American bombers had flown overhead every day, but the only actual attack they'd seen was on the distant Yen Bai Air Base the day they'd set out. The four men had trekked northeast on an old French road that took them almost to the Chinese border, then turned south on mountain trails and crossed over the Song Hong on a decrepit colonial-era bridge. This had all been to avoid American bombers. Had they taken a more direct course, or had they taken a truck rather than the bicycles, there was a good chance the materials would have been destroyed from above.

The circuitous route had made a 300-kilometer trek into one of 500, but the respite from the war had been worth it. Lim had developed a lot of sores on his back and shoulders from years of carrying heavy loads in various oddly shaped backpacks. Pushing the bicycles for those weeks had allowed the open wounds to heal.

The four men had met Lieutenant Sung and two other Dac Cong in So'n La. Sung spoke with both couriers alone, then released Ang to some men with the 559th to work on a northern branch of the Trail. The lieutenant explained to Lim that he had been chosen to stay with the Dac Cong because he had experience carrying loads in the mountains along the Trail, and the platoon might need another courier in the near future.

This was a completely new experience for Lim. Sung had actually explained his reason for the orders, almost as if he were speaking to an equal, unlike any other Vietnamese soldier had done in the previous years. Lim could see that Sung was not of the Viet tribe, and though he spoke the language perfectly, there was an accent that indicated he had perhaps come from one of the smaller tribes. In any event, Lim liked Sung's approach and looked forward to the new assignment. The man was stern and there was something deadly serious in his demeanor, but he didn't refer to Lim as miao—a step up.

Within minutes of meeting with another twenty-three Dac Cong soldiers in the town of So'n La, the platoon had trekked another four kilometers west to a series of small mountains around a village known as Chieng Co. The white limestone peaks were perhaps no higher than 200 meters, but they were very steep and made almost hollow by caves. Huge stalactites hung from the steepest bits of rock, while long streaks of orange and blue ran down the vertical sections. The less-than-vertical sections of dark gray rock were riddled with pockets and sharp edges. Holding little soil, these lower-angle slabs were mostly covered by vines that hung from the summit. It was an environment very similar to what Lim had learned to climb on around the plantation.

The first few days with the Dac Cong were simple and straightforward. In fact, the work was almost restful when compared to ferrying loads on the Trail. He was to have the rice boiled by sun-up in the morning. He was then to open the equipment crates and set out all the climbing gear so it was easily accessible. After that, he would do the dishes and make sure there was a large pot of boiled water cooling so the soldiers would not become dehydrated. He then got to sit and watch the Dac Cong work with the equipment.

For Lim, this latter bit was actually a little frustrating. A couple of the Dac Cong knew the basic knots, and clearly Lieutenant Sung had read a book on how to use the mountaineering equipment, but it was obvious the commandos had never actually climbed with ropes, carabiners, and pitons. Lim didn't dare say anything to them. They were highly respected in the North Vietnamese Army, and reminding the powers-that-be that Lim had grown up on a French plantation could make for trouble. Instead, he simply did his job and offered to help with any chores the Dac Cong needed.

On the fifth morning, Lim had prepared the breakfast and pulled out all the equipment before the other men had stirred. While waiting, he began to play with the Goldline rope, sliding it through each hand and practicing the knots he had learned so many years before. It felt good just to have the gear in his hands. Lim wrapped the slick rope around his waist three times, then rolled the end under the coils so they all pulled evenly. He then tied a bowline knot, creating the traditional rope-harness climbers used, known as a bowline-on-a-coil.

It was a standard method of tying into any rope so the pressure, in the event of a fall, was spread over a wider area of the climber's waist and not just onto one single strand of the thin line. Lim stood over the uncoiled rope and reached down to pick up a hammer. He then put five of the heavy iron pitons on a US carabiner and clipped it to one of the strands of rope around his hips. He reached into the air with the hammer and held up a piton, as if tapping it into an imaginary crack, and was suddenly startled by Lieutenant Sung's voice.

"Where did you learn to do that?" Sung asked sternly as he stepped from a dark recess in the cave.

He had apparently been watching for a few minutes, and there was no getting out of this.

Lim was terrified. "I learned it as a boy, Lieutenant Sung. It won't happen again, sir."

"Lim, I want you to tell me how you learned that," Sung replied. "It appears you know very well how to properly use this equipment. Where did you learn this?"

Lim's life was about to change and he knew it. The

commando leader had seen something that was out of the norm in the People's Army of Vietnam. There was no use in lying, and to date Sung had been fair to Lim, so he told the truth.

"I was raised on a French plantation," Lim replied, untying the bowline. "The owner had lived in the mountains of France as a young man. He took his son climbing on the rock outcroppings in Ninh Binh Province, and my father and I often went with them."

Sung stood watching Lim recoil the rope after pulling it from his waist. "How many times did you climb?" he asked.

"I'm not sure, Lieutenant; I was young. But it was many times. The Frenchman missed the mountains of France and wanted his son to have the childhood of a boy from the Alps."

Sung stood staring at Lim. He didn't blink.

Lim found it hard to look into the dark eyes of the Dac Cong commander.

"You saw us these last days," Sung said. "Why did you not step forward with this information? We could have used it."

"Sir, I'm sorry. It has not been my place to question anything in the army. I'm a porter, not a soldier."

The Dac Cong lieutenant continued to stare at Lim. The young Hmong kept his eyes toward the ground.

"You are Hmong, no?" Sung asked.

"Yes, sir. My family is from Phou Samsoum."

"That's not even in Vietnam," Sung replied with a slight chuckle. As the saying went, you ask a Hmong where he is from and he gives you the name of the nearest mountain, not the nearest town. "Phou Sam-

179

soum is a mountain in Laos, in Xieng Khouang Province where the Hmong General Vang Pao comes from. Are your mother and father there or are they on this plantation?"

"No, sir. My mother died when I was young. My father was taken by soldiers about ten years ago and never returned. My grandparents on my father's side were still there six years ago, but I have not been back since I started carrying loads on the Trail. I don't know how they have fared in the war."

Lieutenant Sung listened intently and nodded as Lim spoke.

"I'm of the Yao tribe," Sung said. "My people come from Ha Giang on the north border with China. For that reason, many officers in the People's Army don't trust me. Some see me as Yao, and others as Chinese. To them it doesn't matter that I was born in Vietnam. I'm telling you this to show you I understand why you did not speak up, but that has to change. You are going to teach me and the other men of this platoon what you know about climbing mountains. Even if it means adopting the ways of the French, these men must know how this equipment works. From now on, for as long as you are under my command, you are Private Lim. Do you understand?"

"Yes, Lieutenant Sung. I will teach you everything I know."

"You will start this morning."

It was clear to Lim that Sung didn't hold the same kind of prejudice against him that most of the Vietnamese soldiers did. However, it was also clear the Dac Cong commander saw Lim as a tool for a job. If

Lim didn't do the job well, the outcome could be worse than the insulting remarks he had lived with for so long.

Sung woke the men and they ate the rice porridge Lim had prepared, then everyone was ordered to gather at the mouth of the cave. Sung reintroduced Lim to the platoon as a private in the Peoples Army, and their teacher. One soldier made a joke below his breath, but the snickers were instantly silenced by a glare from the commander.

"Private Lim, begin today's lesson," Sung said.

"The first thing we have to master is how to tie in to the rope correctly," Lim said as he dropped the Goldline in the dust amid the platoon. "A single strand in a fall could break your back, so we do it like this."

Lim wrapped the rope around his waist three times, then rolled the strands together with the cord and tied a knot called a bowline.

"This is called the bowline-on-a-coil, and we must have it mastered before we can climb."

"You men will know this technique well enough to do it blindfolded," Sung exclaimed. "You must be able to do it in the dark."

The platoon broke down into the five squads they had been training in, and Lim showed each squad leader how to tie the special knot. He then went from squad to squad going through each step so at least one man per group could easily tie in. This man then taught his fellow soldiers. After two hours of practicing how to tie into the rope, Lim explained how a single overhand knot could be used to safely fix a climber to the mountain.

"Take a bit of rope, like this," he said while making a big loop of cord and holding both strands. "Now wrap it around itself and pass it though. You now have a fixed loop that can be slung over a spike of rock, or clipped into a piton. You can even wedge the knot in a crack. This allows you to take your hands off the rock and rest or do other tasks."

The men wandered around the cave, finding ways to affix themselves to the walls. They ate lunch and then returned to learn one of the most difficult techniques.

"To support another climber, we need to use the friction of the rope around our bodies. We call this belaying," Lim said. He sat behind a rock and asked Sung to tie into the rope. He then laid out slack and told Sung to run backward. The rope came taught and began to stretch, but Lim held the bigger man with ease.

"With this technique, we can prevent each other from falling," Lim said. "Even a climber going above can be caught this way if the proper techniques are applied."

The men spent the rest of the afternoon learning how to take in and let out rope when belaying. At dusk, Lim felt that most of them had the systems down. They were now ready to learn how to move over the rock.

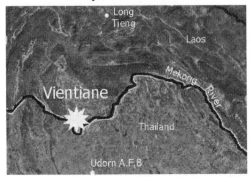

"Good morning, James," Tom Dillon said to his assistant. "I hope that despite Christmas festivities at Madam Lulu's Bar, you got some sleep last night, because we are in for a long day."

"Good morning, sir," James replied as he handed a stack of papers to his boss. "I gathered earlier this morning that we lost some assets in the far south, but I wasn't given the details. What happened?"

"Yeah, well, a lot. This morning's meeting had everyone in the Country Team chiming in," Tom said. Everyone in the embassy was aware that the ambassador liked to refer to the people giving him reports on the war in Laos as his "Country Team."

"The air attaché, the CIA station chief, Richard Milano out of Udorn, and there were cables from Saigon and General Harris at the Air Force Pacific Command in Hawaii," Dillon said. "We have some big problems. It seems that overnight, the NVA hit our TACANs at Muang Phalane and Phou Kate. The Lao army ran. In

183

fact, they may have even known the attack was coming. A couple of American technicians were killed, as well as a few PARU who stood and fought."

"Jesus," James exclaimed. He understood the importance of the TACANS.

"It so happens we also had two USAID volunteers at Muang Phalane last night," Tom continued. "They're either captive or fleeing on foot. A PARU team is looking for them."

"So we can be certain the North Vietnamese know what the TACANS are now," the young diplomat said rhetorically.

"Not only can we be sure they know, but now they have the design," Tom replied. "The thermite charges did not go off, and the North Vietnamese have the important components." He poured some coffee and went to his desk. Both he and James saw the effect on American positions all over the globe. It put a lot of egg on the Ambassador's face.

"Who've you chatted with on this lovely morning?" Tom asked facetiously.

"We're still getting a lot of flak from the pilots for the straight approaches. I got two calls: One from the 355th at Takhli and the other from 44th in Korat."

Expected, Tom thought. On November 18, the men at Lima Site 85 had directed a large formation of F-105s on the air base at Phuc Yen. This was the largest concentration of MiGs in North Vietnam, and they wanted to make a real impression, so four squadrons of four planes each had been put on the mission. The North Vietnamese had wanted to make an impression, too, and they had far more SAMs in place and were ready to launch at the moment of the attack. At one point there were twelve surface-to-air missiles in the air at the same time.

The pilots were under orders not to divert, but when the lead plane and his wingman were blown from the sky, the orders went out the door. The other pilots jettisoned their bombs far from the target and evaded the missiles and associated 57mm gunfire. The hit to the morale of the pilots in 7th/13th Air Force was substantial. They had all begun to complain they were being treated like B-52 pilots, but without the big bomber's advantages of altitude and radar defenses.

"I can understand the tension," Tom said. "The pilots are at the whim of the accuracy of the NVA when they can't evade the guns. I imagine it's a bit like being told you have to storm a trench as an infantryman. You just have to hope the other guy misses."

James nodded at the clarity of the comparison. Neither had ever been in battle, but the two men were well versed with the outcome of those horrors. In November, 1944, Tom's father had been part of the first wave of Marines to storm Orange Beach on the Japanese-held island of Peleliu. Tom remembered being woken, years later, to the screaming nightmares his dad suffered through. American pilots were suffering now over North Vietnam. To date, Commando Club had seen almost seventy successful bombing flights on North Vietnam, but it was coming at a substantial cost. Five brand new F105's, along with their pilots, had been shot down.

"The attacks on the TACANS last night have hit a nerve with the President, and the ambassador has changed my role," Tom said. "That of course means your role has changed, too, James. We are to work with an Air Force lieutenant colonel as the area defender for Lima Site 85."

"OK, so less offense and more defense?" James replied

"Yeah. We'll be constantly reviewing all the intel on truck movement, troops, what the CIA says the Hmong are telling them, everything. We're supposed to ignore everything else in the country for now, and focus entirely on the defense of LS 85 and Phou Pha Thi. This is so we can accurately get bombing attacks on the construction of Road R602. These attacks on Phalane and Kate last night show the NVA are doubling their efforts to destroy our navigation equipment, so we have to double ours to stop them."

10

January 12, 1968, 1315 hours
(18 days later)
Lima Site 85, Phou Pha Thi, Houaphan Province,
Laos

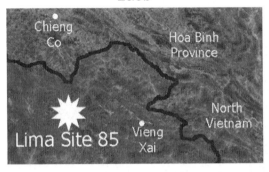

Sunny afternoons were a rare pleasure on Phou Pha Thi, and the men of Operation Heavy Green were taking full advantage of this one. The morning mission had gone well over North Vietnam, and the technicians were happy to finally have a cloud and rain-free day on the mountain. The sky was blue, the jungle green, and the poppies were blooming in the Hmong fields with bright red and white flowers.

Luang and Large were sunning themselves on the cracked slabs of rock near the TACAN. The two of them had created what Large called the Phou Pha Thi Book Club, where he read aloud to Luang and anyone else who wanted to hear the English or American classics. A few of the technicians regularly sat and listened to the Texan's deep booming voice and a couple of the PARU enjoyed it too. A few weeks before, they had started reading Sir James George Frazer's The Golden Bough, then had finished From Ritual to Romance by Jessie Weston the day before. Today, they were beginning Joseph Conrad's Heart of Darkness.

Luang loved listening as it was helping him with his English vocabulary, and Large loved reading aloud as it reminded him of "bedtime" with his two daughters.

Meanwhile, Shep, Alex, and Jum were quietly lying at the mouth of the small cave on the ledge below the Mission Room. Shep's initial fears of the big drop had given way to an appreciation for the view. He and Alex had come up with a safe and easy way down and back up from the shelf and along with a few other guys not at the site that morning, they really liked the big ledge.

Jum, of course, just liked being around the Americans, even though he couldn't garner what the conversations were about. He simply sat quietly and watched the fog and mist roll up from the valley below. If someone said something while looking his way, Jum would politely smile and nod.

All the Americans had one thing in common: They felt lousy. Two of the technicians had unidentifiable, low-grade fevers. Alex had a rash on his waist, but he had no other symptoms. A few of the technicians had come down with dengue fever, which they'd probably picked up in Udorn, and had been bedridden for a few days. This, plus the constant bowel woes that had the crew going through three rolls of toilet paper a day, had changed the assignments. The original plan had been for two teams to alternate in two-week rotations, but the various illnesses had forced members of each team to substitute for the other, so the original composition of the two crews was all mixed up.

They were all friends, but this mixing of the groups did affect morale in one unforeseen way: All the Heavy Green technicians had been instructed to buy their own meals at the Udorn PX. They'd worked out the purchases to produce a big communal meal everyone shared. Doing this on the first rotation, when everyone was in his original group, made dinner one of the highlights of the day. Now that the teams were mixed together, meals had become something of a potpourri of culinary possibilities. Each night one of the techs assumed the task of making dinner; it seemed the new game was to come up with the craziest combination of ingredients possible. Peanut butter and ketchup sandwiches were not a hit, but Weenies a la King were. Shep had declared that tonight they'd dine on tuna-spooj, whatever that was.

The one rule was that under no circumstance were Jum and Burnie allowed to assist with the cooking. Both kids' favorite meal was nsav chiav, congealed pig's blood over rice, and they liked it with every meal.

No one else agreed.

Most of the PARU were in their bunkers that afternoon, and other technicians were hanging out in various spots they'd claimed as their own private space around the installation. Some were writing letters or re-reading those they'd received. Brad, John, and Burnie were leaning against the Dushka bunker wall, staring casually off to the southeast.

189

Construction on Road 602 had reached ridges within six miles of Phou Pha Thi, and with it the destruction of the road had increased in earnest. Word was out there'd be a series of bombing runs on the road that afternoon, and John and Brad were watching the sky, hoping to see the planes as they came in for the attack. The two Americans had actually seen the bombs drop from F-4s and F-105s the day before, with the help of a spotting scope and binoculars. Burnie was great for this activity; his young Hmong eyes could pick up the planes before Brad or John had them spotted.

The two soldiers had come to enjoy sharing the differences in the war as it was fought in South Vietnam and Laos.

"So you were saying yesterday that the villages were coerced into holding weapons for the Viet Cong?" Brad asked John.

"Yeah, it's a pretty shitty place for the locals to be in," John said. "The Viet Cong come in and kill the head of the village if he doesn't store weapons and provide rice for them. The next guy in charge of course agrees to their terms. A few days later, we walk in and find weapons. We then accuse everyone of being in cahoots with the VC. After a month of it, every village in a region has been declared part of the VC effort, so it becomes a free-fire zone for both sides. It's Churchill's Domino Theory, but at a village level."

"You can't win a war that way unless you kill everyone. One of the first things they teach you at the Farm, the Agency's paramilitary training camp, is how to win over hearts and minds. It's why I believe in what we've been doing here in Laos. One paramilitary guy assigned to an area of twenty villages is not going to win by fighting. The local people have to like you. If the NVA comes in and kills the leader of a Hmong or Lao village, we respond by bringing them rice and fruit. It's pretty clear who they're going to like more."

"How'd you end up here in the first place?"

"I got hired by the RAND Corp in 'sixty-one. I had a degree in Asian anthropology from Dartmouth, and for a reason they could then see, but I couldn't, it was a hiring qualification. I'll have to tell you about RAND sometime. Crazy place. Anyway, I went from there to the CIA, which had me stationed in India for six months. Then to the Farm for paramilitary training. The Agency then sent me to Tibet, and I transferred here in 'sixty-five."

"You like this better than Tibet?"

"Yeah, well, this place seems to be harder on the body. I was losing weight for a while, then pulled a twelve-foot tapeworm out of my ass last year. But I like the Hmong. They're a sweet people. They say a prayer for an animal's spirit every time they hunt. They apologize to a dead deer just after killing it. They know they have to hunt to survive, but they really don't want to kill the beasts. It's brutal but sweet at the same time.

"I respect that they just want to be left alone," Brad continued as he stood up to stretch. "I mean, they aren't perfect, and there is a racist component to their world. The Hmong see themselves as racially pure, and the village elders don't want to see the young Hmong assimilate others into the clan, but that's no different from anyone else over here. The Khmer hate the Viet, the Lao hate the Khmer, the Han Chinese hate everybody. They each see themselves as the one pure race. This American concept of pluralism we're striving for is completely alien over here, but given the environment, I can understand where the Hmong are coming from. They just don't want the Vietnamese telling them how to live, and I can get behind that."

"Hell, in South Vietnam it goes a step further," John said. "The Catholics and Buddhists hate each other. I hope LBJ can push through more of these Great Society reforms back home. This place is proof that racism kills." John stood up and stretched too. "I'm gonna check on the bucket under the air conditioner. If we don't save every drop of water we can, it'll be a thirsty week."

"Tud!" Burnie exclaimed as he pointed down the valley. His effort to pick up American terminology had made for some interesting Hmonglish. "Tud" meant he could see a Thud.

John spun his big spotting scope to the east as the hissing sound of the F-105 reached Phou Pha Thi. All the technicians stood and looked toward the sound.

A Raven in an O-1 Bird Dog, essentially a souped-up and scaled-down Cessna 170, had just fired a smoke rocket to mark a target and was now circling above it. John could see the smoke about eight kilometers east of Phou Pha Thi.

The F-105 dove into a shallow canyon as if flying straight at the marker, then pulled up about three hundred feet above the ground. A tiny dot tumbled through the air below the plane, and John watched as the jungle shook with the blast. The bomb had fallen just uphill of the marker. As he watched, he gave the blow-by-blow of the attack aloud so the others could know what was happening. About five seconds after the bomb's blast, when the pilot was in a high-banking turn back toward the target, everyone on Phou Pha Thi heard the rumble of the explosion.

"That's probably only about five miles from here," Brad said. "It confirms what the scouts said last night. They really are getting close."

John nodded to his friend with a solemn look and bent back down to the scope. The F-105 dove back at the target at about a 45-degree angle. The speed of the plane is shocking, he thought, and though he couldn't see the tracers, one had to assume a 37mm gun was firing at the plane from below. At that speed it was no wonder they only hit about half their targets. This time, though, the bombs were pickled at the exact right moment and landed on the original smoke laid by the Raven.

"I think that is one dead bulldozer," John said. He continued to watch the scene to see if the Thud would make another pass. "Our Air Force is doing a good job of slowing a construction project, though I'm not sure how that helps the war effort in South Vietnam."

"Yeah. Do you get the feeling the tail is beginning to wag the dog here?" Brad asked, panning across the valley with binoculars. "We were put here to get the North Vietnamese, but we spend most of our time watching them try to get us."

"It seems to me the proof is in the numbers, man," John said. "Shep pointed it out this morning: We directed a hundred thirty flights over North Vietnam from here, in November. In December, that dropped to ninety-three, but we directed nearly three hundred-fifty over Northern Laos. We were supposed to be here to attack targets around Hanoi, but the Air Force is defending this facility more than attacking North Vietnam."

In just two short months the battle zone had shifted from the outskirts of Hanoi to Northern Laos. According to Richard in Udorn, General Vang Pao had conceded the Bam Bam River Valley and hills just south of Sam Neua to the enemy, which meant harassment from Hmong troops based on Long Tieng was all but finished. On top of that, the mountain had been buzzed by a MiG-21 the day before. The message was clear that the North Vietnamese wanted the Americans out of Northern Laos.

As the F-105 raced off for its home base to the south, smoke rose from the blast site. John watched as another explosion rocked the jungle and noted that its black smoke and orange flame indicated the bomb had likely hit a fuel tank. The technicians slowly made their way to the Dushka bunker to take a look through the scope. A few of the PARU came from their bunkers as well, though Luang stopped them and said they needed one man at the post and one looking through the scope.

"They're getting closer every day, John," Large said in his deepest voice.

"And we are dropping more and more ordnance, too," Alex added.

"Yeah, I know," John replied.

"Tud," Burnie yelled while pointing northeast.

"Four Tud."

There was no hiss of the jets as there should have been, but everyone turned to look for four F-105s. They squinted into the distance and could see tiny dots against the blue sky. Brad turned the scope onto the dots to verify they were actually airplanes.

"What the fuh—?" he mumbled as he stood up. "Those aren't F-105s. It's like we stepped into some time machine set to nineteen-seventeen."

John bent and looked through the scope, then immediately stood straight up. "Everybody into the bunkers. Now!"

January 12, 1968, 1315 hours
(same day)
Chieng Co, So'n La Province, North Vietnam

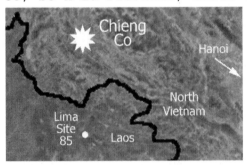

The previous weeks had been pleasant for Lim. His job was still to make the meals, but also to teach climbing each morning. In the afternoon, the Dac Cong would train with their weapons while Lim prepared the evening meal. There were no bombs to worry about, though they could hear planes every morning. It had actually been the most agreeable two weeks Lim had spent since he had left his village a Phou Samsoum.

The commandos had been climbing all morning and into the afternoon, and their hands showed it. The moist air made for soft skin, and every man except Lim and Sung bore cuts and scrapes from pulling awkwardly on the sharp rock. The two more talented climbers moved over the stone with greater control of their body position, which had made for fewer unexpected slips that had to be controlled using their hands.

Today's climbing objective had been quite a challenge. Lim had made it up this one rock face and rigged the rope through two pitons at the top. He had rappelled back down and then gotten the men to climb while belaying each other. Sung was the last to attempt the face; none of the other commandos had been able to reach the top. The atmosphere at the base of the wall was always friendly but competitive, and everyone chided the commander as if there was no way he could scale the new climb. There were reasons why Sung had risen to the top of the Dac Cong, and clearly one of them had been his athletic ability. Other than Lim, Sung had proven to be the best climber of the group.

This particular route was different from the others they'd made that week. It looked easy from afar as the angle was far less than vertical, but the steepness of the rock was only part of the obstacle. The size of the holds was just as important, and this climb had a crux with very small footholds. There was simply no way to pull yourself up it; you had to use balance and footwork to overcome the most difficult section.

Sung tied into the rope and began to climb as one

of the other commandos belayed him. He climbed about ten meters and reached the crux. It was clear this was the most difficult section, and Sung knew he had to step high and left onto a tiny edge to reach another larger hold—his problem was he didn't think he could stand on that edge; it was just too small. As his forearms began to burn, Sung accepted it was now or never: You either get going, or you fall off because you've lost all your strength, he told himself. He placed his foot on the edge and rocked over it, then began to stand. In an instant, his boot folded over, his foot slipped from the limestone edge, he fell and was left dangling on the rope.

All the men taunted him as he was lowered to the ground.

"Lieutenant," Lim said, "I think you should try something different. Put on my boots and do the climb." Sung had specially requisitioned Lim a pair of boots to replace his worn-out sandals, and Lim tossed them to the commander.

"Lim, you have the same shoes as mine, but at least two sizes smaller," the frustrated commander replied.

"Just try it, sir. I put a special Hmong spell on them for you."

The men listened to the little Hmong man. No matter what their feelings for the Hmong, they had learned over the course of the weeks that he knew what he was doing and they'd be wise to take in all his instructions. Sung shrugged his shoulders, sat on a boulder, and removed his tan, Chinese-made boots, then forced his foot into the smaller shoes. He tied himself back into the rope and quickly climbed back up to the crux. This time he stepped out onto the edge and took a deep breath. The foothold felt more secure, so he stood up and grabbed the hold above it. The climb had been the hardest yet, but suddenly it felt easier than anything he'd done that day. Lim lowered the commander down and had him do the same climb again; this time it felt like nothing at all. He could feel every hold through the tighter boots.

"That is amazing, Lim," Sung said as he was lowered to the ground. He untied the boots and handed them back to Lim.

"The extra space in your boots simply folds over when you try to stand on small footholds," Lim said. "You also get a better feel for what your feet are on if the shoe is tight."

"I definitely had a better feel for how well my boot was sticking to the rock. Corporal, come here," Sung said to one of the other commandos. "I want you to write down everyone's shoe sizes and then subtract two sizes. This afternoon you will go to So'n La and get a message to General Giap's office in my name. You will request boots two sizes smaller than we currently have for every man, is that clear? We may not wear them all the time, but it will be useful to have smaller boots for more difficult climbing."

"Yes, sir." The corporal saluted and jogged off toward the cave-camp.

A few more of the commandos tried the route in their standard-fitting boots, but all failed. Everyone was dismissed for a one-hour lunch around 1300. Lim had boiled a chicken to go over rice, which had been carried into the field with them that morning. The commandos each took a share of the chicken broth and rice onto a plate-sized piece of banana leaf and ate the food with their tattered fingers. Lim waited until everyone had their meal before taking his own. At the start of the week, this deferring to the soldiers had made for some hungry afternoons, but the lieutenant had made it clear that the soldiers had to leave food for Lim. His lessons were the reason they were there and starving him was not going to help. The men respected Lieutenant Sung. He was not only their commander but clearly the toughest and most experienced of the platoon, so they did as they were told.

Lim took his rice and chicken to a shaded spot near the edge of a nearby rice paddy and began to eat. He let his feet hang off the muddy paddy dike, just barely above the young, pale green shoots of rice poking through the brown water. This paddy was about fifty feet across, then there was another, and another, reaching all the way to a karst tower that rose from the watery rice farm with steep, dark gray walls.

Moments after Lim sat down, Sung joined him. "This broth is very good, Private Lim," the lieutenant said.

"Thank you, Lieutenant."

Sung sat on the paddy dike and let his legs hang down near the brackish water. It somehow felt good to see the young shoots of rice just beginning to poke through and get their first taste of sunshine. It meant there would be rice on the table later this year.

"When you worked on the Trail, did you make it all the way to the south?" Sung asked. "I mean, to where we are fighting the Americans?"

"No, sir," Lim replied as he smeared a couple fingers of rice through the thin chicken broth. "My binh trams were all north of the fighting, but we did see many American bombers."

"So you have never seen any of the fighting you support in this war?"

"No, sir. Just the planes and the bombs."

"I was a saboteur near Binh Hoa, outside of Saigon," Sung said as he chewed. "We did everything with meticulous plans. We dressed as Viet Cong and wore armbands that said we were from the South, so if we were killed, the death appeared to be from the insurgency. Even in the afterlife we were fighting the Americans' morale." Sung took a sip from his canteen, then continued. "Being a part of the fight for the South really taught me we have to embrace the dan tranh. There is no time for us as individuals. There is no counting days until we are finished with service. We must either come together and win the fight however long it takes, or we die trying."

Lim understood the dan tranh philosophy. It was a belief that, like ants, all the people of Vietnam had to unite and work as a team. He had heard Ho Chi Minh speak of it on the radio one night. Uncle Ho had said that with time and the dan tranh philosophy, the people of Vietnam had an advantage over the Americans. The American soldier came to fight, and on the first day he began counting down until he could leave. Not having that option made the people of Vietnam better soldiers. The problem was, with the exception of these past two weeks, the Vietnamese had made it clear to Lim that he was not one of them.

"I hear what you say, Lieutenant," Lim replied. "I appreciate the respect you have shown me." He wanted to say more on how the changes to Vietnam had affected his life, but it was not a subject that could be taken lightly. Sung was a believer in the revolutionary cause, and though Lim felt empowered by being asked to teach mountaineering to the platoon, there was only so far Sung could go. Lim's anger about the Hmong's place in Vietnam could be taken as treason in the wrong ears.

"I think I understand how you feel, Lim," Sung said. "Do you know the I Ching?"

"I was taught it by the French when I was young, but I remember more about climbing than I do schoolwork," Lim joked.

"My favorite passage from the book is this: 'Times change and with them their demands. Thus, the seasons change in the course of the year. In the world cycle, there is also a spring and a fall, as there are in the lives of peoples or nations. These call for transformation.'" Sung paused a moment in thought, then continued. "I believe there is a future for us in Vietnam, but it will have to come in a different season."

"Perhaps," Lim replied with a smile. "I will get to work on the platoon's dinner now."

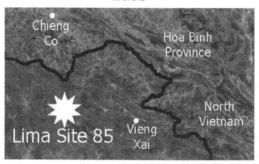

The single-engine biplane design of the four Anton-ov Colts, complete with guide wires running from the cockpit to the top of the tail, and fixed landing gear, made them look like something out of World War I. They had actually been designed in the Soviet Union in 1947, almost twenty years after the Great War. Con-structed in the Ukrainian city of Kiev, the four dark-green aircraft were built to land and take off using short runways. They could also fly at very slow speeds, making them an effective bomber if the pilot dared fly at only 35 knots over his target.

As the planes closed in on Phou Pha Thi, the tech-nicians grabbed helmets and hid in the bunkers, while Burnie and Jum ran for the Hmong trenches. John snatched up his M16 from a bunker and took a posi-tion next to the Mission Room, while Brad and Luang readied the Dushka machine gun. The planes broke formation, with two going into an orbiting pattern high and perhaps a mile south of the mountain. The other

planes came straight on from the east.
***

About this time, Kyle Dramis was very much enjoying the view of the Laotian countryside from the open door of a Bell 204 Huey. The air was smooth, which was always nice when you had a lao Lao hangover, and the helicopter was over territory likely NVA-free, so a crash wouldn't mean certain death. He knew the pleasantness of the day wasn't going to last the moment the young Air America pilot turned with a distressed look and tapped him on the leg.

"Sir, someone at Alternate just said your boys at Phou Pha Thi are under attack," the kid said. "It's some sort of aerial bombardment."

"Okay. Change of plans, Craig. We might be doing a rescue," Kyle said. "Tune the radio into Lima Site 85's frequency and head that way."

Kyle put on the rear headset and began loading another thirty-round clip for his AK-47. Two days before, his M16 had jammed for the third and final time. He'd thrown it out of the helicopter and switched to the more dependable communist weapon.
***

On the mountain, the technicians were in a panic after the first strafing run by the North Vietnamese planes. As soldiers fighting with the American Air Force, Brad and Luang were used to total air supremacy, so they were befuddled when the biplanes passed overhead. The two men fired the big machine gun, but clearly missed the target.

On the first run, each plane dropped four small bombs from a tube that extended from the belly of the aircraft. The shells went off down the ridge, and the technicians could hear yells from the Hmong between bursts of gunfire. Either the camouflage paint on the buildings was working or the pilots were focused on the cleared landing zone and silver tin roofs of the CIA hooches. The second attack was also focused a few hundred meters south of the radar equipment. Brad and Luang fired with the Dushka, but again missed the moving targets. Neither man had ever fired at an aircraft before.

John ran back into the radio room and called Udorn. It was his second call for help and he wanted it to sound a little less stressed than the previous message.

"This is Lima Site 85. We are currently under attack from the air," John said in his best pilot impersonation.

"Well, get back out there and shoot at them, Bradley," the voice on the radio replied.

"Kyle, is that you?" It wasn't exactly safe radio communication, but Kyle rarely followed the book.

"Affirmative. We are in a Huey and have you in sight. Do you need casualties taken out?"

"We haven't had the chance to assess that yet. I'd say hold back and wait for fighters to knock these guys down. We'll know more soon."

"Roger. We might be able to help. In any event, the message has gone through and two F-4s are en route from Udorn. You get back out there and give 'em hell."

John dropped the microphone and ran back out with his M16 as the planes came in for a third pass. This time they were coming straight at the radar buildings. Everyone ducked as the aircrafts' machine guns raked the cliff side just below the Mission Room and Dushka bunker. The moment the guns quit firing, the PARU fired with their M16s and Brad and Luang opened up with the big machine gun. The first plane was flying so slow and so low it was almost impossible to miss. Bullets ripped into the underside of the lumbering biplane as another bomblet dropped through the tube. It hit just left of the TACAN, knocking the machine off its foundation, then black smoke puffed from the plane's engine cowling. There was no time to cheer as the second plane passed overhead, dropping three more bombs. Somehow they all managed to hit between bunkers and buildings, and shrapnel passed over the cowering technicians. As the second plane gunned its engine for another pass, the first turned for the North Vietnamese border with its engine sputtering and smoke pouring out of the cockpit windows.

The second plane turned out over the valley west of Phou Pha Thi to begin its run, but ran into unexpected trouble. The men on the mountain watched as the Air America Huey took position above and behind the plane. The North Vietnamese air crew had clearly not noticed there was another player in the air and had kept their air speed slow so they could get another accurate strafing and bombing run.

"This is a brand new, taxpayer funded Bell 204-D," Kyle yelled to the helicopter pilot. "It's gotta be faster than that piece of shit. Pull right above him and try to stay there."

Kyle clipped himself into one of the cargo floor mounts, leaned out the side window, and stood on the

205

landing skid. He fired about fifteen shots with the AK into the top of the plane. This woke the pilot up, but as he was passing over the south ridge of the big peak there was no way for him to dive and gain safe speed. The pilot tried to evade to the east, but the helicopter was far more maneuverable, and Kyle got off another ten shots. The pilot turned for the North Vietnamese border, but something was wrong with the plane: It was losing air speed. The young Air America pilot was able to bring the Huey right over the top of the Antonov Colt, and Kyle emptied his second magazine into its cockpit. He was close enough to see blood and brain spatter on the windscreen. The plane began to lose altitude faster, and soon it was in a dive. It crashed into a ridge a few miles north of Phou Pha Thi.

Back on the mountain, John ran into the radio room to find out where the fast-moving jets were. Two planes were down, but there had been four in the original formation.

"Well, that's somethin' you don't see every day," Kyle said over the radio. "You boys on the ground better be happy with the show. It's rare for a drunk CIA paramilitary guy to shoot down a bronze-age biplane from a moving helicopter."

The building rocked with the thunder of two F-4 Phantoms buzzing the ridge.

"Yeah, too bad we aren't here," John said into the microphone. "You boys would get some medals if we were just over the border."

John dropped the microphone and stepped back outside.

"Luang and Brad ran down to the Hmong line,"

Shep yelled to him from a bunker. "They said the bombing could be a set up for a ground attack."

John gave a thumbs-up, then turned to scan the sky where the other two North Vietnamese planes had been flying. They were nowhere to be seen. Apparently, the pilots had bugged out at first sight of the Phantoms. John began checking the damage to the buildings while the PARU reloaded the Dushka.

A few minutes later, Brad walked back into the radar area and sat on the Dushka bunker wall. "The Hmong already had scouts out. There is no coordinated attack," he said. "Those planes were dropping 120mm mortar shells. A couple of them didn't go off, but about fifteen did." He took a deep breath and sighed. "Four Hmong are dead," he said to no one. "And Burnie is one of them."

11

February 1, 1968, 0315 hours
(20 days later)
Lima Site 85, Phou Pha Thi, Houaphan Province,
Laos

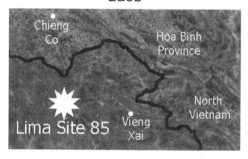

"John, God knows you need yer beauty sleep, but I think you better get up," said the deep, soothing voice.

John Lilygren opened his eyes to see Large leaning over his bunk. The light was on at the far end of the staff quarters, but the bunks were so close together it was hardly disturbing. John then noticed no one else was in their bunk, and he glanced at his wrist watch.

"Large, Jesus man, it's still last night," John mumbled. "Unless this is an emergency, wake me when the boys receive the operations order."

"We think it's an emergency, but no one is sure," the big man replied. "There's some pretty serious shit goin' down. We're in the radio room. Coffee's brewin'."

John stood, slid on a pair of fatigue pants and

grabbed a jacket, then followed the big Texan to the door. He could hear the patter of heavy raindrops on the exposed sections of the building. Rain had been nearly constant in the previous two weeks, and the nighttime temperature could drop into the low 40s. It may be Southeast Asia, but the conditions were anything but warm. He staggered out the door and into a deluge, then down the ladder and into the first door on the maintenance and communications building.

The inviting scent of coffee was overpowered by stale cigarette smoke. The technicians, smoking and looking serious, were all gathered around the telex desk where Alex was wearing radio headphones and taking notes. Jum sat on one of the crates of TACAN replacement parts, calmly watching everyone but without the usual smile on his face.

"Ignorance is bliss," John said to the group. "I was happy when I was asleep. In ten seconds I'm going to be very unhappy. Who wants to fill me in?"

Shep handed John a cup of black coffee. The cigarette looked out of place in his hand, like he didn't really know what to do with it.

"What the hell, man, you don't smoke," John said, after taking a sip of the brew.

"Well, I do tonight. We came in to get started on today's mission and found out South Vietnam is on fire. The communists have hit everything. Even the embassy is under attack."

John had discovered over the previous three months that the technicians were hardly military-savvy. Their jobs in the Air Force were in electronics, not combat, so the extent of their tactical understanding of war was limited to one class in basic training and various John Wayne movies. However, the tension in the room was as thick as the cigarette smoke, so John knew the situation had to be serious.

"What exactly have they attacked?" John asked the room.

"Everything, John. Seriously, everything," Alex said. "New attacks are erupting all over South Vietnam."

John nodded. The fog of war made sure that what exactly was happening would not be fully understood for some time, but it was clear the North Vietnamese were up to something big. He and his men needed to be ready for anything.

"Jum, go get Captain Luang, then go tell Mr. Brad to get up here," John said in broken mix of Thai and Hmong. If there was a concerted offensive by the North Vietnamese, an attack on Phou Pha Thi was likely.

The entire intelligence community knew the North Vietnamese had been threading a political needle with two divergent allies for years. The Chinese, who provided huge amounts of small arms and food supplies, had pushed for a long, protracted guerrilla campaign to slowly wear down the will of the South Vietnamese and their American allies. For the most part, this was how the war had been conducted. The Soviet Union, which had provided the air defenses and more sophisticated weapons, had pushed for a series of set-piece battles where their modern equipment could be pitted against the American's modern army. North Vietnam had to keep both allies happy, and to appease the

Soviets, they had attacked the South en masse.

"I have to admit, fellas, this is a total surprise," John said. "And it's a bad thing when the enemy can pull off a big surprise. No one expected an attack on the Tet New Year. It's like Christmas, New Year's, and everyone in Vietnam's birthday rolled into one night."

In fact, the South Vietnamese Army and US intelligence had received some warning of an impending attack. However, the importance of Tet in Vietnamese culture had led the Americans to believe the battle would come later in the month, and no one foresaw the scale of the fighting. From a military standpoint, the Americans didn't believe a coordinated attack the size of the Tet Offensive was possible. They believed the North's forces lacked the supplies and the tactical ability to put together a coordinated battle throughout South Vietnam. The Americans were wrong.

According to the reports the men at Lima Site 85 were receiving, mortar shells and Katyusha rockets began raining on bases in South Vietnam shortly after midnight. Hue was overrun by an estimated force of 7,000 Viet Cong and North Vietnamese, and the firebase at Khe Sanh was encircled by another estimated 40,000 NVA troops. Over thirty battalions on the outskirts of Saigon struck South Vietnamese and American bases at Tan Son Nhut, Long Binh, and Bien Hoa. In total, communist forces attacked thirty-six of the forty-four provincial capitals in South Vietnam. Perhaps most damning, just before 0300, Viet Cong sappers blew a hole in the fortified wall of the American Embassy and poured onto the Marine sentries. As the holy grail of American power in Southeast Asia, this enormous building was the starting point of every operations order in the war theater.

The technicians were startled when Captain Luang, draped in a soaking wet green poncho, came through the door.

"Pi John, what is happening?" he asked, while trying to catch his breath.

"There are attacks taking place all over South Vietnam," John said. "We could be next."

"Kop," Luang said. "I will wake both squads and make sure my men are on alert."

Luang turned and ran out the door as Jum came in. The young Hmong went to John as the technicians turned back to Alex on the radio. "He say no cha gee, no problem." Jum handed John a crinkled note that had been wadded into the palm of his hand. John unfolded it and had a look.

"Hmong recon teams report no new movement. Nothing new here. Will come after dawn. Be vigilant. Hugs and kisses, Brad."

"Okay, guys. Brad says they have no reports of anyone prepping for an attack here. We'll stay on it, but so far, so good."

"With the North Vietnamese inside the US Embassy, do you think we might get an order telling us to bomb Washington?" Shep asked and everyone chuckled. His light sense of humor was good at breaking the ice of a scary situation.

John convinced them it was safe enough to stop chain smoking; the air quality of the cramped building improved. The men monitored the radios and telex machine until the sun was lighting the overcast sky from above. About 0900 the rain stopped and everyone stepped outside for fresh air. The mountain summit was shrouded in dense clouds that muffled all sound. Brad silently strolled up the trail with his M16 in hand.

"There's nothin' happening here," Brad said as he walked up to the Dushka bunker. "It appears we are safe, but I would not want to be in the land of leeches right now."

As the morning grew brighter, a cold and gusty breeze carrying banks of fog and cloud blew up and over the rim of the cliff. Thin sheets of white vapor sprang from the fog-covered valley, dancing past the bunkers and the Mission Room. It was a cold wind, reminding everyone the storms would rise and condense soon, sending another torrent down on the facility.

Jum and the technicians went back into the radio room, while Brad and John stepped into the Dushka bunker. They had refortified the area after the Colt bombardment, which included a small roof that could not only deflect some shrapnel, but also held back the rain. The two men nestled under the roof as the drizzle began.

"This looks like the largest single offensive of the war, by either side," John said. "Tactically, I would not have thought they had the ability to put something like this together."

"Yeah, if they can pull this off throughout the South, what can they do here?" Brad asked rhetorically. "At this point, we know there's been movement of troops all over Northeast Laos. The NVA could hide an entire division under the jungle canopy and we'd never see it."

"Maybe we need to improve our offensive capabilities a little," John said. "We can't have the Hmong and Air Force do all the fighting. I'm going to ask for more PARU to be stationed up here."

"That's a good idea," Brad said. "I'm gonna try to get the Hmong to start doing hit-and-run engagements on these NVA forces near the road construction. Maybe it will make them more wary and slow the tide."

Brad had brought in some more captured equipment and stationed it around the landing zone and his hut. There was a Soviet "Hail" rocket launcher in pieces but theoretically fixable, and an 81mm mortar that Vang Pao had captured from the NVA. They had also flown in a 105mm howitzer under a Chinook helicopter and now had it aimed into the valley bellow Phou Pha Thi. The Hmong were still dug in deep, and they'd been instructed in the use of the larger weapons.

The biplane bombardment had been a wake-up call. It was, to date, the only aerial bombardment by North Vietnam of the war and showed just how desperate they were to destroy Lima Site 85. Since then, NVA forces had been picked up on sensors and by Hmong recon patrols all the way around Phou Pha Thi. The American, Thai, and Hmong forces on Phou Pha Thi really were on an island in a sea of enemy fighters.

"Last week the Air Force flew over a hundred attacks on the forces around this mountain. That's a lot of bombs, and here you and I are saying we have to raise our game to protect ourselves. This place was supposed to direct bombs on North Vietnam, not spend all its energy defending itself."

"Yeah. The tail is definitely wagging the dog now."

"You think we're doing any good with all of this?" One of the technicians had posed the question earlier in the morning, but John was asking Brad's opinion on a different level. "I mean, not just here at Phou Pha Thi, or even in Laos, but the entire war."

Brad sighed and stared out into the mist. "Before I was with the Agency, I worked at the RAND Corporation," he replied. "I think I told you that."

John nodded.

"So in 'sixty-one, the Pentagon had us set up a top secret war game. I think we called it the Omega Program. We took everything we knew about the region and the players and put it on the table: strength of North Vietnam, strength of Viet Cong, reliability of South Vietnamese forces, weapons the NVA would get from the Soviets, everything we could think of that could affect the outcome of a war. There were two dozen of us running this game, all playing the role of different people in the war. We broke into a red group, the Commies, and a blue group, good guys. It took about a week to do it, and that was working twelve hours a day, but we finished with a pretty certain understanding on the outcome of the war."

"What happened? Are you saying you didn't see this attack and that it's changed everything?"

"No. Quite the opposite," Brad replied. "We could see that by the early 'seventies the South Vietnamese had lost, the North had won, and the US had been pushed out of the region with thousands dead and a disgraced place in world opinion. It also cost us bil-

215

lions, and the Russians came away with more knowledge of our capabilities."

"Holy shit. What did the Pentagon say?"

"They didn't like it. They paid us to play it out again, but this time we switched who was on what side. I got to be General Nguyen Giap in that one. We also lowered the amount of aid China and Russia put in the game, and raised American assistance and troop levels and the involvement of the South Koreans, Australians, and Thais. It took another week to do it."

"And?"

"And we lost again," Brad said frankly. "It just took another year."

"Jesus. And now here we are running it again."

"Yeah, but this time with real bullets and real bodies."

"I've lost twenty-six men under my command," John said. "Twenty-seven if you count Burnie. If you take a step back and look at this, none of it makes any sense. I'm not talking about the war in Laos and Vietnam, I'm talking about all war. Twenty-five years ago you would have had a hard time convincing anyone in America we'd be allies with the Germans and Japanese, but we're the best of friends now. That came after we united with the British to destroy them, and that's keeping in mind that a hundred and thirty years before, we were fighting the British and getting support for it from the Germans. I wouldn't be surprised if thirty years from now we are over here with the Vietnamese to fight the Chinese."

Brad chuckled at the thought. "I suppose we're forced into the parameters of our time. For me, despite what we found with Omega, I believe in what we are doing here in Laos. I don't believe in communism. I believe it's wrong, and I believe if their economic and political approach were that good, they wouldn't have to kill so many of their own people to force it on them. So I accepted the position because you have to draw the line somewhere."

"Yeah, and I agree with you in principle. I mean, once I spent some time with the Hmong, I understood why the CIA was trying to draw the line at the Vietnamese border. But now, hearing what kind of attack the North Vietnamese were able to put together last night, I don't think we're cut out for this kind of war. The North Vietnamese are willing to do things to win that we're not. It may be time to pull back to the other side of the Mekong."

The rain continued to patter on the tin roof for the rest of the day.

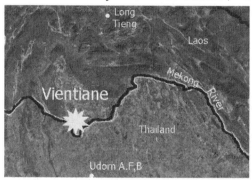

"Sullivan said he wanted them out by February first," Richard Milano said bluntly from the doorway to Tom Dillon's office.

The ambassador hadn't returned his phone calls for the last three days, so Richard had flown to Vientiane to get his own audience. So far, the best he could do was the ambassador's assistant.

"As it turns out with hindsight, that would have been a pretty good day to safely close down Lima Site 85," Richard said. "Then we wouldn't have to be worrying about them during this Tet-offensive in South Vietnam."

On the day before the North Vietnamese had launched the attacks, Richard had received a copy of a report detailing how Military Assistance Command of Vietnam (MACV) had reassessed the Hmong. They were now certain the guerrillas could hold off an NVA attack for as long as it took to get the technicians off Phou Pha Thi. The report disgusted Richard. Every bit

218

of intel on Phou Pha Thi went across Richard's desk, and he knew nothing had changed to bring sudden light to the issue. On top of that, there wasn't anyone in the American military who knew as much about the Hmong as he and his operators did, and they hadn't been contacted about the report. It was obviously created for political reasons.

"What can I tell you, Rich?" Tom replied. "This is above Ambassador Sullivan's pay grade. Remember, he didn't even want to do this mission. Yesterday he told the White House the technicians have to be out by February twenty-fifth, and he thought he might have gotten removed for saying it."

"So is it coming from Secretary McNamara, or from General Harris in CINCPAC? Who's calling the shots now?"

"McNamara has the President's ear, so this is coming from the White House. Our hands are tied here."

Richard walked into the office and took a seat across from Tom, then let out a big sigh. The convoluted and politicized command structure had always been a problem in Vietnam, but none of the CIA operatives ever thought it would make it to Laos. The CIA knew that as long as they kept American soldiers off the ground in Laos and the war remained a secret, Military Assistance Command of Vietnam, the US Embassy in Saigon, the Joint Chiefs, and the President would stay out of it and the spooks would close the deal. Now the military establishment had a foot in the door, and the slow gears of political bureaucracy were taking over.

"Look," Richard said. "The intel is like this: They-have Road 602 built within three miles of the base of the mountain. On the nineteenth, I got a report from a Hmong recon patrol that five battalions had moved west of Sam Neua along the road. That's two weeks ago, and they've only added to it. That's a force substantially bigger and better trained than what we have defending the site."

Tom listened to Richard explain the situation, even though he had already seen the same intelligence reports. He liked the career CIA man, and there was no questioning his knowledge on fieldwork in Laos. He also saw that Richard was frustrated and was simply not willing to look at the bigger picture.

"We're going to start having the technicians direct bombers from Lima Site 85," Tom said. "The Air Force says their bombers can hold back the Vietnamese with pinpoint accuracy."

"Oh, yeah, this is the same Air Force that said we'd win this war with Rolling Thunder. 'Bomb 'em into the Stone Age,' and all that. It's a load of crap, and you know it."

Tom rolled his eyes. He'd stepped into that one. "Yeah, but I want you to see it from their position. The weather has been atrocious this year. In the last few months there've been only four days our bombers could fly visual strikes on North Vietnam. Right now, nearly thirty percent of all the strikes for Operation Barrel Roll and Operation Rolling Thunder are being directed by Lima Site 85. At the same time, we've just been attacked on virtually every front in South Vietnam with weapons that've come in from the north before we started directing the bombing raids from the Site."

"I get it: We've slowed up the supply line, but do we really want to fight the coming battle for Phou Pha Thi?"

"The President is worried we may lose the entire Khe Sanh firebase just like the French lost Dien Bien Phou," Tom said. "If we don't stop the supplies flowing south, a few thousand US Marines may die."

Both men paused in the argument and stared sullenly at each other. They were each preaching to the choir. The die had been cast when Lima Site 85 became effective.

"Look at the big picture," Tom said again in a calm voice. "Slowing the North Vietnamese supplies to Khe Sanh only seems to work with the bombing directed from Lima Site 85. This whole war may suddenly be dependent on those eleven technicians directing flights over North Vietnam."

Tom is right, Rich thought. For now, the technicians have to stay.

February 13, 1968, 1215 hours
(11 days later)
Southern So'n La Province, North Vietnam

The trekking had been hard from the start, even for Lim. Years of working on the Ho Chi Minh Trail had given him the strength to carry heavy loads, but the speed the Dac Cong moved at was difficult to maintain. To make it just a little harder, a couple of the commandos had added ammunition to Lim's load. If Lim complained he was overloaded, the other commandos would know, and then anything was possible. They'd listened to Lim teach, but they didn't like him. It was safer to just carry the ammunition and keep his mouth shut.

On February 9th, the night before they began the trek, Sung had finally given Lim and the Dac Cong a short explanation of where they were going. The objective was to destroy an American base on a mountain in Laos. The Dac Cong would work in unison with a division of men from the North Vietnamese Army that was already taking a position against the Americans. He had then pulled Lim aside and explained it in more detail.

"Two months ago I told you I was keeping you with my commandos because you had carried loads on the Trail," Sung had said. "That was true then, but it is no longer the reason you are here. Our assignment is to destroy a base high on the mountain, which means we must climb the mountain. I have been there, but I still don't know how we will make this happen. We may need you to lead the climb, so that is your job now. For now you are a porter, but we may need you to climb."

Lim had never been a soldier and was a long way from being a Dac Cong commando. He also wasn't sure he believed in the cause.

"Lieutenant Sung, I have not fought in this war," Lim said. "I have only shot a gun when hunting, and I don't know how you and your men fight."

"I know," the Dac Cong commander had replied. "You are not Dac Cong, so you will not have a gun. We just need you for the climb."

A cold fear swept over Lim when he heard the words. As he marched behind the soldiers, Lim thought of Sung's words. "We just need you for the climb," the commander had said. Sung was a committed revolutionary. He was willing to die for a cause and expected it of all the soldiers in his command. But for Lim, if the North Vietnamese had shown him anything, it was that this was not his cause. Even after his help, the Vietnamese in Sung's command still hated him for being Hmong.

The respite from carrying loads on the Ho Chi Minh Trail had perhaps put him in a far more dangerous spot. Now it seemed he might be leading a charge up a fortified mountain with no means of defending himself. Perhaps worse, Lieutenant Sung's demeanor had changed. His face had grown stern in appearance, without even a hint of a smile, and he had spoken very little to Lim or the other commandos. Sung had been relatively approachable for two months, but he was a cold instrument of war now. It was clear the mission was all that mattered, and that meant Lim was only as important as he was useful.

12

February 18, 1968, 1300 hours,
(five days later)
5.2 km ESE of Lima Site 85, Phou Pha Thi,
Houaphan Province, Laos

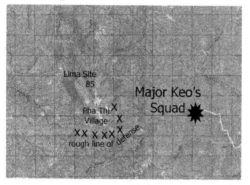

There was just a small gap in the trees. Major Keo looked through the foliage and across the valley to the east in an effort to get his bearings. With all the seasonal rain, the smell of rotting forest filled the air around the mountain. He heard the honking of a great hornbill, then the flapping of wings as a pair of the giant birds flew by, just above the jungle canopy. Somewhere thousands of feet above that, a small, propeller-driven aircraft, probably flying from the American base near Long Tieng, was looking for targets in the dense jungle. Keo knew he and his men had done a good job hiding the forward-most sections of the road, and they were safe under the cover of the forest.

Despite the American bombers' best efforts, construction of the Road 602 had gone well to this point without Keo being forced to leave his position at the forward staging area. However, they were now within comfortable range of his 122mm howitzers, and the proper placement of the weapons was paramount. Keo had gotten reconfirmation that he would be in charge of the artillery attack on Phou Pha Thi. For that, he needed to find a location that hid the guns from the American planes but could be reached from a forward observation post via an 800-meter field telephone line.

Keo had the battle plan, including the targets for the opening salvo from the artillery, and for all to go as planned, the aim of the big guns would have to be true. He simply couldn't trust anyone else in his command to put the artillery exactly where it needed to be so he could see the target and they could fire in relative safety.

Both Lieutenant Dao and Captain Tung, the two ranking field commanders, had vehemently stated that the major should not come this far forward. For two weeks miao patrols had been harassing the road crews, and losses in the associated battalions had been significant. The miao had put together hit-and-run attacks on both a daily and nightly basis that kept everyone on edge. It was difficult to sleep at night, and thus hard to stay focused during the day. The filthy barbarians did seem to know their forest, and considering the statements of his two senior officers, there was no denying it was affecting the men. Keo had finally put his foot down and given them an order not to discuss the fact he was working in the field. He would be leading the force out to find the correct artillery locations, and he would not hear another word about it.

The riflemen of the two squads accompanying him had been hit the day before by the miao, and they were quite nervous. The men knew the area and how the attacks were often arranged, so for much of the morning Keo had focused on finding the right place for the road and let them worry about the enemy. But at that moment, he needed to confirm their current location. Reading the battle plan and then comparing it to the map revealed some irregularities, so he called for another opinion.

"Sergeant, come here," he said to a nearby soldier. "Do you agree that this point here"—he pointed to the map—"is that point there on that ridge?" Keo pointed through a break in the foliage to a tree-covered ridge.

"Yes, sir, Major. I think we are right here," the young cadre whispered.

Keo looked at him in slight disgust for the whisper. The soldiers clearly had not been shot at as many times as he had and needed more seasoning before they were sent south.

"Okay, do you recall how steep this ravine is?" he asked as he pointed at the map.

The sergeant leaned over the map to verify the position. As they both focused on the location, crimson blood and pieces of tissue splashed across the paper and the sharp report of an American M1 cut through the forest. Keo realized the soldier's head had just exploded, and the moment he did, a bullet hit him in the right shoulder. As the major spun and instinctively began to dive for the safety of the ground, he heard the jungle erupt with the fire of the American rifles. Before his body reached the dirt, another round had entered his abdomen just above the belt line, and a third went into his left eye and exited behind his right ear. Major Keo never felt himself hit the ground. Someone else would direct the artillery.

February 28, 1968, 1100 hours
(ten days later)
4.6 km SE of Lima Site 85, Phou Pha Thi
Houaphan Province, Laos

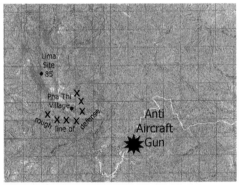

Tom Sears had woken early that morning, gotten his coffee, and lifted off from Alternate before dawn. General Vang Pao had thrown a big party the night before, with his preferred wife, their enormous Hmong family, and all his favorite Ravens and CIA operatives. A pig had been slaughtered, and lao Lao was served by the bucketful. Tom had bowed out early, around 0200, so he could be well rested for the day's fight, but there was still a bit of a fog between his ears. The fresh cold air blowing into his O-1 Bird Dog helped to clear his head.

When Tom Sears was in the air, which was usually about ten hours a day, he went by the call sign Raven-86. He and three other Ravens had been flying above the newly constructed road for a month, picking targets and handing them off to various fighter jocks to decimate. He had been shot at while returning home the night before, and it had kind of pissed him off. Shooting at a guy who had been at work all day long was low, and Raven-86 knew the gunner knew he'd been in the sky since morning. It was rude, but a well-placed bomb would no doubt help the NVA gunner's manners. Tom flew over the area he'd been shot at about 800 feet above the jungle, but could not spot the gun. He came at the broken ridge from a different angle and a little lower, but still no luck.

"Raven-86, this is Wizard-1, do you have a target for us yet?" the deep voice asked calmly over the radio. He was a new guy. Tom could just feel it. The F-4s had been circling overhead for fifteen minutes or so, but that was part of their cushy job. They were safe up there and had plenty of fuel to burn.

"Hold your horses, Wizard-1," Tom responded. "I'll have a nice, juicy triple-A gun for you in just a minute or two."

The NVA gunner was there and Tom knew it, but it would take a little bit more coaxing and skill to get him to reveal his exact position. This was what Ravens did that no one else even considered. Tom dropped the Bird Dog to about two hundred feet above the jungle canopy and kept his air speed at seventy-five knots, then flew right over a break in a ridgeline. It was the kind of partially protected spot the anti-aircraft crews of the NVA liked, complete with a rock outcropping on one side of a shallow ravine. Keeping his left hand on the throttle and right on the stick, Tom cocked his head to the side window so he could use his peripheral vision to see either the gun out the side or gunfire in the plane's path. He passed over the ravine and, just as predicted, a line of green tracers shot skyward just right and in front of the Bird Dog.

There he is, Tom thought as he heard the gunfire. A ZPU-4 with a 12.7mm gun. Probably assembled by our friends in Beijing.

Tom knew the gunner would adjust his fire back left and had planned to use the terrain to his advantage to evade the lethal bullets. He threw the throttles forward, pushed the nose down, and turned directly into the fire as the plane dove for the canopy. Though this action would actually take the plane closer to the ground, it would also add speed. The added benefit the Ravens understood was the closer to the canopy, the harder it was for a gunner to keep his eye on you.

The Bird Dog's airspeed jumped up to a hundred knots in just a few seconds, and Tom smiled as he watched the line of tracers spiral into the sky to the left of the plane. He dove over the ridge and picked up more speed, then went to a thousand feet above the ground and armed one of the white phosphorous targeting missiles. As he did so, he noted a lone, aging, propeller-driven T-28 coming into the area from the south. As soon as he saw the aging plane, he was certain this gunner was going to have a bad day.

"Wizard, did you see the tracers?" Tom asked over the radio. "Let me put down some smoke and you can teach him a lesson."

"Roger that, Raven-86," the pilot replied. "You are earning your paycheck today."

"Yup, all of six bucks an hour, Wizard-1," Tom replied.

Ravens didn't do their job for the money.

"Raven-86, this is Superchild," an accented and excited, higher-pitched voice said through the radio. Tom knew Superchild well and a smile beamed across Tom's face. The F-4 pilots might miss, but Superchild was like a Raven's insurance policy. If this gunner didn't run from his position right now, he was going to die.

Tom triple-clicked his microphone to let Superchild know he had heard the transmission and rolled the plane over and into a 45-degree dive straight at a large tree about a hundred meters west of the gun emplacement. A few seconds into the dive, the green tracers began to stream up toward the tiny Bird Dog, so Tom adjusted his direction and flew straight at the gun. He triggered the missile and watched it shoot straight into the ravine next to the gun. A bullet or two might have caught the tip of his left wing, but nothing vital had been damaged and the Bird Dog zoomed out over the valley east of the gun.

"Wizard, the gun is about ten meters east of my smoke," Tom said into the radio. "He is protected in a tight ravine that runs west from that ridge. You'll need to put it right on him to make the kill."

"Roger that, Raven-86. We've got this."

Tom went into a holding pattern over the southeast ridge of Phou Pha Thi as it was Hmong territory and he could be sure no one would shoot at him. He passed over the radar installation at Lima Site 85 and watched as the first Phantom dove on the target. Wizard's angle to the target looked right, but his speed was too high. Moving at just under 600 knots, it would take more luck than any one man had to make the hit. The Phantom pulled out of the dive and dropped his bomb, but the device overshot the ridge and fell harmlessly into the valley to the east. Its detonation instantly condensed the air, throwing a shockwave of white fog out as the canopy shook in the blast. The gunner, having not even been able to hear the plane approach until too late, fired blindly into the sky a second or two after the Phantom passed. Neither man had hit his mark.

"Wizard, you got monkeys and ants on that run," Tom said.

"Roger, Raven-86," the flustered voice replied. "My wingman is going to have a shot at it."

The second Phantom came in at the same angle but a bit more from the west. He pickled his bomb earlier, but it fell down the ridge and a couple hundred meters west of the gun. The blast and shrapnel of the 2,000-pound Mark 118 explosive passed over the gunner with no effect. It was going to take a more accurate shot than that to get the guy.

"Gentlemen, it may just be me, but it appears you need a little more time on the bomb-range," Tom said snarkily. He loved putting fighter jocks in their rightful place. "Let me show you how a talented pilot gets this done."

"Roger that, Raven-86. We have two more, if need

'em," the pilot replied.

Tom shook his head. I know how many bombs you have, rookie, he thought.

"Superchild, I need you to kill that son of a bitch," Tom said into the microphone. "Make me proud, Lin."

Tom Sears had been sipping lao Lao with Superchild at Vang Pao's party. Superchild's real name was Lin Lee, and he was a legend to the Hmong. Lin had been a schoolteacher in Long Tieng before the war had intensified. He had gone through the CIA's Waterpump Program and come out as the most gifted flier any of the trainers had ever seen. The Hmong ground forces called him Choa Fa, the Prince of the Sky, for his uncanny ability to destroy enemy positions. He flew more missions than any other pilot in the war and almost never missed his target. While American fighter pilots received a commendation if they completed a hundred missions in a year over North Vietnam, Lin Lee was flying a hundred and twenty a month over Laos. The Ravens all knew that Lin was not flying by the seat of his pants, but was simply a different kind of pilot. Lin Lee didn't fly the T-28 like a man who had studied aeronautics in a school, but more like a falcon, with the airplane just an extension of his body.

Tom watched as the T-28 barrel rolled downward into a vertical dive. The gunner had a perfect view straight up at the airplane and immediately began to fire. Lin instantly shut him down with a quick blast from .50-caliber machine guns, then focused back on where the bomb would go. He pickled a single, World War II-surplus, 750-pound bomb, perhaps two hundred feet directly above the target. It fell straight into the ravine and pieces of the gun exploded into the sky. Tom could see the tops of the trees quiver as the plane passed barely above the canopy. It flew out over the valley and began to gain altitude.

"I empty now, Tom," the Raven and Phantom pilots heard over the radio. "Superchild return to Long Tieng for more bomb. See you in afternoon."

Tom triple-clicked his microphone again. Superchild flew off to the south, but Tom noted the Phantoms were still circling. Their silence made him giggle.

"Raven-86, uhh, was that Lin Lee?" Wizard-1 asked.

"That's affirmative, Wizard-1."

"Well, I guess the legend is true," the F-4 pilot replied.

The radio was quiet for a few very long seconds. It was amazing how Superchild could silence the cockiest American fighter jock.

"We are low on fuel and returning to Udorn," Wizard-1 finally said. "If you would, thank Mr. Lee for the lesson in humility."

"Roger that, Wizard-1," Tom said. "Before you go, put the rest of your ordinance on my previous smoke. You can't return to base with it and I know Charlie is somewhere around that road."

The F-4s took another run along the ridge, dropping their bombs in a steady line, then sped off to the south. Tom took the Bird Dog up to 2500 feet and began looking for another target.

February 28, 1968, 1300 hours

(same day)

Lima Site 85, Phou Pha Thi, Houaphan Province, Laos

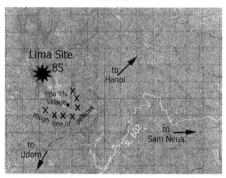

John and Brad waited for the new technicians at the landing zone. The twenty-fifth of February, Sullivan's most recent "pull-out day," had come and gone, and Lima Site 85 was directing more strikes than ever. In fact, 7th Air Force was sending in the four extra radar technicians so they could more effectively bomb around the clock. In fairness, the ambassador had fought to pull the men off the mountain, but pressure from the White House and the Air Force had overruled him. Now there would be fifteen technicians on Phou Pha Thi, all of them civilians surrounded by what had become a combat free-fire zone.

Perhaps the best piece of intel on the enemy's intentions was found by the Hmong after they'd ambushed an NVA major and two rifle squads. The plans were detailed, even giving exact positions of NVA units just prior to the attack. The only troubling part was that it was so detailed, and of such importance to the North Vietnamese attack, that everyone questioned its authenticity. The possibility that the map had been planted as false information had to be considered. It was simply a blunder for the enemy to have let a ranking officer wander into combat with the plans of a future fight, but until they were proven otherwise, the defenders of Phou Pha Thi would assume it was real.

Richard Milano had argued for two Air America choppers to be stationed at Lima Site 85 so the technicians could be pulled out immediately in an attack. The ambassador had shot that idea down, perhaps correctly saying it would present too juicy a target for the NVA. He felt they would likely lose the helicopters to a sapper on a suicide mission long before anyone could mount a real attack against the radar. Instead, the new plan was to keep two Air America Hueys and three US Air Force MH-53 Jolly Green Giants at Lima Site 20/Alternate. The choppers would be fueled and ready so they could be at Phou Pha Thi in thirty minutes or less. Everyone assumed the Hmong could hold on for half an hour.

The new plan was for the men to stay at Lima Site 85 until the tenth of March. Not one day longer. Sullivan had pushed for an earlier date, but without a clear forecast for exactly when the attack would come, the White House would not budge. The technicians had to stay on Phou Pha Thi until March 10th, unless a battle erupted.

The big helicopter set down in a cloud of red dust and the rotors kept turning while the four men unloaded. More water, food, and sleeping bags were brought in, plus a few special crates Richard had included against the ambassador's wishes.

Brad and John shook hands with the new arrivals, Large, Shep, and Alex being among them, then each grabbed an end of a crate and hauled them out the rear hatch of helicopter. Four Hmong ran in the back of the helicopter and grabbed other supplies, including a brand new Weber grill. Large had been saying for a month that with the view they had, there should be steaks and beer. Apparently he'd spoken to the right person, probably Richard, and gotten his wish. As the MH-53 lifted off and headed south, a squad of Hmong soldiers took the boxes from the Americans and followed the group up to the radar site.

Despite the NVA tightening the noose, the month had not been all bad. As part of the Hmong New Year's celebration, the technicians had joined the villagers of Pha Thi for the Baci festival. The ambassador had forbidden this kind of "fraternizing with the locals," as it would truly give away there were Americans on the mountain, but John and Brad were in charge at L.S. 85, and they didn't care. Everyone but the US press corps knew there were Americans on Phou Pha Thi, and if anything, the attendance of the Americans would harden the Hmong defenders' resolve. By meeting the Americans, the locals would not only be fighting for friends, but would also know that American war planes could be counted on for close air support.

The technicians had loved the festival. The Hmong women had dressed in their most colorful clothing and wore large strings of silver beads around their necks. Both the men and women had sashes around their waists, red or white, depending on their clan. Throughout the night, different groups would get up to perform a particular dance. The technicians were also asked to dance, and they made the most of it by pulling their shirts over their heads and doing The Twist.

Because it was a special occasion, a pig and a buffalo had been slaughtered for the Americans (everyone was thankful they were not expected to eat the congealed blood), and lao Lao was passed around all evening. The highlight of the night was a game where all the single Hmong boys and girls lined up across from each other. They then tossed wicker balls back and forth. It was explained to the Americans that if a ball was passed from a boy to a girl it was considered an advance. If the girl liked the boy, she would pass the ball back, and if not she might pass it to someone else in the hopes it would be reciprocated. The older Hmong watched in approval as these first stages of courtship were performed.

The evening culminated with the Americans having threads tied around their wrists as a symbol of friendship. The thread was intended to protect them from the few bad spirits that lived in the forest around Phou Pha Thi and hundreds of evil spirits down in the land of the leeches where the technicians traveled every two weeks.

Everyone woke the next morning with a hangover but still managed to put together a successful mission against the Phuc Yen rail yard on the outskirts of Hanoi.

Security at Lima Site 85 had been bumped up the previous week. With John's request, fifty more PARU commandos were brought in and placed under Luang's command. A few had taken positions near the radar site, but most had built a more solid perimeter around the landing zone. The Hmong had fortified their trenches and were continuing daily raids on any NVA platoons that got too close to the mountain.

Security in South Vietnam had improved too. The attacks by the NVA and Viet Cong had, for the most part, been pushed back. The city of Hue, near the North/South Vietnam border, had been retaken by American and South Vietnamese forces, and the siege at the US Embassy in Saigon had ended by the morning after the attack. However, the siege of Khe Sanh had not been stopped. For the first time in history, B-52 bombers were dropping their entire load on enemy troop positions around the perimeter of an American base. NVA troops were close enough to the fence to lob mortar rounds onto the runway, and the Air Force was dropping over a thousand tons of bombs a day on the surrounding forest to hold them at bay. President Johnson had told the MACV commanders that the base had to be held at all costs, while the North Vietnamese battle plan for the Tet Offensive had been to take it no matter the cost. With that, Khe Sanh had become a symbol of the war, and both sides were putting everything they had into the battle. Its future was still in the air.

The new technicians followed John and Brad up the trail to the radar site. Two of the radar techs were directing a flight over Road 602 just west of Sam Neua, and the rest were watching the show take place on a nearby ridge. From the Dushka bunker, all the men could clearly see two F-4 Phantoms attack a gun placed on the small mountain to the east. The daily jet show had become a relief, not only because seeing and hearing the bombs gave the technicians a sense that something was being done about the approaching enemy forces, but it also broke the monotony of waiting their turn to direct the next mission. Since the Baci festival, no one had dared stray farther than the landing zone. The NVA was out there, and the radar technicians knew they were the target.

"I guess we're gonna be in pretty tight quarters considering there are more bodies than beds," Large said to all over the roar of an F-4 streaking through the valley below.

"Yeah, I'll stay in the bunker with the Luang," John replied. "That will free up a bed. We have enough bags for everyone to have their own, but you guys will need to share bunks according to the rotations."

Another bomb blast rumbled in the distance as a Raven circled above in an O-1 Bird Dog. Everyone turned to the east to watch the second Phantom attack the target. As the bomb detonated, they could see the jungle blow apart, then a couple seconds later feel the rumble of the air. The technicians had directed almost five hundred airstrikes around Phou Pha Thi in February. Add to that the attacks being orchestrated by the Ravens, the NVA was really taking a beating. Still, they were inching closer, and everyone at Lima Site 85 felt an attack could come at any day.

"We brought you guys something," Brad said as the Hmong set the wooden crates down behind the bunker. "The ambassador said 'no,' but he wasn't there when the helicopter took off, so here you go."

Brad popped the lid off the first crate to expose

eight brand-new Colt M16s. Everyone stared at the guns as another blast rocked the heavy air.

"I'm a little foggy on this, guys," Shep said. "We need military guns to be here, but we aren't allowed to wear military uniforms because it will show we are in the US military? I mean, don't get me wrong. I'm glad I finally have something to defend myself with, but as I understand the Geneva Conventions, we can be executed by the enemy for this. That wasn't in the travel brochure."

The whole group snickered. Shep's humor always put a nice light on a bad situation. Large liked to refer to his friend's dark sense of humor as "adding mustard to our shit sandwich."

"I know you guys liked the pay with this job, but I think every one of you has said you wanted to do something that could really affect the war," John said. "According to Richard Milano, the White House feels this operation may be helping keep those Marines at Khe Sanh alive. They are completely surrounded by nearly forty thousand NVA, but the enemy doesn't seem to have the equipment to put together an attack. The White House and the ambassador think it's because of the work you're doing here."

"All of us are nervous," Brad added. "Things are coming to a head. No question. But we know what the NVA is trying to do. Those plans the Hmong took off that NVA major last week were detailed. They intend to mass troops down below, artillery in the valley, and on the ridge to our east. That hasn't happened yet, so they can't attack."

"You guys are the last shift," John said. "Ambassador Sullivan has said that no matter what, we will pull out on March tenth. The Hmong and PARU have built two consecutive lines of defense, the helicopters are on standby at Alternate, and the Hmong and Ravens are hitting them constantly. On top of that, you're defending yourselves daily by directing strikes right here. Let's just do our jobs and then bug out next week. By this time next month, you'll be home with your families."

13

March 10, 1968, 1710 hours
(ten days later)
1.7 km SSW Lima Site 85, Phou Pha Thi,
Houaphan Province, Laos

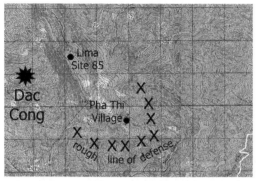

The huge limestone face rose menacingly over the commandos. Lim had heard of this mountain, Phou Pha Thi, ever since he was very young. It was revered by all the Hmong clans, but he had never even seen a picture of it. Now, through a gap in the forest, he was looking up at its most impressive face. Long streaks of white and gray rock ran between vine-covered ledges. Jagged gendarmes of stone poked into the sky along its highest ridge. For the first time in six days, the sky was clear and the setting sun bathed the upper headwall in a golden light that Dominique's father had called "alpenglow." The mountain was beautiful, but the idea of climbing it was terrifying.

They had trekked for almost a month to reach Phou Pha Thi, and Lieutenant Sung had said little along the way to explain the mission to his men. The commandos had followed an old French road south from So'n La the first day in a steady rain. They had been ordered to wear the traditional sandals made from old tires and carry the tighter-fitting boots so the new boots would not be damaged or rub blisters on their feet. The cold rain washed mud through their toes, and each man had to be diligent to keep the leeches off his ankles. They had camped in the open on many nights and been woken by the carnivorous worms. After a couple days of hiking, the road passed into a steep canyon with a large stream. Mudslides had destroyed the road in many places, and the men were forced to make stream crossings with their heavy loads. One commando had almost been swept away.

They'd reached the confluence of the stream and the great Song Ma, or Ghost River, a week into the trek. This river flowed through North Vietnam only fifty kilometers south of the plantation where Lim had grown up; he had seen it numerous times. The commandos crossed the Song Ma on a log bridge, and then turned southwest over very steep mountains. From then on, the platoon had avoided any trail or road, which had made for much harder walking. The pace slowed dramatically just a few kilometers before reaching Phou Pha Thi, and Lieutenant Sung kept the men totally silent while they marched. American jets roared overhead, and they could hear blasts to the east, but were never actually threatened themselves. To make sure Hmong patrols didn't detect them, Sung scouted the area they'd hike before allowing the commandos to pass through. The platoon had arrived below the southeast ridge of the mountain in darkness on the night of March 9th. While the men lay quietly in a field of elephant grass, Sung and another commando, Corporal Kinh, quietly met with an NVA captain. The platoon woke before dawn and traversed to a position below the west face where they sat silently throughout the day. As dusk approached, Sung had finally explained their mission:

"There is an American base near the summit of this mountain. Our mission is to destroy it and kill everyone there. We have been given this mission by General Giap himself. Very few in the People's Army even know of our existence, much less that we are here to kill these Americans. Get on your boots, unload your packs to fighting weight, and stay silent. I will be back in ten minutes. Lim, you come with me."

The ordered isolation scared Lim, but he followed Sung through the forest to a clearing that had obviously been a poppy field earlier in the year. From the edge of the poppy field, the evening light provided an impressive view of the big mountain.

"I climbed much of the south ridge of the mountain last night," Sung said in a whisper, pointing to the obvious ridge. "I found a small break in the lines by rock climbing to the west. The mountain is heavily fortified by the local villagers, and there are Thai Special Forces near the summit. We would never be able to take it, and that is why you are here. You are going to get me and my men up that face."

Lim looked up at the big wall. It was far higher

than anything he had ever attempted, but there were weaknesses climbers could follow. The most obvious was a large cleft to the left, or north, of the highest part of the face. That would be the best approach.

"Lieutenant Sung, it appears to me the best way to ascend the mountain is by the couloir on the left," Lim said. The commando probably understood climbing well enough to see that, but Lim made his opinion clear.

"The American base is about a hundred meters right of the top of the couloir, just above the biggest part of the face," Sung said. "Getting us to the top of the gully will work fine, but there is something else. There can be no noise. No pitons, no hammers, and you cannot knock down rocks. If the Americans hear us, they will be able to drop grenades from above, and the mission will fail. That cannot happen."

Lim nodded. "If I am going first, do I need a gun?" He'd never wanted to fight the war but there was a sense of self-preservation with the mission. He might need to defend himself.

"You get a rope. Nothing more."

Sung had been solemn for the entire trek and hadn't spoken a word with Lim in three weeks. It was clear the mission meant everything to him and individuals involved meant nothing. Lim knew he meant nothing more to this man than he had to the commanders along the Ho Chi Minh Trail. The two quietly walked back to the rest of the commandos and Lim took a seat off to the side.

"In The Art of War, Sun Tsu wrote 'Avoid what is strong and strike what is weak.'" Sung said in a low tone. "We are going to destroy this base by avoiding the enemy's fortifications and attacking him in the way he least expects, that being via the steepest part of the mountain. That is why you have been training as climbers for the last month. Once we reach the summit, we will break into our five squads and separate. All of us are going to be close enough to hold onto the enemy by the belt so he cannot use air support. I want everyone to get some sleep. Be ready to fight. We leave in four hours."

March 10, 1968, 1725 hours

(same day)

Lima Site 85, Phou Pha Thi, Houaphan Province,

Laos

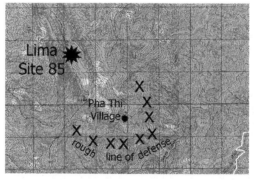

The first ten days of March had gone exactly as expected for everyone on Phou Pha Thi: The Ravens and technicians directed bombs on targets around the mountain, the Hmong harassed the enemy day and night, and the North Vietnamese inched closer and closer to the Hmong front line. While the site directed a hundred fifty-three strikes around the mountain in their own defense, they managed to get in only three strikes against North Vietnam.

The irony that only two percent of their efforts were directed toward the mission they'd originally been assigned was not lost on anyone. All the powers-that-be in the American Embassy, Udorn, Saigon, and Washington, D.C. had finally recognized that the North Vietnamese knew what was on the mountain, and they had relaxed the rule that all radio transmissions had to go through a plane flying over the Gulf of Tonkin. This official declaration meant nothing to the way the technicians worked at Lima Site 85, but it showed the men calling the shots were paying attention to them and not just focused on the Marines at Khe Sanh.

Though most of South Vietnam had been retaken after the initial Tet Offensive, the siege of the combat base at Khe Sanh had not improved. Around-the-clock bombing, much of it right outside the perimeter of the base, had destroyed or pushed back a number of North Vietnamese regiments. However, the base was still only able to be fully supplied from the air, with the Marines and Air Force dropping an average of sixteen tons of equipment and food per day.

The North Vietnamese still controlled the region around Khe Sanh, and if anything, their use of artillery had increased. In one day, over a thousand shells had landed inside the base's perimeter. General William Westmoreland, the commander in charge of all US forces in Vietnam, had even considered the use of tactical nuclear weapons in the rugged terrain west of the base, and he had formally requested the weapons be armed and delivered to the area. To his credit, Secretary McNamara had replied that the use of nuclear weapons was "inconceivable." Nevertheless, the siege continued with no end in sight. Slowing of the flow of weapons by bombing the supply lines from North Vietnam was recognized as a big part of the US Marine's defense.

Ambassador Sullivan's pull-out order of March 10th had held right up until the morning of March 9th. MACV intelligence in Saigon had confirmed that on March 10th, a large shipment of arms would be going through the Thai Nguyen Rail Yards forty miles north of Hanoi. The White House wanted it destroyed. As usual, the weather was predicted to be atrocious over North Vietnam, so the only way to hit the target was through radar-directed bombing. Sullivan was told that, based on enemy troop estimates, their locations, and the accuracy of the bombing that had been directed by the Ravens and from Lima Site 85, the local Hmong would be able to hold long enough for the helicopters to get in and pull out the technicians. With that, he caved in again, and decided to keep the technicians on the mountain for one more day. The re-re-revised plan was that the raid on the rail yard would proceed, and helicopters would be in the air at 0600 the morning of the eleventh to take the Americans and PARU out. The Hmong would disappear into the jungle and perhaps make their way to General Vang Pao's forces at Alternate. Whether or not the villagers of Pha Thi moved to Alternate was up to them.

While the technicians directed their last strike on North Vietnam, Brad and John began to work on their own counter-attacks. The very latest intel had estimated there were eight battalions of NVA soldiers, or perhaps thirty-five hundred cadres encamped around

Phou Pha Thi. Hmong patrols estimated there were about a thousand NVA within half a kilometer of their lines, and they had seen field crews laying communication wire to facilitate field telephones the NVA used during attacks. Brad and John had the latest information from the Hmong patrols, and knew the location of the highest concentrations of enemy troops.

The two men stood on the roof of a bunker next to the helipad and watched planes whiz over the jungle canopy in the valley below. A Raven had just come overhead and was working with two Thai pilots flying A-1 Skyraiders.

"Raven-86, this is Lima Site eight five," John said into a large, handheld field radio. John had called in artillery strikes and adjusted their fire for a couple of years with the same equipment, and it felt good to be back in the fight again. "We estimate your target should be about forty meters west of your smoke and on the edge of that large poppy field. Be advised: Much closer to the mountain and you will likely open up the Hmong line."

"Roger that, L S eight five," the Raven replied. "I'll bring 'em in parallel to the front line. Just tell the Little Guys to keep their heads down. This is gonna be big."

The Hmong knew the protocol for close air support, but sometimes the temptation to watch the cha gee take a beating was overwhelming and a soldier stood up to see the bomb do its work. Over the years this had resulted in more than one headless Hmong, and the defenders could not afford to lose anyone around Phou Pha Thi. Brad had repeatedly drilled it into the

Hmong leaders that they had to keep everyone down during the airstrikes.

The A-1 Skyraider was an amazingly effective aircraft for close air support. The plane could fly in a steep dive on a target or slow down and drop bombs from just above the trees. With a single 2700-horsepower radial engine, it could carry almost eight thousand pounds of ordnance along its wings and fuselage. It carried two CBU-2 bombs, as well as four .50-caliber machine guns for attacking troop concentrations. The big guns were capable of penetrating most of the armor the North Vietnamese put in the field. The CBU, or cluster bomb unit, was actually a single canister filled with smaller bomblets, each roughly the size of hand grenades. When the CBU opened, the bomblets scattered across the battle zone in hundreds of shrapnel-filled smaller explosions. Napalm was perhaps the only weapon that inspired more fear in the NVA than a CBU, but the cluster bomb was far more effective.

The Thai pilots preferred coming in as a dive-bomber, but Raven-86 let them know the best approach was low and fast along the Vietnamese front line. On their initial pass, the first of the two Skyraiders strafed the enemy position with his machine guns, which kept the North Vietnamese from firing. The second took advantage of the hiding infantry to drop both cluster bombs. They made a second pass and reversed roles, and Brad and John watched from the ridge above as hundreds more bomblets sprayed hot shrapnel through the jungle. The two Thai planes then sped off to the south, empty of bombs and with the sun setting soon.

"Does that look about right, fellas?" Raven-86

asked over the radio.

"Affirmative, Raven-86," John replied. "We probably won't be able to get a body count for you, but we heard a cheer from the Hmong front line, so I think you put it right where it needed to be."

"Roger that," the Raven replied. "I'm gonna go high and wait a bit. I think we may have two more fighters in before sundown. Raven-86 out."

The O-1 Bird Dog gained altitude to about five thousand feet above Phou Pha Thi and began to circle. John figured the pilot was having a sandwich and a beer while he waited for the next bombers.

"John, I think we should add a bit to what they just did," Brad said as he walked to the improvised rocket launcher. The explosive-firing contraption had been sitting there for weeks and no one had gotten to fire it.

"We're bugging out tomorrow morning," Brad said. "And this thing isn't gonna get to go with us, so let's have some fun. It will inspire the NVA to eat dinner just a little faster."

"Might as well," John replied. "No reason to give rockets to the North Vietnamese just so they can shoot them at us next month."

"Maa nee, kop," Brad said to three of the PARU who were watching from the roof of a hooch.

They walked up to Brad, who was pulling a green tarp off the launcher, and began arming the rockets. The CIA's technical division had taken time away from making cigar bombs and poison pens to put the launcher together. It was based on the working components of a captured Chinese rocket-launcher, but made functional by various American surplus gear taken off damaged Raven aircraft, and a few pieces of a captured NVA rocket-launcher. No one had ever actually seen it fire, or even knew if it would, and that was part of the intrigue for Brad.

John grabbed his radio and backed off the helipad as Brad and the three PARU got in a bunker. The CIA operative then yanked the cord, and instantly a series of 2.75-inch rockets hissed out of the tubes and streaked over the Hmong lines and into the valley. The five men watched for the impact of the projectile, knowing it would only be puffs of smoke emanating up from the trees. As the first rocket exploded, everyone saw a strange parting of the jungle just south of projectile's impact. Suddenly there was whistling overhead, and John dove for a bunker.

"Incoming!" Brad screamed at the top of his lungs.

A pair of 105mm howitzer shells, probably from guns captured from General Vang Pao, impacted on the helipad. John looked up from the muddy floor of the bunker as four more shells whistled overhead and then exploded somewhere near the radar site. The PARU and Hmong were suddenly racing all over Lima Site 85 to find a sheltered but defensive position.

"How the hell did they manage that?" Brad yelled as another shell whistled into the trees behind the Hmong front line. "This isn't return fire. It started before our rockets even detonated."

"I'd say they had the exact same idea you did," John yelled as he tightened the strap on his helmet. "You both wanted to ruin the other's dinnertime conversation. They are just better at it than you."

John crawled from the bunker and began running

up the trail to the radar site as two more shells fell in front of Brad's position. He heard a couple more higher-pitched shells, probably from a 120mm mortar, drop somewhere down the ridge. Another shell sailed overhead toward the radar site but failed to detonate.

Two things were already clearly discernable about the attack: The North Vietnamese had multiple artillery pieces within point-blank range of Lima Site 85, and they knew exactly where they should shoot. Clearly the area had been scouted for range certainty. As John reached the staff quarters, he heard the concussion of another shell exploding behind it and then steel pellets showering and clanking on metal. He looked down to the landing zone to see Brad's 105mm howitzer toppled on its side. So much for shooting back.

"Everybody out, get to the bunkers," John screamed into the thin-walled staff quarters. He ran up the steep steps and saw two technicians huddled in the first bunker with two PARU protectively standing over them. The technicians had their helmets on, but one was wearing his backward. John looked to the two bunkers along the ridge and saw the tops of PARU helmets, then ran to the Dushka bunker. Large and Kevin, the computer specialist, were under the roof of the bunker with the PARU again watching over them. One of the shells had left a crater less than ten feet from the bunker and all four looked terrified.

"Where are Shep and Alex?" John yelled as another shell detonated in the small trees between the landing zone and radar site.

"They're in the Mission Room trying to direct another strike on whoever's shooting at us," Large said.

John hopped up and ran into the Mission Room as a mortar round impacted against the east side of the staff quarters building. He watched it rock on its foundation as the projectile detonated.

"I'd love to tell you guys to stop what you're doing, but I don't think you guys should to stop what you're doing," John said to Shep and Alex.

Shep held his left hand up as if to hold John back, while his right hand held the earpiece to his head. He had a flak jacket on but couldn't wear his helmet and the headset at the same time.

"Yeah, whatever you got, we need it now, and keep it coming!" Shep yelled into the radio.

John crouched in the doorway as two more shells whistled over the building.

"John, we're gonna stay here and direct the strikes," Shep shouted. "If you could figure out exactly where these things are coming from, I have two A-26s and two F-4s inbound. We might be able to get the guns if the planes get here before dark."

John stepped into the building and to the radar desk and picked up a pencil. He leaned over Shep and put an "X" on the exact location of the howitzers. The mortar positions were still a mystery.

"You hit that, and a lot of this is going to stop," John said as he turned for the door. Realizing he'd left his gun somewhere near the helipad, John grabbed three of the five M16s in the corner. He ran to the Dushka bunker and jumped in with the technicians and PARU. Two more shells, again fired from the howitzers, sailed over the radar site and down into the valley below. Between shots, he could hear the Raven in his

Bird Dog flying just south of the site. Another plane, a single T-28, then came in from the south.

"John, are we going to be overrun?" Large asked in a low voice. The big man was clearly distraught.

John thought how consistent it was that the guys with families always had a look in their eyes more sad than scared when under attack. Maybe this phenomenon was a matter of John overthinking the situation. Or maybe men with families felt worse for their kids and wives than they did for themselves. John took in a deep breath and let it out.

"No, Large, we're all right. This artillery is aimed at us, not the Hmong. If the NVA was going to try to attack the mountain, they'd soften up the front line first. They're just letting us know they can see us. It'll be dark soon and a lot harder for these assholes to aim."

The truth was John didn't know if an attack was coming, but there was no reason to give Large and Kevin more to worry about. He turned on the radio to listen to Brad as the paramilitary man orchestrated the defense. Another shell landed in the trees near one of the PARU bunkers and a second flew over the ridge.

"Luang tee ny?" John asked one of the PARU of his captain's location. The young Thai soldier stood and pointed at the bunker near the trail down to the landing zone. John had run right past Luang without noticing him.

"Guys, can you all hear me?" John yelled from the rim of the bunker. He heard a few guys say "Yes".

"Okay, these dickheads are firing from the east of the mountain. That means it's pretty much impossible for them to hit anything on the west side. As a matter of the angle of the gunfire, the safest place to be is down on the ledge above the west face. When there's a lull in the shelling, you might think about getting there. Got it?"

He heard a few murmurs from the bunkers. Clearly, no one was excited about getting out of the fortified holes.

John stood and looked south to the Raven circling over the valley. He then noticed that a few two-inch-thick steaks, the ones brought in on the supply helicopter with the new grill, were laying in the dirt.

"Large, why are all the steaks you worked so hard to get scattered around the TACAN?" he asked.

"The Weber took a direct hit in that second round of shells. The blast blew it off the cliff."

"That's a shame. I'll buy you a steak at the B-29 Bar in Udorn tomorrow night." John was trying to keep things light, but the big Texan was clearly not taking the shelling well.

Two more shells hit down near the helipad as a pair of F-4 Phantoms roared over the mountain. It would be dark in minutes, and John wasn't sure the planes would have enough time drop their ordnance. He turned the radio's volume up so it could be heard over the circling jets. No one at the radar site could see the area the artillery was being fired from, but they could hear Brad calmly chatting with Raven-86 about the bombs.

"Actually, I don't think I need to mark with my missiles," they heard the pilot say. "The smoke and flames from your shots are visible. Would you say the gun is about a hundred-fifty meters south of the southernmost fire?"

"Roger that," Brad replied as a mortar landed along the trail between the staff quarters and landing zone. "Again, Raven-86, be advised no farther west or you are on the Hmong line."

"Roger, eight five," the Raven replied. "This guy doesn't miss. Lin, you heard the man. You are cleared to the target."

"Superchild is inbound," a higher pitch voice said over the radio.

The men ducked as two artillery shells approached with a horrifying scream. One sailed over the ridge and into the valley below the west face, but the other landed between the latrine and one of the PARU bunkers. The NVA was clearly trying to hit the site, but its location on the crest of the ridge made for a very difficult target. After the first shell burst, everyone stood in their bunkers and watched as the T-28 seemed to stall above the big peak. For just a moment they wondered if it had been hit, but as the pilot rolled the plane into a perfect 80-degree dive, everyone realized that the unorthodox aerial move was part of the plan. There was a quick burst of machine-gun fire, and then the plane went just out of sight of the technicians. They heard and felt the bomb blast a second later. The T-28 sped over the ridge to the east and climbed then turned to the south in the very last rays of light.

"Nice drop! There are a couple of pieces of artillery that won't be firing anymore," Brad said. "Raven-86, we aren't exactly sure where the mortars are firing from."

"Roger that, L S eight five," he replied. "I've got two

F-4s with CBUs. We'll put ordnance just east of that last blast. Hopefully, that will do it."

The radio went silent as the Raven dove into the dark valley. They could only barely make out the airplane until the missile launched, then watched a yellow streak shoot into the black forest and light up the area with a white flash. About twenty seconds later, both Phantoms streaked over the forest high enough for the men to see the orange flames shooting out the aircrafts' exhaust. The ground lit up in yellow as hundreds of smaller bombs, concentrated in two balls of fire, exploded through the trees. Everyone on the mountain listened to the jets scream toward the orange line of sunlight on the horizon. The shelling had stopped.

"L S eight five, I'm gonna go up above and hold," Raven-86 said. "I think we may have some more for you in an hour or so, but you are cleared to do whatever you had planned earlier. I'll be here if you need me."

John had started listening to the radio conversation a little late. Clearly, Brad had planned to attack with the Hmong to mop up whatever the airstrikes didn't destroy, and the Raven was letting him know there were no more inbound bombs that might kill the friendlies. The technicians probably wouldn't hear from him until he got back, but they left the radio on in case he needed help.

Shep and Alex came out of the Mission Room and surveyed the scene. The TACAN had been damaged, and there were a lot of little holes in the east wall of the staff quarters building, but no one had been injured or killed.

"We aren't using any flashlights tonight," John yelled to all. "Let your eyes adjust to the dark. You'll be able to find your way around."

It was clear the NVA knew exactly where the radar site and landing zone were, so it was generally decided that there would be no sleeping inside that night. The men got out their olive green sleeping bags and went back to the bunkers. Alex went to the cleft in the rocks just below the TACAN, and Shep went to his cave on the ledge below the Mission Room and above the west face. They lay down, knowing the helicopters would be there at first light.

14

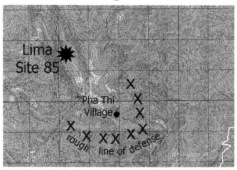

Lim didn't sleep at all. He had been going over his mental picture of the face, trying to come up with a way of leading the climb and not making noise. He knew the couloir would have loose rock, but the face presented more difficult climbing. If he climbed the face he'd have to find solid points to tie off for the commandos to belay from, and that would eat up time. If he climbed the couloir, someone in the platoon would no doubt knock off a rock or two and potentially alert the Americans. Either way, he would face the dark side of Lieutenant Sung, and that would possibly be fatal. The Dac Cong leader only cared about the mission. Everything else, including Lim, didn't matter.

Artillery rounds had been soaring over the moun-

tain in the early hours of the evening and landing about half a kilometer north of where they had
camped. Even if Lim had not been worried about what
lay ahead of him that night, he wouldn't have slept
with the shells bursting just five hundred meters
away. On top of that, American jets had been flying
overhead almost constantly through the evening. A few
of the Dac Cong had somehow slept through it.

The shelling abruptly stopped an hour after dark,
and the other concern of the night had entered Lim's
mind. Once he did get these men onto the crest of the
mountain, there would be a battle. Lim wasn't a soldier, and he had never wanted to be part of the war.
Without being able to see the summit of the mountain,
he had no idea if there would be hiding places or not.
Even if there were, was that his fate? Or did Sung have
some other reason to send him up the mountain first?

With no other option, he focused on the job he'd
been ordered to do. A month earlier, Lim had taught
the commandos how to coil a rope to wear it over one
shoulder, like a bandolier of ammunition. Lim carried
one rope over each shoulder to keep his hands free to
climb. The other commandos each carried their AK-
47 and a rope, plus a few grenades, and one man had
only a B-40 rocket launcher.

They began the trek up the slope below the big face
at 2200 hours. The platoon quietly made its way to the
base of the huge west face, about half a mile directly
below the American base, and then began traversing
along the rock toward the gulley. At the bottom of the
big gully, Lim had all the commandos tie into their
ropes so they had their hands free to climb when the

terrain got steeper. The men went another five hundred meters up the gully, moving silently over solid rock or areas where vines held the broken fragments of stone together.

About four hundred meters below the summit ridge, Lim decided there was too much loose rock to continue in the couloir, and he led the platoon up the rock wall while staying parallel to the couloir. The stone was incredibly featured with a choice of huge handholds at all times so he could pick the route to climb purely based on keeping the men quiet. Ledges were common, and he set up belays regularly and had each man bring up the man behind him while the climber in front continued to ascend. This allowed them to always keep moving up. His fears about the difficulty of the climb soon subsided. Falling off the mountain was not going to be his undoing, but reaching the summit might. The thought nagged at him as he ascended.

The men made some noise. It was difficult to keep twenty-six people from tipping over a stone or breaking a branch, but the war was working to mask the clatter. There was the rumble of shells randomly falling on the ridge above, but also the drone of aircraft overhead. A small plane had been flying for hours over the peak, and a much larger aircraft with multiple engines circled at a higher altitude. This plane was dropping phosphorous flares to light up the battlefield, and the wind occasionally carried the burning white lamps into the valley below the west face, giving the commandos enough light to make out the features of the rock. From time to time, bombs detonated in the distance, some big enough to actually shake the mountain.

The angle had gotten less steep after three hours of climbing, and Lim guessed they were nearing the ridge. Using a small palm tree to fix his position with the rope, he belayed Sung to the ledge, then continued into the dark as Sung brought up the man behind him. No one had held the rope for Lim all night, and that was just as well. He wasn't going to fall on this terrain. About fifteen meters above the ledge, Lim came within sight of a strange bush. He paused to take a more concentrated look at the shape in the faint light. The shrub was very thin and seemed to grow in circles across the rock. After a few seconds he realized it was not a bush, but concertina wire. They had reached the edge of the American base. Lim climbed back down to Sung and the ledge as the third commando was putting the man behind him on belay.

"Lieutenant, about fifteen meters above there is wire across the face."

The Dac Cong leader looked up but couldn't make out the concertina wire so far away in the darkness. A bomb rumbled somewhere on the other side of the mountain.

"I will take care of it," Sung replied. "We are lucky you didn't trip a mine and give away our position. Wait here."

As the fourth commando reached the ledge and began to belay the man behind him, Sung took a tool from his shirt pocket and placed it in his teeth, then began climbing into the darkens. The commando moved silently, but after a few minutes Lim heard the faint sound of wire being snipped. Another commando reached the ledge, and then a sixth. The ledge was only about five meters long and Lim realized that as everyone came up they would run out of space. He traversed farther right onto the steep wall where he found good holds, but was also farther from the widest part of the rocky shelf. Another man came up from below, and then another, filling the ledge and pushing Lim farther and farther out onto the big face. Everyone was packed together on the ledge when Sung climbed back down. The lieutenant untied from the rope, whispered something to the commandos about removing mines, then started back up the face. Lim only heard Sung's last command clearly: "Kill everyone." Each of the commandos untied and dropped their ropes on the ledge, then followed Sung into the darkness.

Lim was suddenly alone on the big west face of the mountain, holding onto large holds but with no clear direction. There was a battle about to take place above him, and he knew the face was not the safest place to be. Rocks, grenades, even bullet fragments could come down the mountain. It was obvious there was no way to climb back down the mountain before the battle erupted, and he had no urge to go up and be part of the fight. He could traverse back to the ledge but reasoned that since it was directly below where the Dac Cong had just gone, it would probably be the most dangerous place on the face.

After a couple minutes of thought, Lim decided the safest course of action was to traverse away from where the commandos had gone and away from the big gully. He untied from the rope and moved out over the big face on good handholds. After perhaps fifty meters, he found another ledge that seemed safe. The level section of rock continued off to the right, but Lim curled up against the wall and waited in exhaustion for the fight to begin.

He didn't have to wait long.

March 11, 1968, 0240 hours
(same time)
Phou Pha Thi, Houaphan Province, Laos

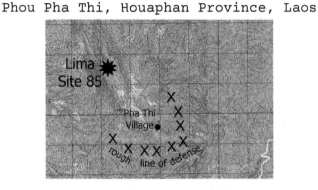

Just a little farther up the mountain, a completely different night had evolved. The initial shelling had come to an end around 1830 hours, and the technicians had taken their sleeping bags and water bottles from the damaged staff quarters and moved to the various bunkers. Shep and Kevin had both kept their bags down on the ledge and in the cave as it was the safest location if the shelling were to resume. Shep reasoned it would also have the best view with the morning sunrise, and he looked forward to seeing the big helicopters approach. Brad had stayed at the bunkers near the landing zone with about half the PARU, while Luang had spread the other Thai soldiers along the ridge between the radar site and helipad.

Raven-86 had refueled and returned to circle overhead in case he was needed, and John made sure everything was ready for the coming evacuation. The main radio they used to communicate with Udorn had been damaged, so messages were being routed through Air America at Alternate. The call sign for the morning flights had been set as "Compress."

At 1930 hours, a C-130 Hercules, call sign "Lamplighter," had begun to circle the mountain. Lamplighter dropped flares every few minutes and the burning white phosphorus bathed the whole mountain in a strange white light that flattened away all color. The technicians watched as the hissing fire ignited under a parachute, then slowly descended, making an odd thumping sound as its glow revealed parts of the mountain. Eventually each flare burned out or fell into the jungle below, and the big plane would release another. The noise of the C-130, the Raven in the Bird Dog, and the flares offered a strong sense of the American military's presence, and that gave the technicians comfort.

Then at 2005 hours the shelling resumed, only this time from larger batteries below the south ridge of the mountain. The guns had a better angle on the radar site, but much to the technicians' surprise, they battered the landing zone and the lower flanks of the mountain. What the technicians hadn't realized, but Brad, John, and Luang did, was that the NVA's tactics had changed. Rather than try to blow up the radar site with a shell, the NVA was now softening up the Hmong front line. There was going to be a real battle after all, and the big question was whether the Hmong would hold back the attacking army.

John and Luang had been with Brad at the landing zone when the battle began. Two F-4s streaked through the darkness above Phou Pha Thi, and flares dropped over the village and south ridge. Shells rained down on the village and Hmong front lines for about an hour, but the soldiers had dug in deep and there were minimal casualties. Raven-86 marked an area south of the village with a phosphorus missile, and the Phantoms dropped CBUs right on top of the white flames. The Hmong held their position for the first hour of attack.

About that time, Brad ran back up to the radar site to the Mission Room. Shep had taken Alex's place at the radar station, and four of the other technicians were manning their posts so radar-directed night bombing could be conducted around Phou Pha Thi.

"You want this," Brad said to Shep as he circled sections of a Soviet map. "This is the map we took off that dead major, and the positions are corresponding exactly to the way the North Vietnamese are attacking. Hit these spots, and you hit them."

Shep took the map with a nod, then asked, "Are they gonna be able to hold?"

Brad smiled back. "Yep. We have to assume yes. It's war. You do your job, the guy next to you does his, and we take care of each other. If you bomb those positions, the Hmong will hold their line through the night."

Ten minutes later, a pair of twin-engine A-26 Invaders passed over the mapped positions of the NVA battalions. Cluster bombs tore through the enemy force and thwarted a second wave of the attack. The Hmong were holding.

Shep directed bombing runs until around midnight, then Alex took his seat with four other technicians. Artillery shells continued to fall in the Hmong village and occasionally around the helipad, but it had been four hours since any had been fired at the radar site. To be on the safe side, Shep and Kevin curled up in their bags on the ledge; it was still the safest location. They dozed off between blasts and flares, praying the Hmong could continue the fight and dreaming of the plij ploj sounds of the rescue choppers.

At 0248, Wee, one of the original PARU to be stationed on the mountain, was on watch from the high bunker on the ridge. His best friend, Boon, was napping down in the hole. The bunker was dug into a softer area of dirt high on the hillside, but had a stout wall of stone along its downhill side. Wee was watching the valley to the southeast in the eerie white light of the flares, anticipating the bright yellow blast of cluster bombs exploding through the trees. He heard a quiet thump on the dirt to his right, then the bang of metal on metal at his feet. Glancing down, he saw Boon curled up in the corner, then the dark, checkered texture of a Soviet-made F-1 hand grenade. There was a yellow flash, and the two PARU were gone.

Shep was startled awake by the grenade blast. He sat up, instantly aware of small arms fire from two different kinds of guns erupting above the ledge and perhaps fifty meters north of the Mission Room. The Thais were screaming, and then they heard John yell a command in Thai. More small arms fire erupted as the technicians grabbed their M16s. Kevin climbed up above the ledge and peered across the open ground behind the Dushka bunker and between the two buildings. One of the PARU was slumped over the bunker wall, and another man in dark clothing lay face down on the limestone slab.

Injured men's high-pitched screams filled the night between gunshots, now almost constant. Kevin heard two muffled blasts from inside the Mission Room and saw orange flames inside the building through a series of holes that had instantly been blown in the thin metal walls. He watched as Large jumped up from the Dushka bunker and ran toward the TACAN. A series of five or six shots rang out as a dark figure appeared from the door of the communication room, and Large fell forward, face down. The dark figure, now clearly a Vietnamese soldier, ran to Large and stood over him, then fired three more shots into the Texan's back. The big man's body shook, and then was still.

Kevin pulled his M16 off his shoulder, balanced himself on the small ledge, then took aim at the soldier. As he did, another shadow moved from around the Mission Room and along the cliff. Two shots rang out and Kevin tipped over backward. He landed next to Shep on the ledge, dead.

John Lilygren began running up the trail from the landing zone the moment he heard the grenade. He knew instantly what had happened. The attack on the Hmong was a feint, and the real battle for Lima Site 85 would be fought from the west.

"They are behind us!" he screamed in Thai as he reached the staff quarters building. A grenade detonated inside, and John peered around the building as a Vietnamese soldier started up the steps. John took aim and shots from his M16 rang across the ridge. The NVA soldier fell dead.

John started up the stairs, then shot another dark figure who appeared from around the communications building. Shots from the various PARU bunkers were almost constant, and he could hear Luang yell, "Watch the right side!" in Thai. John stepped up to the next level as a Vietnamese soldier fired into someone lying on the ground. He dropped to one knee and squeezed off two rounds into the attacker's side, then ran toward the Dushka bunker as two more shots were fired from behind the Mission Room. Just before he got to the bunker, he realized the dead American was Large, then searing pain ripped through his shoulder and thigh as a blast from a grenade blew one of the bunker walls apart. John was knocked high into the air and came down on the slab of limestone headfirst. He didn't move.

At the helipad, Brad was coordinating the Hmong defense as the NVA surged behind the artillery fire. He knew, with the number of men the North Vietnamese had in the area, the Hmong had to hold. The PARU would stand no chance against that many troops. He also knew there was a major attack going on at the radar site and that without help John and the PARU would have a difficult time defending the technicians. A few of those guys hadn't even fired a rifle since basic training. Basic Air Force training. Still, everyone had a job to do, and his was to keep the Hmong holding the line.

As a jet screamed overhead and Luang's PARU moved up from the helipad, Brad saw the flash of two grenades detonate near the bunker just north of the radio room. There was gunfire from M16s and AK-47s in the trees beyond it, then only two shots, both from an AK. He knew another of his men was dead. He yelled for the PARU to harden the right flank and watched as five PARU ran into the shrubs and took positions behind rocks. As predicted, a group of two and then a group of four NVA in black uniforms came hopping down through the boulders and ledges below the radar site. Luang watched as his men all stood in one motion and killed the NVA in a hail of gunfire.

There was a surge on the left side, but the PARU held there, too, then five more men charged down the trail. Two were killed, and the others were pushed back, but another group had followed the first surge and taken strong defensive positions in the boulders just below the staff quarters. Suddenly, they were in a stalemate. Like a World War I battlefield with two trenches, neither side could push forward. They were both in perfect defensive positions.

Lim was startled from an exhausted trance with the blast of the first grenade. It sounded like it was right above him, and a few rocks rained off the limestone face above the ledge, indicating his position wasn't as safe as it had first appeared. He traversed farther right, and the ledge soon widened, but there was more shooting above. He continued across, then ducked behind a large block when multiple machine guns opened up. There were more grenade blasts, and the fighting seemed to spread across the ridge faster than a man could run. Lim heard someone stepping along the edge of the wall just over his head and felt he should move again. He stepped out from a notch in the wall and considered going back left to find a safe place.

"Jum, get over here," a man said.

Lim was startled by the voice and it took him a moment to realize he was hearing English.

"Come here before you get your head blown off," the man said. He was standing at the mouth of a small, dark cave with an M16 in his hand. Lim recognized what the man wanted, and did exactly as he was told.

"Get in the fucking cave, Jum," the man said as he grabbed Lim's jacket. "Wait, you aren't Jum. Who the hell are you?"

Lim finally understood something and could answer.

"I am Lim. I am Hmong," he replied.

"Okay, I'm Shep. Now get in there before you get shot."

Lim stepped over a man's body, crouched in the back of the cave, and watched the American waving to someone above. Silhouetted against the pale white light of a flare, the dark-skinned American panned his rifle back and forth. It did not look like a natural motion for the man. Lim stared at the man's face in the light of the flare; he had never seen anyone with skin that dark.

A Phantom screamed over the ridge as the two other radar techs climbed down to Shep. It was Luke Valdez, a radar technician from Tucson, and Charlie Guarino, the TACAN mechanic. Of the two, only Charlie had a gun. All three cringed as two AK-47s opened up just above the rim of the cliff. They heard a grenade detonate by the TACAN, then many more shots.

"How many of them are there?" Shep asked in a whisper.

"I don't know. They're everywhere. They got Large, and I think they got John. The Mission Room was blown up," Charlie said as he crawled into the cave. "Who's this?"

"His name's Lim. He's one of the Hmong," Shep said. "Where is everyone else?"

"There's a bunch of guys over by the TACAN," Valdez said. "I don't even know if they have guns."

Shep shouldered his rifle and climbed back up. He could hear the gunfire coming from the area near the TACAN, and the radar technician realized he might be able to shoot the attackers from behind. As he peered over the rim of the cliff, the shapes of four men standing on the ledge next to the TACAN fired shots into the ground beyond his sight, presumably executing his friends. Shep raised his gun and aimed for the man on the right. He pulled the trigger and heard the pop, then watched as the man twisted and dropped off the ledge. Instantly, the other commandos spun and fired, and bullets and rock shattered in front of the radar technician. He jumped backward to get away and fell onto the ledge. Valdez grabbed him before he rolled into oblivion.

Within seconds, the Dac Cong were at the rim above, and a grenade rolled down the wall. All three technicians dove onto Lim in the cave as the grenade, now lying against Kevin's body, detonated. The lifeless corpse flew into the air as fragments ricocheted through the cave. Shep felt Valdez wince and saw blood run from his neck. A second grenade exploded, but Kevin's body had landed on it and the men in the cave were spared.

Kevin's torso and arms leaned against the wall next to the cave; his legs had been blown off the ledge. The smell of blood and opened bowels mixed with burned cordite filled the air, and Valdez vomited in the cave. Machine gun fire sprayed along the rock just beyond where the men huddled. Shep stared into the distance as the last flare faded out. He pulled what was left of Kevin's body in front of the cave entrance and waited for the Vietnamese to attack.

Looking through a gap above Kevin's tattered remains, the three men could see a line of orange and purple light just forming along the eastern horizon.

***

At 0420 hours and in total darkens, two MH 53 Jolly Green Giants departed Udorn for Phou Pha Thi. They were equipped to refuel in the air along the way, and the journey would take almost two hours. A couple of A-1 Skyraiders also left Udorn for the big peak, fully loaded for close air support.

At Alternate, Kyle Dramis had been awake all night with a few of the Ravens listening to the communication around the battle. They could hear Brad giving commands to the Hmong, then orchestrating bombings through Tom, better known as Raven-86. Tom had returned twice for fuel, but took the lead through the night rather than share it with another Raven as he understood the lay of the battlefield.

There had been no radio response from the technicians all night, and the men at Alternate assumed they were either dead or the radio had been destroyed by a shell.

Kyle knew the rules of engagement for the Air Force, and he knew the mountain was a free-fire zone. The Air Force would not risk the crews and the choppers for whoever was left up there. He grabbed his M16, rousted his two favorite Air America pilots from their dreams, and ten minutes later all three were in a Huey and en route to Phou Pha Thi. When they came within clear view of the mountain, the sun was just high enough to light up the battle site. Smoke and flames rose from huge areas around the base of the mountain. As they got closer, they spotted more fires in the Hmong village and on the landing zone.

"Kyle, there are two A-1s about to strafe the ridge. Apparently it's crawling with NVA," the helicopter pilot said to Kyle who sat pensively in the back of the Huey. "We're going to hold out over the valley to the west of the mountain and see if that puts the fear of God into the gooks."

As the heavily loaded planes descended on the mountain, Kyle watched out the open side door of the Huey. Sheets of fog rose quickly over the huge west face and past the radar site. He saw the two planes coming from the east, an advantage that blinded any NVA gunners on the ridge. As the first plane passed over, maybe no more than a hundred feet above the limestone and trees, shots were fired into the air from a Dushka machine gun in a bunker at the radar site. Clearly, the site had been overrun. The NVA fired late and missed the plane, but they had telegraphed the punch.

The second Skyraider opened up on the Dushka, and Kyle watched as dust flew and bullets ricocheted through the battered equipment. Men in black shirts ran up the ridge to the north, and when the dust settled there were two more NVA bodies lying next to the toppled machine gun.

"Okay, we're going in," the pilot yelled.

High above, the pilots of "Compress" had reached the mountain and were listening to Raven-86 talk with Brad at the landing zone. They knew there were dozens of injured PARU and at least one American who needed to get out and that the Hmong were falling back into the jungle. It was so desperate that the Raven had even tried to set down on the lower airstrip in the hopes he could get two people out, but he'd been shot back into the sky by ground fire. The mountain was falling to the enemy, but the rules of engagement from 7th Air Force clearly stated they were not to land on a hot landing zone in Laos.

"To hell with the rules," the pilot mumbled to himself. "The time is now."

As billows of fog rose from the valley, Compress-1 touched down on the helipad with its rear gate down. The landing zone was flooded with wounded Hmong and PARU. They watched as the CIA operative and a PARU officer organized the wounded to be moved to the chopper, then, fully loaded, the helicopter barely lifted off and dove along the ridgeline to the southwest. As it did, Compress-2 touched down and the remaining men loaded onto the plane. The last aboard were the CIA operative and the PARU officer. They lifted off and flew just above the radar site, then the flight engineer grabbed the pilot's shoulder. Someone was still moving near the staff quarters at the radar site.

The pilot slowed, knowing he was an easy target for an NVA soldier, but no one fired. It appeared the strafing runs by the Skyraiders had pushed them safely away from the radar installation, but he couldn't see a landing site to put the helicopter down with all the debris scattered about. The pilot pointed at the flight engineer and gave a thumbs up, then pointed to the rescue specialist. With his M16 in hand, the rescuer slipped out the side door of the hovering helicopter and was quickly lowered to the ground.

There were numerous bodies on Phou Pha Thi, but only one was right there and moving. He rolled the injured American over, noting he'd been hit in the shoulder and leg and had a deep gouge in his head. The man was alive but drifting in and out of consciousness. The young rescue specialist strapped the wounded man onto his own body, then gave a thumbs-up to the flight engineer and together they were lifted off the ground. As the Jolly Green Giant flew over the south ridge of Phou Pha Thi, the rescue specialist's M16 strap broke and the gun dropped down the west face of the mountain. He wouldn't need it again that day.

Meanwhile, Kyle Dramis' Air America Huey had buzzed over the top of the ridge and banked hard to the right. Bodies were strewn everywhere, but no one fired up at them. They flew out over the valley and then came back toward the west face. As they approached, a man emerged from a small cave, pushing a body out of his way as he did so. He waved his arms in the air to get the crew's attention, and they flew in the direction of the injured Americans. Making a quick estimation on the size of the cliff based on the man standing on the ledge, the pilot speculated he could approach the mountain and hover. The rotors would be just above the rim, while everyone in the ship was below it, thus shielding them from ground fire. It was a dangerous move, but it might save a few of the radar technicians.

When the helicopter's wind screen was about twenty-five feet from the ledge, the pilot rotated the machine counterclockwise, thus facing the open door toward the cliff. Updrafts of mist blew along the wall, but he focused completely on the tiny wobbles of the helicopter and managed to just touch the right skid onto the ledge.

"Let's go," Shep yelled over the rotor wash. He helped lift Valdez to Kyle who stood on the Huey's skid. Charlie climbed in as well, then Shep dove onto the chopper's floor.

"What about the Hmong?" Kyle yelled.

"He's a dead man without our help," Shep yelled. "The NVA are all over the mountain and he's cut off from the village."

Kyle waved for the little soldier to step across the void and into the helicopter.

"C'mon, Lim," Shep yelled. "You have to go now."

Lim looked along the ridge of the mountain and down into the valley below. There was smoke everywhere. The men in the helicopter looked almost as if they came from another world, but their faces were truly beckoning. Lim took a deep breath and stepped into the American helicopter. They pulled away and dove for the safety of the west.

Epilogue

March 11, 1978, 7:00 PM

(ten years later)

The Stardust Hotel and Casino, Las Vegas, Nevada

The Ravens could throw a hell of a party. No one had ever questioned that, and this one, on the tenth anniversary of the battle for Phou Pha Thi, was obviously not going to be an exception. John Lilygren walked toward the ballroom with a sense of apprehension. He'd seen a couple of the men and had spoken to almost all of them a few times on the phone since the end of the war, but this was the first time most of them had gotten together since the battle. He had learned he loved everyone who had gone through Operation Heavy Green, but for some reason he was a little afraid of the moment when the survivors would see each other again. Eleven technicians had died, not to mention many Hmong, and in the end it had all been for nothing.

Many of the memories were painful, and perhaps his apprehension was about having all those mental images rushing back into his mind at once. John stepped through the heavy metal doors and his fears instantly faded away with the sight of Brad Drakely's smile. The two walked past everyone else and bear-hugged.

"You look great, John. Mountain living in Wyoming

is obviously good for the body as well as the soul," Brad said.

"So do you, man. It looks like you've put on a couple pounds, too. I guess those tapeworms have moved on to more fertile fields."

"Well, they have me pushing a pencil in Langley these days; the bourbon adds up around the waist. Hey, before you get pulled away by some of the other guys, I want to introduce you to someone. You have a lot to talk about with this guy."

"A guy on Phou Pha Thi?" John asked as Brad waved someone over from behind.

"Well, sort of. I'll let him explain it to you," Brad said through a sly smile. "Really nice guy. Teaches history at the University of Montana. We use him as a resource from time to time. Here he is. John Lilygren, this is Professor Phou Samsoum."

John turned and looked down, then offered his hand. "Hello, Professor Samsoum. I'm John Lilygren; my friends call me John."

"Hello, John," the young Hmong replied. "I have heard a lot about you. Please call me Lim."

Afterword

In the hours after Lima Site 85 and Phou Pha Thi were overrun by the North Vietnamese Army, American planes dropped bombs all over the mountain. The goal was to help the Hmong retreat, but also to keep the advanced communications and TSQ-81 radar equipment out of the opposing army's hands. Nevertheless, that technology did eventually make its way to Hanoi and then on to Moscow.

Eleven American technicians died on Phou Pha Thi. It was the largest loss of Air Force ground personnel in the war. For many years after the war was over, the American taskforce assigned to try to identify men missing in action in the war were not allowed to visit Phou Pha Thi. This helped fuel theories that the men had been taken captive and were POWs who were never returned after the war. In the early 1990s, the taskforce was allowed to visit Phou Pha Thi for only a few minutes and thus not able to make a search. Then in 2003, the taskforce was granted access to the site again and able to do a more comprehensive search. They have now identified most of the Americans who were lost in the battle of Lima Site 85. It is generally accepted that the Dac Cong killed the men and threw the bodies off the cliff.

The loss of Phou Pha Thi came hand-in-hand with the Tet Offensive, a time that can now be seen as pivotal in the Second Indochina War. The United States was never again able to direct radar-guided attacks on

North Vietnam, and despite an easing of the rules of engagement to allow bombing of more targets around Hanoi, was never able to stop the flow of arms down the Ho Chi Minh Trail.

The Tet Offensive was a complete military failure for the North Vietnamese and Viet Cong, but it showed the American people the NVA's resolve to win the war. Public opinion of the war fell further, and America began to downsize its role in South Vietnam. By 1973, the US had pulled out and left the South Vietnamese forces to fight alone, and by April of 1975, the North Vietnamese had taken control and united the two countries under one flag.

For most of us, the war in Vietnam has become ancient history in the light of so many more battles that have been fought since. The youngest Vietnam veterans are in their late sixties now, and sadly watching as their grandchildren are fighting wars in entirely different parts of the world. Relations with Vietnam have been normalized, and the US and the Vietnamese actually enjoy a healthy level of trade. In fact, business is so good between the two countries, it has led one Vietnamese government official to say, "You won. We became capitalists."

It is perhaps a bit of an exaggeration, but the fact remains that modern Vietnam would like to be friends with the United States. In an ironic twist I allude to in the book, the Vietnamese have indicated a wish for a greater US military presence in the region to help thwart the ambitions of their traditional enemy to the north: China. China invaded Vietnam in 1978, and though they pulled back, the country has clearly shown it considers Vietnam and the South China Sea to be in its sphere of influence.

For the Hmong, the loss of Phou Pha Thi was the worst disaster of the war and led to perhaps the worst period of their history. The North Vietnamese occupied the peak and used it as a forward base for attacks in central Laos. Due to the spiritual importance the mountain held with the Hmong, General Vang Pao felt he had to retake the mountain to lift the morale of his people. He put together numerous offensives, but all were thwarted by the North Vietnamese and Pathet Lao. Vang Pao's army of Hmong grew much younger and much older as his main battle troops died and their children and grandparents took up the fight. He eventually accepted that the fighting had to stop.

An exodus of nearly 300,000 Hmong fled to Thailand amid reports of "re-education camps" and genocidal policies by the communist government. Tens of thousands made their home in the United States, originally settling in Southern California and the mountains of Western Montana. There are now nearly 300,000 Hmong in the United States, with the largest communities in California, Minnesota, and Wisconsin.

Despite the scars left on America by the Vietnam War, many of the people of Thailand believe it saved them from a darker future. The Mekong River became the new wall against communism as the so-called Bamboo Curtain. While re-education camps and killing fields became a part of life in Vietnam, Laos, and Cambodia, Thailand came away in relative prosperity. For many years following the war, the King of Thailand was known to throw an annual party for the CIA men who had trained and worked with the PARU and Hmong. Many of those men still live as ex-patriots in Thailand.

Despite nearly sixty years of time passing since the battle, the subject remains very sensitive for many veterans of the war in Laos and the surviving families of those lost in the battle. I hope this book does not reopen those wounds, but instead educates a much younger public on a little-known aspect of the Vietnam War.

Remember, though the military action of the story is real, the characters depicted here are fictional. I specifically wrote the book that way so the survivors could continue to heal from the war without being bothered by the rest of us.

***

The Hmong believe the first clothing you wear in life is the most important. That garment is the placenta you're born in. For your soul to go to heaven, you must return to the place where the placenta was taken off and your body was exposed to the cold world. You can then put the placenta back on, and move on to a comfortable place in the afterlife. The Hmong who have fled their ancient kingdom have not had that opportunity, and it is believed their souls wander the Earth in despair.

However, the Kingdom of Laos has very much opened up in the last fifteen years. Tourism to the city of Luang Prabang and to the Plain of Jars has helped to show the world the beauty of the Land of a Million Elephants. As it further opens up, perhaps the Hmong will be able to safely return so their souls can move on.

Terminology/Glossary/Places

A-1 Skyraider: single-engine propeller-driven attack plane developed during WWII

AK-47: automatic rifle designed in the Soviet Union in 1947. Still in use today, still most common rifle in the world.

Alternate: name given to Lima Site 20 at Long Tieng in Laos. Main base for the CIA, Ravens, and Vang Pao's Hmong army. Name was said to have been chosen as "20 Alternate" to throw off the press as they would never look for a base at an "alternate" site.

Anti-aircraft artillery: AAA or triple-A, guns designed to fire explosives shells at opposing aircraft. Most common sizes of shell fired in Laos and Vietnam were 37, 57, and 85-mm in diameter.

B-40: Vietnamese-built rocket-propelled grenade launcher based on Soviet RPG-2.

B-52: largest USAF bomber during Cold War. One B-52 could drop 75, 500-pound bombs, or 50, 750-pound bombs.

Barrel Roll: code name for bombing campaign in Northeast Laos in the early years of America's involvement in war. Intent was, in combination with Steel Tiger, to disrupt flow of mili tary supplies from North Vietnam to South Vietnam.

Bell UH-1 "Huey": Bell helicopter. Has become symbol of war in Vietnam.

Bin tram: geographic section of command on Ho Chi Minh Trail. Each binh tram had men assigned to its maintenance.

C-123: wide-bodied transportation aircraft; precursor to C-130.

C-130: known as Hercules, this aircraft had a wide, round fuse
lage and four engines; could land and take off with heavy
loads on very short runways.

Cadre: soldiers of a military unit.

Call sign: name an aircraft takes for a given mission. Fighter
pilots often given a call sign as a permanent nickname.

Cambodia: one of four countries of former French Indochina.
Once ruled by the Khmer; most famous site is Angkor Wat.
Millions killed by Pol Pot, the leader of group known as the
Khmer Rouge, after the American era of the Vietnam War.

Cha gee: a nasty and somewhat racist term the Hmong use
for Vietnamese. The Vietnamese, in turn, used the term miao,
or barbarian, for the Hmong. Both terms are similar in acceptance and use to the "N Word" in American nomenclature.

CINCPAC: Commander in Chief, Pacific region. Based at Pearl
Harbor, Hawaii. Admiral oversees almost all military operations in Pacific theater.

Couloir: steep, usually narrow gully on a mountain.

Dac Cong: the special forces of the North Vietnamese army.

Dan tranh: concept put forward by leaders of North Vietnam:
The war must be approached by millions of individuals acting
in concert for one finish.

Democratic Republic of Vietnam: see Republic of Vietnam

Dien Bien Phou: valley in Northern Vietnam on border with
Laos. French lost decisive battle here that ended tenure in
Indochina.

Domino Theory: first put forward by Winston Churchill, then
made popular by the Kennedy Administration, theory that
one country falls to communism, which knocks the next
country "down" to communism, and then the next, like domi-

Dushka 12.7mm: common machine gun built by the Soviet Union based on American .50-caliber design. The guns are so similar Dushka can fire .50-caliber rounds.

Duster: helicopter that came in to remove wounded GIs.

Dvina S-75: most common Soviet radar-guided surface-to-air missile of Cold War. US military referred to it as SAM-2. Could move at three times the speed of sound and go as high as 60,000 feet. Warhead had proximity fuse, meaning it detonated near target and did not have to go through target. Commonly referred to as a SAM.

F-105 (Thunderchief): US attack aircraft developed in 1950s; kept in use until mid-1970s. Also called a Thud. Capable of supersonic flight and able to deliver large bomb loads.

FACS: Forward Air Controllers.

Fragmentary Order (Frag): operational order given to a military unit with changes from original form.

French Indochina (Indochina): French colony in Southeast Asia made up of modern countries of Laos, Vietnam, and Cambodia.

Geneva Agreement (1962): agreement made by all parties involved in Second Indochina War that Laos would not be drawn into the conflict. Agreement was: North Vietnam, South Vietnam, and the United States would pull all military forces out of Laos.

Gomers: like dink or gook, a somewhat racist term used by American GIs to identify the enemy. Use of term started in Korean War.

Green tracers: one in every five bullets fired from a 12.7 mm machine gun, burns green with phosphorous. Allows the gunner to know where his stream of bullets is going and adjust his fire.

Hanoi: capital of North Vietnam, and now capital of Socialist Republic of Vietnam.

Hmong: (pronounced: M-mong) an ethnic group from the mountainous region of Southeast Asia and China. They have also been referred to as the Moob and the Meo.

Ho Chi Minh: Born in the late nineteenth century or ear ly 20th century, was the revolutionary leader of North Vietnam and chairman of its communist party. Served as leader of North Vietnam from withdrawal of the French in 1954 until his death in September, 1969.

Ho Chi Minh Trail: Known as the Truong Song, or Truong Trail to the Vietnamese, because it traveled through and along the Truong (Annamite) Mountains, supply route for military equipment from North Vietnam to South Vietnam during the American years of that war.

Hooch: small house or hut.

Huey: see Bell UH 1. Standard helicopter of the United States during the Vietnam War.

Initial Point (I.P.): the point of contact and where aircraft went into formation for a radar-guided attack from Lima Site 85.

KIA: killed in action.

Karst: a rock formation, generally limestone, in which softer rock has eroded away, leaving behind spires, towers, and mountains. The Katchenaburi Karst Formation of southeast Asia is the largest karst formation in the world. It runs roughly from Guilin, China to northern Borneo.

KC-135: based on the same platform as the Boeing 707, standard tanker aircraft for aerial refueling of United States Air Force attack aircraft since the early 1960s.

Khe Sanh: in the Quang Tri Province of central Vietnam, the American Khe Sanh Combat Base was a major installation that came under attack during North Vietnam's Tet Offensive.

Klick: one kilometer.

lao Lao: fermented grain alcohol made from rice and a host of various exotic ingredients the distiller wants to add.

Laos: Lao People's Democratic Republic, more commonly referred to simply as Laos; one of three countries that had been part of the French colony of Indochina.

Lima Site: landing strip in Laos built by the CIA and USAID to deliver aid to various tribes in the more remote parts of the country. Lima was taken from the NATO phonetic alphabet, as in Lima for L. Site was for strip. Thus Lima Site means landing strip.

Lima Site 20/Alternate: main base for Hmong resistance during the war, as well as the base of operations for the CIA and Ravens. See Alternate.

Lima Site 36: large landing strip near the Lao town of Nha Kang just north of the Plain of Jars. Was used by Air America rescue helicopter crews to more quickly reach downed American pilots in North Vietnam.

Lima Site 85: landing strip, and later radar site, on Phou Pha Thi mountain in Northeast Laos: A land-locked, mountainous country in Southeast Asia bordering Thailand, China, Viet nam, and Cambodia.

Loadmaster: a person who handles the cargo of an Air Force helicopter or airplane. Air America loadmasters were referred to as "kickers."

Long Tieng: see Alternate or Lima Site 20.

M16: standard 5.56-caliber infantry rifle used by American forces from the early 1960s to present. A manufacturing defect in the ammunition during the 1960s gave the gun a reputation for jamming.

MACV: Military Advance Command in Vietnam.

Mark 84: 2000-pound bomb. One of the largest bombs dropped by US forces during the Vietnam War.

Mekong River: one of the largest rivers in the world, the Mekong begins in China and runs through Southeast Asia draining into the South China Sea in Southern Vietnam. It naturally creates much of the border between Laos and Thailand. For that reason, many American pilots during the war referred to it as "the Fence."

Meo: a catch-all term for minority tribes of Southern China and former Indochina; translates to "barbarian" in one Chi nese dialect.

Miao: stemming from the word above, in this text this word is used as the derogatory racial slur of the minority tribes of Vietnam.

MiG 17: developed in the early 1950s in the Soviet Union, commonly used by the North Vietnamese during the war.

MiG 21: developed in the late 1950s, super-sonic aircraft; most advanced plane flown by the North Vietnamese during the war.

Montagnard: catchall French term that directly translates to "mountain people"; was used in French Indochina to describe a number of hill tribes, including the Hmong in Vietnam and Laos.

Muay Thai: lethal martial art practiced by the Thai. Also Thai land's national sport.

Nakhon Phanom: city in the far east of Thailand on the Lao tian border. The Royal Thai Air Force Base there was used by a number of American units during the war.

National Liberation Front (NLF): also known as the Viet Cong, the NLF was the revolutionary force in South Vietnam during the war. It was common for North Vietnamese soldiers to dress as NLF so if they were killed they'd be counted as a part of the insurgency.

North Vietnam: technically known as the People's Democratic Republic of Vietnam, but commonly referred to as North Vietnam, the section of the French colony of Indochina known as Vietnam north of the 17th parallel. It came into existence with the 1956 Paris Peace Accords. Simply became Vietnam when the countries were united after the fall of South Viet nam in 1975.

North Vietnamese Army (NVA): technically the People's Army of Vietnam, this was the common American and allied name for Army of North Vietnam.

Operations Order (OPORD): detailed plan for a military action. Generally made up of five parts; situation, execution, sustain ment, logistics, and command. If any of that is altered after it is introduced, the OPORD becomes a fragmentary order, or frag.

PARU: Police and Aerial Reinforcement Unit. A Thai elite mili tary unit created with the help of the CIA in the 1950s. Goal was to stop communist insurgency in Thailand, but was later used for various military operations during the Vietnam War.

Pathet Lao: Communist Party of Laos. Based just east of Sam Neua in Houaphan Province during the war. The Pathet Lao and North Vietnamese shared goals, and it is widely accepted they generally followed the orders that originated in North Vietnam.

People's Army of Vietnam (PAVN): see North Vietnamese Army.

People's Republic of Vietnam: see North Vietnam

Phou Pha Thi: (pronounced "Poo Pah Tee") a large and rugged mountain in the Houaphan Province Northeast Laos. Was considered somewhat sacred to the Hmong, and became the location of a TACAN and then a radar guidance center for aircraft flying missions over North Vietnam and Laos. Com monly referred to by Americans as Lima Site 85.

plij ploj: term the Hmong used for the sound of a birds' wings flapping. During the war, it came to mean the sound of a helicopter rotors.

Plain of Jars: largest open plain in North Central Laos at roughly 15 miles across. The jars are megaliths scattered across the plain in various sites that date back to circa 500 BC. Their exact usage is not known, though one theory says they were burial urns.

Rangers: elite special operations unit of the US Army based out of Fort Benning, Georgia.

Rappel: Using friction to descend on a rope. The word abseil is also used for this action.

Ravens: CIA-hired forward air controllers based out of Long Tieng, or Lima Site 20 Alternate, in Laos.

Recon: commonly truncated word for "reconnaissance." Ap plied to the gathering of information on areas a military unit does not have control.

Republic of Vietnam (Democratic): commonly referred to as South Vietnam, was one portion of the former French colony of French Indochina. South Vietnam was created in 1956 through the Paris Peace Accords as the portion of Vietnam south of the 17th parallel. Was dissolved as a country and made part of the People's Socialist Republic of Vietnam in 1975 with the forces of North Vietnam overtook the capital of Saigon.

Rolling Thunder: technically "Operation Rolling Thunder." A bombing campaign conducted by the American Air Force,

Navy, and some parts of the South Vietnamese Air Force against North Vietnam. Began in 1965 and continued through 1968.

RPG-2: A rocket-propelled grenade designed by the Soviet Union. Precursor weapon used in World War II was known as a bazooka. The RPG fires an explosive charge on a small rocket, has an effective range of about 100 meters. Is still in use today.

SAM: surface-to-air missile. See Dvina-S-75

Sam Neua: capital of Houaphan Province in Northeast Laos

Sapper: catchall term for military personnel who construct or destruct military installation. Term was commonly applied to members of the North Vietnam Army and Viet Cong who placed mines or infiltrated American and South Vietnamese bases.

Sheep-dipped: being removed from the military by the CIA to work as a civilian. Also used for taking off a military uniform so a soldier can pose as a civilian.

South Vietnam: common term for the Republic of Vietnam. See Republic of Vietnam

Souvanna Phouma: prince of Laos who took the position of Prime Minister when French Indochina was broken into four countries of Laos, Cambodia, North Vietnam, and South Vietnam. Was in power from 1972-1975. His most notable acts, intended to appease both sides in the war, gave both the North Vietnamese the right to pass through the country and then later gave the United States the right to attack (from the air) any military unit of the North Vietnamese Army. Led to Laos being the most heavily bombed country in history.

Soviet Union: often abbreviated as the USSR for Union of Soviet Socialist Republics, was a communist country cre ated from numerous nations in Europe and Asia in 1922. Its

largest state, and most populous state, was Russia. TheSoviet Union was allied with the United States during
World War II, but the two nations became adversar-ies
in what is commonly referred to as the Cold War. It supported numerous Marxist and communist movements around the world from the 1940s until it dissolved in 1991.

Spook: common slang term for someone who works in the American intelligence network, most commonly with the Central Intelligence Agency (CIA).

Steel Tiger: bombing campaign conducted by the US Air Force in Southern Laos to disrupt the flow of weapons on the Ho Chi Minh Trail.

Surface-to-Air Missile: see SAM or Dvina S-75.

TACAN: Tactical Air Navigation System. Emits signal with in formation to help pilots discern his/her bearing or distance from its fixed location.

Thud: common term for an F-105 Thunderchief American at tack aircraft.

Triple-A: see Anti-aircraft artillery.

Trail, the: as used in this book, an abbreviation for the Ho Chi Minh Trail.

Udorn: city in Northeast Thailand. The Royal Thai Airbase at Udorn became one of the largest bases for the United States Air Force, specifically the 7th/13th Air Force, during the war.

USAID: United States Agency for International Development. Agency tasked with giving foreign aid to civilians outside of the United States. Often worked alongside the CIA during the Vietnam War.

Vang Pao (General): leader of the Royal Lao Army/Hmong mi litia in Laos during the Vietnam War. Born in Xiang Khoung Province of North Central Laos, Vang Pao's military career began by fighting Japanese occupation of French

Indochina during World War II. 1945: began fighting the North Vietnamese and Pathet Lao communist forces with the French; continued that fight through America's in volvement in the war. Immigrated, 1975, along with thousands of other Hmong, to the United States following the loss of the war to communist forces. Became social leader of the American Hmong community. Vang Pao passed away in 2011 in Fresno, California.

Viet: commonly referred to as the Kinh in modern times; largest ethnic group in Vietnam.

Viet Cong: see National Liberation Front

Viet Minh: organization began by fighting the Japanese in their occupation of French Indochina, later was leading organization opposing French rule in the colony. Eventually rolled into the communist party when North Vietnam came into existence with the Paris Accords.

Vietnam War: A catchall term for the First and Second Indo china Wars commonly applied now to the American period, or Second Indochina War. The First Indochina War began in 1945 when Viet Minh forces began fighting the French for control of the colony of Indochina. Could be argued that there was a pause between the two wars between 1954 and 1956, though skirmishes in the future South Vietnam were already taking place. The Second Indo china War began in 1956 when North and South were separated at the 17th parallel, which escalated into America's involvement in the 1960s and early 1970s. The Second Indochina war ended in April, 1975 when Saigon and South Vietnam fell to the communist forces of North Vietnam (see People's Republic of Vietnam).

Wild Weasel: the call sign for an American aircraft designed to draw, then evade, and then destroy the source of enemy fire over North Vietnam.

Bibliography

Having been born only a year before the Battle of Lima Site 85, I did not serve in Vietnam or Laos. That means writing this book required an enormous amount of research. Fortunately, I did this research for fun through many years of my life as I love the subject. A simple bibliography rarely tells us what we need to know, which is "What did you draw on for that information?" The books I pulled information from are listed below, as are other sources, but I feel the need to single out a few of them.

The single best historical accounting of the events around Lima Site 85 is Timothy Castle's One Day Too Long. It is an impressive display of research, and is quite readable. Tragic Mountains, by Jane Hamilton-Merritt, is, in my mind, the most enjoyable book about the Hmong and the CIA programs in Laos. There are dozens of stories in that book that could someday each be a book in themselves. Back Fire, by Roger Warner, also gives a good explanation of the CIA's actions in Laos. The same could be said for The Ravens by Christopher Robbins. The Ravens were brave, and they were wild, and he does a great job of showing how the combination made them effective as a force in Laos, as well as how strongly they felt for the Hmong.

The Ten Thousand Day War by Michael MacLear is an excellent source for understanding not only the war, but also how America ended up involved in the war. After you read it, read In Retrospect by Robert McNamara. The former Secretary of Defense comes clean on every level and does a great job of explaining the decision process that led to the debacle. A Bright and Shining Lie by Neil Sheehan does a good job of explaining how it all happened, but In Retrospect comes straight from the source when late in life McNamara was trying to make amends for past mistakes. For what it's worth, McNamara also did a documentary film called The Fog of War during the lead-up to the Second US Iraq War that details how he saw the same mistakes that led to the Vietnam War being made by another generation.

There are excellent Web sources that I called on for this book.

Interviews with the people involved can be found at http://limasite85.us. This site also has a lot of photographs that one can view for visualizing scenes. The CIA has a report on the fall of Lima Site 85 on its website. There are numerous military sites that give graphic information on the weapons used in the war. A great example of these would be Craig Baker's site on the F-105 Thunderchief.

I have been fortunate enough to have lived much of the last twenty-six years in Thailand, and have traveled extensively throughout Southeast Asia since 1990. A huge amount of what I could write about here was based on my own travels and exploring the jungles of Thailand, Laos, and Vietnam.

I thank my climbing partners for those trips, but also thank a few men whom I will never know by name because they spoke to me on this subject. They were traveling, too, and were clearly coming back to Laos and Southeast Asia to see it in a time other than that of the war.

I should also mention Soong, our guide-guard on my first trip to Northern Vietnam in 1991. He had served in the NVA for six years, and had excellent descriptions of the war from that side's perspective. On the American side, I thank Khun Dick Balsamo for the jungle hikes we have done together in addition to his graphic explanations of his "forced all-expenses-paid vacation" in Quang Tri Province in 1970. I also drew from the memories of my friend Andy Gramlich, a forward air controller over Vietnam and Laos, and from Carl Wattenburg Jr., my father-in-law, who worked in Army Intelligence during the early years of America's involvement in the Vietnam War.

Barnes, Ian and Robert Hudson, *The History Atlas of Asia*, McMillan, New York, 1998

Bray, Gary W., *After My Lai: My Year Commanding First Platoon, Charlie Company*, University of Oklahoma Press, Norman, OK, 2009

Broughton, Col. Jack, *Thud Ridge*, Crecy Publishing, Manchester, U.K., 1969

Castle, Timothy N., *One Day Too Long: The Secret Site 85 and the*

Bombing of North Vietnam, Columbia University, New York, 1999

Cat, Allen, *Honor Denied: The Truth about America and the CIA*, iUniverse LLC, Bloomington IN, 2011

Chandler, David P., *A History of Cambodia*, Silkworm Books, Chiang Mai, 1993

Davidson, Phillip B., *Vietnam at War 1946-1975*, Oxford University Press, Oxford, U.K., 1988

Fadiman, Anne, *The Spirit Catches you and You Fall Down*, Farrar Strauss Giroux, New York, 1997

Fitzgerald, Frances, *Fire in the Lake: The Vietnamese and the Americans in Vietnam*, Little, Brown and Company, 1972

Hamilton-Merritt, Jane, *Tragic Mountains: The Hmong, the Americans, and the Secret Wars of Laos, 1942-1992*, Indiana University Press, 1993

Harrison, Marshal, *A Lonely Kind of War*, 1997

Heidhues, Mary Somers, *Southeast Asia: A Concise History*, Thames and Hudson, London, 2000

Herring, George C., *The Pentagon Papers Abridged*, McGraw Hill, 1993

Karnow, Stanley, *Vietnam: A History*, Penguin Books, New York, 1997

Lansdale, Edward G., *In The Midst of Wars*, Fordham University Press, New York, 1991

Linder, James C., *The Fall of Lima Site 85, 1995 Edition*, Central Intelligence Agency, 1995

MacLear, Michael, *The Ten Thousand Day War: Vietnam 1945-1975*, St. Martin's Press, New York, 1981

McNamara, Robert S., *In Retrospect: The Tragedy and Lessons of Vietnam*, Vintage Press, New York, 1995

Osbourne, Milton, *Southeast Asia An Introductory History*, Silkworm Books, Chiang Mai, Thailand, 1997

Polifka, Karl L., *Meeting Steve Canyon: and Flying with the CIA in Laos*, 2013

Robbins, Christopher, *The Ravens*, Crown Publishers, New York, 1987

Roddy, Ray Jr., *Circles in the Sky*, Infinity, West Conshohoken, Pa., 2009

Roper, Jim, *Quoth the Raven*, America House, Baltimore, 2001

Sheehan, Neil, *A Bright and Shining Lie, John Paul Vann and America in Vietnam*, Vintage, New York, 1988

Stuart-Fox, Martin, *A History of Laos*, Cambridge University Press, Cambridge, U.K., 1997

Warner, Roger, *Shooting at the Moon: The Story of America's Clandestine War in Laos*, Steerforth Press, South Royalton, Vermont, 1996

Warner, Roger, *Backfire, The Secret War in Laos and its Link to the War in Vietnam.* Simon and Schuster, New York, 1995

Young, Marilyn B., *The Vietnam Wars 1945-1990*, Harper Collins, New York, 1991

Zumwalt, James G., *Bare Feet, Iron Will: Stories from the Other Side of Vietnam's Battlefields*, Fortis, Jacksonville, Florida

Thank you...

I need to thank a number of people for helping me out with this project. Carl Wattenberg Jr., Larry Lightner, Dick Balsamò and Andy Gramlich all served in some capacity in Vietnam/Laos and helped out with technical questions. Ed Gunter with the Ravens post-war organization helped with some facts on those elite pilots, as did Gary Baker on the F-105. There were numerous other people I discussed the war with while in Laos, Vietnam, and Thailand, though their names now escape me. Mike Lilygren, Suzanne Lilygren, April C. Hughes, Joan Dillon, Carl Wattenberg Jr., and Larry Lightner all helped in some capacity with the overall concept of the story, Theodorra Bryant and Deanne Musolf did some developmental copy editing, and Sara Jung proofread the manuscript. Elyse Guarino and Joan Dillon get a big thank you for their artwork.

About the Author

Sam Lightner, Jr. is a life-long writer and climber who lives in Lander, Wyoming. He is the author of multiple works of fiction and non-fiction, including All Elevations Unknown, his widely praised book that tells the story of a series of battles fought on the island of Borneo during World War II.

He has been published in Outside Magazine and most of the world's climbing magazines. Sam was featured in an article in National Geographic in January, 2000.

He lives with his wife Liz and dogs Lexi and Moki in Lander, Wyoming. This is his ninth book.

Sam can be contacted through www.samlightnerjr.com.

photo by Shep Vail